Golden Horse

A Samantha Steele Mystery

Sandra J. Howell

WEST RIDGE FARM PUBLISHING
Hampden, Massachusetts

Golden Horse Copyright © 2016 Sandra J. Howell

Published by West Ridge Farm publishing
Cover Design: Amy Rooney

Publisher's Note: This novel is a work of fiction. Names, characters, places and incidents are either products of the author's imagination or used fictitiously. All characters are fictional, and any similarity to people living or dead is purely coincidental.

ISBN-13: 978-0-9845582-6-1 (West Ridge Farm Publishing)
ISBN-10: 0-9845582-6-8

Printed in the United States of America

Dedication

This book is dedicated to horse lovers everywhere. The beauty of majestic horses still takes our breath away.

Chapter 1

July

The Palomino mare stood quietly at the crossties as Parker Thomas tapped the last nail into the horseshoe on her back hoof. Parker gently set the horse's hoof on the ground, reached over and placed the hammer on the stool next to him. He groaned as he stood up and stretched. Each time he shod a horse, he understood why blacksmiths ended up with back problems and was pleased he hadn't made it his career choice. Parker rubbed his hand down the mare's side and murmured, "Good girl."

As he stretched side to side, then backward and forward, trying to get the kinks out of his back, he let out a low grunt. The summer morning was becoming increasingly hot and humid. The air seemed to envelop everything around it with heaviness. Although the mare had stood quiet at the ties, she too was showing signs from the heat, her sides beginning to glisten with sweat. Parker leaned over and ran his hands under the horse's belly. "There you go, Magic," he said as he stood up again. "You're feeling the heat as much as me. It's gonna be a hot one today." Parker ran his hand down the yellow mare's head and then scratched around her ears. The mare raised her head, stretching it as high as possible waiting for Parker to scratch her favorite spot.

Parker scratched and Magic enjoyed. "How's that, big girl? You like that don't you?" he murmured to her. He stepped away from Magic and ran his eyes over the flashy mare, patiently waiting to be let out of the barn. Magic was one gorgeous mare.

A sudden quiver of anxiety ran through his body as he thought about the planned trip to trailer his prize mare from his farm in New Hampshire to his large horse farm in Florida. He usually didn't give a second thought to having sale horses transported down south, but this was his *favorite* mare.

To allay his unease, he reminded himself that this was not a one-way ticket for this quarter horse, and she would be back at his farm by the end of the month. Parker had shipped many horses to his farm in Florida where they were sold at a prestigious auction house in Ocala. He was a horse breeder and bred and sold the best American Quarter Horses this side of the Mississippi. His name and his farm, Saddleback Quarter Horses, were well-known throughout the quarter horse world, and his horses brought in big dollars.

Parker believed any horse foaled on his farm was a sale horse, but from the first time the yellow filly had stood on her wobbly legs, he knew he would never sell her. It was love at first site, and he knew immediately that the foal was something special. That was two years ago, and next year, Magic would begin his new quarter horse line. He had a long list of interested buyers waiting for her foals, and this trip to Florida would be the last time she'd be off the farm. Parker's love for Magic went beyond her monetary value. He had a special attachment for the stocky golden quarter horse, born at Saddleback, and although he had been offered top dollar from several buyers, Magic was *not* and would *never* be for sale. Parker had bonded with Magic as if she were his only child. Maybe that's the way it was with men without a family, and Parker, a bachelor, fit that mold perfectly. Although Parker had a farm manager and a team of workers at Saddleback, Magic was his pet project, and he handled her daily. He had traced Magic's pedigree all the way back to the Billy Horse line dating back to the 1800's, and he planned to carry on the prestigious genes through her. Parker's great grandparents had been Texans and their love for the American Quarter Horse was in his blood. He vowed that someday he would become a celebrated breeder of quarter horses, and now that dream would become a reality. Parker only bred the best bloodlines, and he had paid a hefty price for Magic's dam, but it was all worth it when Magic was born. Magic was now a huge part of Saddleback's future breeding program, and through her, Parker would begin an amazing line of quarter horses.

Parker grunted as he gave one last stretch to his aching back. It was time to turn Magic out with her friends. He pulled the red bandanna off his forehead and wiped his damp face. The headband was soaked with salty sweat, but it had done its job and stopped the flow of sweat from running down his forehead and into his eyes. He ran his fingers through his damp, thick brown hair, and then picked up his tools and walked to the back of the barn. Even the barn, always cooler inside, was slowly filling with the heat from the ever oppressive day. Large fans standing at both ends of the isle whirled full blast, but seemed to give little relief as the hot air settled into every corner. The heat wave had rolled in like molten lava, and as predicted, there wasn't a hint of a breeze in the air. Even the nights were hot and humid and offered little respite from the oppressive air. Climate change was on everyone's mind and people wondered if this was a bleak look into the future.

Holding the toolbox, he reached over and turned the knob of the tack room door. Pausing, he looked back at the golden horse, who acknowledged him with a low nicker. If horses could talk, Magic's nicker would have meant "bad idea," and for just a millisecond, those exact words passed through his mind as his hard blue eyes caught the liquid brown eyes of Magic.

Parker had learned the trade of blacksmithing as a teenager, working as an apprentice for a local farrier. At the time, he was always on the hunt for odd jobs, and he was an eager student and quick learner. He was obsessed with money, and as a youngster, he loved the jingle of coins in his pocket or the feel of a roll of bills tucked in his jeans, just itching to be squirreled away. Oh, how he relished the idea of having a stash hidden in a place where no one but he knew where it was or how much was there. It was a thrilling fun game when he was a youngster, but the obsessive compulsive behavior persisted as he grew older. The jingle in his pocket and a secret stash, that continued to accumulate, gave him the rush that spurred the behavior on. His youthful obsession with money created a desire for more and soon he was skimming money from every job he had. They were small amounts and never missed by the employer, but this criminal activity shaped him into a man who thrived on danger.

As a teenager, it was a challenge to see just how much money he could skim off a job, and a thrill to never get caught. Like any addict, his brain became hardwired for the risk, and then the reward. The longer he got away with skimming money, the more proud he was of the exploit. The adrenaline rush that came after the skim created a game he never tired of, but as an adult, the game generated riskier behavior and required more planning.

During his formative years, Parker believed he was entitled, and if no one noticed, so be it. He viewed other people as too ignorant or incompetent to even entertain his slick ideas, never mind have the chutzpah to do it. More than that, he consoled himself with the idea that he wasn't stealing. He deserved the extra money because he worked harder than other people. After all, it was only a few dollars. Parker wasn't greedy. He didn't live high, and the amount was so small that no one missed it. To his way of thinking, "If they don't miss it, they don't need it."

Although he had a fondness for horses and loved the hard work, he soon realized that his obsession for skimming would either lead him into a life of crime or a legitimate high-paying job. If anything, the back-breaking work gave him the incentive to excel in school, study tirelessly and kill the SAT's in high school. He graduated with honors and his penchant for math was rewarded with a full scholarship to a prestigious university where he majored in finance.

In college, his good looks and winning smile went a long way to build a trustworthy appearance. No one would suspect that behind the smile and the steely deep blue eyes lurked a man whose brain never rested as he planned the best way to skim money from his job. He worked several part-time jobs, and the challenge was always to find inventive ways to skim money. Whether it was a wait-staff position at a restaurant, a salesman or a landscaper, Parker's intent was to skim a little money here and there. As the years passed, his secret stash grew larger, but he never spent any of it. Just knowing it was there was enough for him. The skimmed money wasn't something he needed and the game was in the risk. To spend any of it would have made him feel like a common thief, and he never thought of himself as that. He consoled himself with the fact that it was only a game and not his way of life or who he really was.

Parker rationalized his obsession with skimming with the

belief that he didn't hurt anyone and it was only a game to him. What the heck. Politicians, bankers and millionaires did it every day and got away with it.

He did much more than a full day's work and asked for no more than a full day's pay. More importantly, he honestly believed he could stop at any time, but the quick release of adrenaline and the high after the skim, kept him going back for more.

After earning his MBA, Parker was recruited by a government agency, and after a short tenure, he was approached by the large financial firm Jefferson and Rooker. He became the rising star at the firm, and within a year, was elevated to the lofty position of Portfolio Manager for a group of major corporations.

It was the ideal career and cover for Parker, and it wasn't long before he was skimming small amounts of money from the large portfolios. More importantly, he learned how easily it could be done. His investment in horses, his skill as a farrier, and his boyhood friend had set the foundation for his audacious scheme to work. It was all too good and all too clever.

Chapter 2

*S*amantha Steele brought her white SUV to a stop at the top of the long, winding driveway that led to her farmhouse. She turned the car off, stretched her shoulders and, with a big sigh, opened the door and stepped out. She was tired and wondered what had ever possessed her to book the flight for her twins, Justin and Kristy, for 8 a.m.

Her daughter and son had asked her to book the early flight to Las Vegas, and she had conceded. The twins, in their second year of college, stayed with their dad Larson for the month after haying season and would return home the week before the college semester began. Sam hated booking flights early and vowed this would be the last time she did so. For one thing, her farm was an hour from the airport and with the required security checks she had to be sure the twins arrived well before the flight time, which meant they had to be out the door by 5a.m.

Flying used to be so much simpler, she thought as she walked towards the farmhouse. *And now, there are so many security checks, creating a long, tedious wait before the flight boards and you lose half the day.* She suddenly felt very tired. Yawning, she asked herself for the tenth time, "Why book early flights anyway?"

The minute she stepped out of the car, her goats Rudy and Roger called to her from their fenced in pen.

"Okay, Rudy. I hear you," she yelled to the goats, now bleating loudly. "I'll be right back and let you out."

She needed to pull herself together and wake up. The goats would have to wait. As she opened the kitchen door, a strand of blonde hair fell out of the red tie wrapped around her pony tail, and with one hand, she moved the wisp behind her ear. It seemed no matter how tight she tied her hair back, one strand was always slipping out, and rather than taking her hair apart and fixing the tie, she habitually pushed the loose strand behind her ear. Still grumbling to herself, she thought, *You have to get up early, drive to the airport, check in and wait. Oy! Never again!*

Hearing the door open, her dogs ran to greet her, jumping up and down in a frenzied state, each one demanding her attention. Tired as she was, she was in no mood to be pummeled by excited dogs, and she yelled, "Off! Sit! Stay!" Astonishingly, the dogs stopped their ruckus and obediently sat and waited for her next command.

"Well, that's something. Finally, you're listening," she said in amazement as she walked to the door and opened it for them to go out into their fenced in yard. They sat patiently, waiting for her command to release. She paused for a moment and then said, "Okay," and in a flash, they raced out of the house, onto the porch, down the stairs and into their large play area. In one quick move, Ranger picked up his ball and raced ahead of the other two frolicking dogs. Sam let out a sigh. It was Denver's idea to fence in an expanded area of their pen so that the three playful dogs could run off their energy. Watching Jazz and Sally chase after Ranger gripping the ball with his teeth, she said a silent, "Thank you" to Denver.

The early morning rush had been crazy, and she knew the twins would sleep on the flight. However, she was not able to go back to bed. She had a list of things that needed to be done, and number one was to phone her grandmother and let her know the kids were on the plane and she was home. Exhaustion was seeping through her body. A sleepless night was par for the course when she had to be up for an early flight. During the night, she had awakened every few hours thinking the alarm was ready to go off or that it had gone off but she hadn't heard it. Denver had offered to drive the twins to the airport, but she always wanted to see them safely on the plane and give them one last hug.

Sam walked to the refrigerator and took out a large pitcher of lemonade, wondering if she would ever think of her son and daughter as independent grownups. Rubbing her eyes, she opened the cupboard and took down a tall yellow glass from the shelf. Her mind was racing as she poured the cold lemonade from the pitcher, and for a moment she stood mesmerized watching it swirling in the glass. *I hope they're all set*, she thought. *And that they packed everything*. She took a large drink of the frosty lemonade, trying to wash away the queasiness that always filled her when the twins left home. The ice cold drink made her wince but it was just what she needed. *Is this the way all parents feel when their kids leave the nest?* She had often talked about her concern with her grandmother Minnie. Minnie had said that it wouldn't matter how old Justin and Kristy were, they would always be kids to her. Where did the time go? It seemed like only yesterday they were in grade school, and then, in a blink of an eye, they were noisy teenagers. Memories of those years flashed through her mind. Time seemed to have passed so quickly, but in her eyes they would always be just that—her kids. College students or not, she could not shake the feeling that if she just blinked, she would see them running through the kitchen door calling her name, "Mom, Mom where are you?" She blinked, feeling the tears beginning to fill the corners of her eyes. *I must be tired*, she thought.

"Stop!" she said aloud. "You are being overly sentimental. You have a new life and a new husband and the twins are living their lives. Be happy." She wiped her eyes and thought of Denver, and a rush of love swept over her. Denver was at a meeting in Boston. He would be gone for the day, but before he was on the road, he had taken care of all of the farm chores. Horses out, dogs fed, chickens out of coop, and her goats Rudy and Roger were fed and watered. *Husband*, she thought. She never dreamed she would say that word again, but she knew it was one of the best decisions she had ever made.

Last fall there had been a wedding at the farm. Samantha and Denver had tied the knot and the party went on 'til the wee hours of the morning. Sam's mother Marcel, who lived in Florida, attended the wedding with a new romantic interest on her arm. She introduced him as "Ben" and even though Sam had reservations about the dapper, gray-haired man, he appeared to be very attentive to Marcel, and Sam could not help but warm up to him. Her mother lovingly called Ben 'my big guy', and he seemed to bring out the best in her. She was warm and chatty and even Denver's parents enjoyed the wedding festivities with the Florida couple and Sam had to admit that this time her mother had chosen wisely.

Sam and her mother never had a close mother-daughter relationship. Although Marcel provided her with life's necessities, she was definitely not a warm, cuddly woman. As Sam grew older, she often wished she had a brother or sister to share her life with, but children were not something in which Marcel found pleasure with.

After all, as Marcel had told her countless times, "You were not a planned baby, but I made the best of it and hope you will always appreciate that you have had a wonderful home and a fabulous mother."

Sam could laugh about it now because she always had her grandmother Minnie in her life. She was the one who gave the big hugs and was Sam's best cheerleader. And it was she who insisted that Sam fill her life with what made her happy, and if that was horses, so be it.

As a grown woman, Sam realized that not every woman was meant to be a mother and even if Marcel hadn't planned on having a child, she had done her best to care for her. Marcel believed her responsibly for Sam was completed when she saw her off to college. Sam majored in journalism and after graduation; Marcel continued to voice her disappointment with Sam's chosen life style. Sam had woven pieces of what made her happy into a career that supported her family, but Marcel thought she should have aspired to be more than just a horsewoman, a journalist, and a part time college professor.

"Think big and focus," was Marcel's advice. "Horses are fine when you're young, but strive for more than that for your children. Set an example." Marcel would never understand Sam's goal was to live a simple life, and that included horses. "She takes after her father," Marcel told everyone. "Always on a horse or at the barn with a horse. I thought she would outgrow it, but like her father, she never did."

Sam's father, the love of her life, had passed away when she was twelve years old. Immediately after his death, Marcel sold their riding stable and moved to a condo. To help Sam work through her grief, she paid for the upkeep and board for her favorite riding horse Ginger. Eventually, Sam found peace with the loss of her father, but her love of horses continued and became a large part of her life. "Don't you think she should have other interests?" Marcel's friends had asked on several occasions.

"No, it's good therapy for her," Marcel had replied. This ended any conversation regarding her parenting skills. Marcel loved her daughter but it was always in her own way and on her own terms, and she didn't take kindly to anyone who questioned her relationship with her daughter. Marcel moved to Florida as soon as Sam left for college but Minnie, Marcel's mother, remained steadfast and was Sam's rock. Their love for each other filled all of Sam's needs. As reserved and self-absorbed as Marcel was, Sam was just the opposite. Minnie had passed on the silly gene to Sam and subsequently she could find something funny in most things. Marcel found Minnie outlandish and eccentric, whereas Sam found Minnie strong and funny. Minnie lived her life without caring what people thought, and found humor in most everything and everyone. She was positive and self-assured and people were not only attracted to the eccentric older woman, they honestly enjoyed being with her.

When she was a young girl Sam had asked Minnie where her mother was born and Minnie replied with a wink and grin, "I found her in a cabbage patch."

Sam giggled. "What? Did she look like my cabbage patch doll"

Minnie rolled her eyes. "No, it's just that she is foreign to me. You will understand why when you are older. She was either born in the patch or she was switched with another baby at birth. She's not like me, and you're certainly nothing like her."

As she grew older, Sam had to stop a smile from forming on her lips when she looked at Marcel. Once in a while her mother caught the look, the half grin on Sam's face. "What's so funny now?" she would ask. Sam had to look away because she could never tell her mother that she had the face of a Cabbage Patch Doll and that Minnie had told her she was born in a cabbage patch. Marcel would never find that amusing and it would give her one more reason to be annoyed with Minnie.

Unlike Marcel, everything about Minnie was fun. Whether it was her fashion style or the constant attention that elderly men gave her, she danced to her own music. She was quirky, quick on her feet, and she found that in most situations there was always something to laugh about. Marcel thought Minnie was embarrassing and out of control, but others found her fascinating. She loved being a fashionista, dressing in wild colored long shirts and black tights, and she owned a closet full of colorful sneakers to match the ensemble of the day. When not in sneakers, she donned a pair of flashy western boots and for good measure wore a fancy cowboy hat over her unruly curly hair.

The grand lady was always accompanied by her two best friends, Dottie and Doris. Doris, christened with the name 'the princess' by Minnie, was perfectly groomed for every occasion. From her shoes to her earrings, every piece of her apparel was the same color. She painted large clip-on button earrings with nail polish to match her dress of the day, and wore shoes the same color as her dress. If the shoes were too large for her tiny feet, no matter, she stuffed them with newspaper. Her hair was gray and puffed up high and each perfect wisp was held in place by a thick shot of hairspray.

Minnie and Doris, although best friends for years, loved to bicker. Doris harangued Minnie about her lack of dress style and Minnie found it amusing to call Doris "the princess."

Of the three women, Dottie was the most laid-back. Her loose, shoulder-length gray hair surrounded a pleasant face, and she wisely stayed in the background when Minnie and Doris were in a tiff. Dottie's outfit consisted of loose faded blue jeans and a simple shirt. Her only change of style in fifty years was sneakers. She switched from flat shoes to sneakers when Minnie showed her the AARP article featuring shoes, accidents, and the elderly. Less falls meant a longer life without fractures and Dottie agreed with Minnie and Doris that on most days they should wear sneakers. Unlike Minnie and Doris, Dottie owned only five colorful pair of sneakers. She was not and never would be a fashionista like her friends.

Every week, for as long as Sam could remember, the ladies came to lunch at the farm. And when needed, they were at horse shows or helping Sam with the twins at the farm. Eager to give advice and encouragement, they were always there, during good times and the not so good times. She called them "her other mothers" and each cherished the title Sam anointed them with.

Although Sam and Denver's wedding was supposed to have been a small affair, the plans had taken on a life of their own and Addie, Sam's best friend and wedding-planner, finally gave up.

The wedding celebration began at three in the afternoon and continued past midnight. Denver's family from Texas remarked they had such a great time and they vowed to return sooner than planned so they could visit with all of their new friends.

Sam and Denver had photos taken sitting on 'Yellow Beast', the tractor that was the bane of Sam's life, and everyone had photos taken with horses and barnyard pets.

The music kept everyone dancing on the wooden platform that Denver had built for the occasion, and the scrumptious food and never ending drinks made the celebration complete.

Lyla Bernhardt, Sam's friend, took over the preparation of

food, and long tables were filled with a smorgasbord of culinary delights. A three-layered wedding cake, filled with vanilla cream and strawberries, was the center of Lyla's presentation and there was much oohing and aahing over the abundance of mouthwatering desserts.

Minnie, Sam's matron of honor, was a smash hit in her long lacy pink dress and fancy pink western boots. Her hair was held back with a large pink bow threaded through loose curls. She looked as pretty as she felt and she danced the night away. What Sam admired most about her grandmother was that she was youthful in person and young at heart. Minnie stopped counting birthdays when she turned sixty-eight, saying that birth years allowed people to pass judgment on the elderly and create expectations that were ridiculous. She said she would prefer to look old for her age of never-ending sixty eight, rather than young for her age at seventy plus. Minnie lived by her own rules and that was that. To keep her weight at a number she was happy with, she exercised at the Senior Center several times a week and swam laps at the YMCA, believing the water kept her skin supple and young. Minnie was the perfect example of a woman who lived in the moment, and let the devil be damned.

Sam looked like her father. She was a slim, agile woman with a speckle of freckles across her nose. Her large blue eyes, bloodshot from lack of sleep, were set in a small face and fine lines next to her lips showed signs of a woman who laughed easily. She was dressed in her usual attire of jeans, a plaid shirt and short brown boots. Unlike Minnie, she was a casual dresser who made her statement with her inquisitive eyes and quick smile.

Walking to the cupboard, she pulled the tie from her ponytail and ran her hand through her loosened hair. She was tired. Her blond hair hung down to her shoulders and she scratched the back of her head where the tie had been. "Coffee," she said. "I need coffee." She reached in, took a yellow mug from the shelf and placed it under her single cup coffee maker. It was time for her favorite beverage and she needed it now more than ever. The lemonade had quenched her thirst but now she needed a caffeine kick. Next she popped a bagel into the toaster and took the cream cheese from the refrigerator. She was hungry.

Chapter 3

*C*arrying her coffee and bagel, Sam pushed open the kitchen door and stepped out onto the large wrap-around porch. She carefully set her yellow mug filled with hot brew onto the small table next to her favorite rocker. Once again, she stretched, and then, with a huge yawn, sat down and leaned back. Her mind was filled with visions of her beautiful fall wedding day, and she remembered promising herself to concentrate on those moments and store them in her memory bank.

Her mind drifted back to Minnie, the ladies, her mother, and her beloved twins. She thought about Denver, how well he fit into her life, how her twins adored him, and how much she loved him. She drew in a deep breath and slowly exhaled.

All is well in my part of the world, she thought as she sipped the hot nectar. As if on cue, the horses grazing in the upper fields whinnied and she turned her head towards them, then back to the dogs who were staring towards the flower beds that lined the fence. Sam focused her eyes in the direction of the dogs and sure enough, two gray bunnies were feeding on tender shoots of clover.

Her eyes followed the dogs and then moved to the bunnies. Sally was frozen in place staring at the intruders and lying next to her, Jazz and Ranger were not moving a muscle. Suddenly one of the dogs moved, and sensing danger, the bunnies quickly scooted under the fence and hopped towards the back yard.

"Well, kids, I guess bunnies win the battle of wits, and I can't help but be happy about that," she said.

The dogs, hearing her voice, cocked their heads and trotted back to sit next to her. She stretched again and looked beyond the large expanse of green grass where the bunnies had scampered to safety. Her eyes focused on the distant mountains that rose up beyond the pastures. The day was promising to be everything the forecasters had predicted. Warm, dry, slight breeze, wispy clouds and perfectly delightful were the words of the day. Sam placed her hand above her eyes to shade them from the sun and watched the clouds slowing floating east. Small puffs of clouds were taking on the shapes of animals. She caught the outline of a cat drift by melting into the shape of a bird, and then another smaller cloud bumped into the bird and formed the shape of a fox. Smiling she recalled the young girl, lying on her back in the tall grass of her father's hay fields , watching as the clouds took on animal shapes. When the twins were young, she showed them how to find animals in the clouds. On warm summer days she laid a large blanket on the ground and pointed out clouds moving across the sky melting into animal shapes. It became a favorite game to see who could find the most animals floating overhead.

The sharp bark from Sally yanked Sam from her daydreaming

and she sat up to see what caused the alarm. "Leave the bunnies alone," she said sternly. Sally stopped and immediately came to sit by her side. "Good girl," she said, patting the dog's head. "It's time to get going." She gave a weary shake of her head and glanced at the flower bed where the bunnies had been, then got up from the chair and picked up her empty coffee mug. "Life is good," she murmured. "But if I don't move, I'll sit all day and never get anything done."

Chapter 4

*I*t was Saturday, and Sam and Denver had just finished dinner when Sam's cell phone rang.

It was her friend Jan.

"Hi, Sam. Is this a good time to talk?"

"Sure. We just finished dinner. Is there a problem? You sound breathless. Is something wrong?"

"No, no. Nothing's wrong, but I have a huge favor to ask of you and Den." Jan paused.

"Go on," Sam replied, mouthing to Denver, "It's Jan."

"Well, one of my horse friends, *Phoebe*, I think you've met her, is friends with a state police officer. Last week, he was called to check on a horse someone reported running along the edge of Tinicut State Forest. It ran into the road and was almost hit by a pickup. The driver swerved just in time to avoid hitting it. He pulled over to the side of the highway, along with another car that had been following him, and called the state police."

"Wow! Lucky for him, and the horse, that he was able to stop. What a deadly thing that can be," Sam said catching Denver's quizzical look.

"I know," Jan said. The horse had on a halter with a broken lead line dangling from it. Anyway, they stopped and caught the horse, and she quieted right down and seemed happy to see people. They tied her to a tree and called the State Police. Once the trooper arrived. he phoned Phoebe to see if she could trailer the horse to her farm until they found the owner. When Phoebe got there, a palomino mare was quietly tied to a tree. Can you believe that?" Without waiting for a reply, she continued, "Phoebe loaded the mare onto her trailer and brought her back to her farm to wait for the owner to contact the police."

A past experience with a similar situation passed through Sam's mind. "Wow. That's insane! I'm sure someone was crazed to find their horse missing. I can relate. I remember when we searched the backside of the mountain for Tom's missing cows, not to mention chasing after my own. Remember how my cows made a habit of pushing through the fence to get to my neighbor's apple orchard. And everyone in this town has had a missing horse or other farm animal at one time or another, but I wonder how this horse ended up there."

The conversation had Denver's full attention. He had been leaning against the back of the chair sipping coffee, but moved forward and whispered, "What's she talking about? A run away horse?" He had a pretty good idea of what happened, from listening to the one-sided conversation, and it didn't sound good.

"Jan, I'm going to put you on speaker phone. Den is sitting across from me, and I think he's wondering what the heck we're talking about. Okay?"

"Sure, since my favor will also need his go-ahead," Jan replied.

She was actually relieved to know that Denver would be in on the conversation. He needed to be on board and she was glad to have his input. If they said yes, that would be a huge help for Phoebe.

"So what exactly do you need from us?" asked Sam as she pressed the speaker button on her phone.

Before Jan had time to answer, Denver said, "Hi, Jan. This sounds like quite the story. Tell me more."

"Hi, Den," Jan said without skipping a beat. "Well, a runaway horse will certainly pique your interest. It's a mystery to all of us how the horse got there. Have you heard anything about it?"

"No, this is the first time, but I've been busy and out of town for a few days. If anyone would have heard something it would have been the lady sitting across from me." His speech still held its southern drawl, although now it was showing signs of a New England twang mixed in. He winked at Sam.

As usual, she felt a flush spread to her cheeks. He loved to tease her. There was something about his blue eyes that captivated her, and whenever he winked at her, it always created the same response. The blush!

Sometimes she felt like a Pavlov dog in a lab. Denver winked and she blushed. She turned her head away, trying to hide her pink cheeks. Her hand moved unconsciously to pull a strand of hair away from her face and she tucked it behind her ear. For a millisecond, she lost the whole conversation. She reached for her cup of coffee and took a sip. A distraction. That's what she needed.

Denver's brows knitted in concentration. "So, are you saying, this horse was probably running free in the state forest for who knows how long and no one has come forward to report it missing?"

Jan took in a quick breath. "Yes, and that's why I need you and Sam to help out. Phoebe really needs to find another farm to keep the mare until the owner contacts the authorities. I've been out to Phoebe's to see the mare and she's one gorgeous animal, and for sure someone must be looking for her."

"Wait a minute," said Sam. She was right in her initial assumption. Jan wanted them to take the runaway. "Jan, before we say yes, Denver's right in wondering what this is really all about. Are you telling me that this happened last week and no one has reported the horse missing and that this horse could have been loose in the forest for longer than a week?" Sam was aghast. "You mean this horse just appeared out of nowhere?"

"Yes. Crazy huh? But this is what I was told. Phoebe thought she would have the horse for just a day or two, but now it looks like it could be longer. And this is where you come in."

"I see where you're going with this," Sam said, frowning as she pondered the bizarre story.

Denver had on his serious face. He was more interested in the runaway horse and who the owner was than reading into what Jan was asking. "What do the police say?" he asked.

"Well, Phoebe's been in touch with the State Police but no one has reported a missing horse."

"That's just plain weird," Sam interjected. "Someone owns this horse."

"I know," Jan said. "Phoebe thinks it's only a matter of time before she gets a call from the owner, or the police. Someone from the local newspaper interviewed her and took photos of the horse, but Phoebe is thinking that the horse is not from around here. And who knows how long she was running wild in the state forest. She was pretty scratched up but must have found some open grass areas to graze on because other than a little down in weight, she looks good. Phoebe had her vet check her out and he said she could have been lost in the forest for a couple of weeks. It's amazing, but the only thing she needs is a farrier. One of her shoes is loose."

"So, how do we fit into the picture?" Sam asked, knowing full well what the favor was.

Denver looked across the table at Sam and grinned. He knew where this conversation was going.

"Well, Phoebe did her good deed and brought the horse to her farm, but she has too much on her plate to keep her any longer. She has seven horses of her own, a riding school, and a herd of kids. I was thinking," Jan paused, "I know every now and then you take in a rescue horse. Would you have a place for this mare until someone claims her? It's a lot to ask, but it can't be much longer till the owner shows up."

Denver's mind was racing. A beautiful horse and no one has come forward? It just didn't sound right. "So, what's going on now with the search for the owner?"

"I wish I could tell you more, Den. You know anyone who's missing a horse usually calls the local police first. Word gets around pretty fast. I can't imagine that the owner isn't looking for the mare. We're thinking she's traveled further than we thought. Maybe this horse came from out of state. Who knows?"

"So, tell me again. How long has she been at your friend's barn?" Sam asked as she looked at Denver and mouthed, "Can you believe this?"

"A week," replied Jan. "Phoebe asked me if I could find someone else to take her. She thought she would only be at her barn for a few days."

Sam was silent, her mind racing trying to think of something else to say.

Jan took that for a yes, and rushed on. "For sure it can't be much longer before someone inquires about her. Someone owns this horse and I bet whoever it is, is really concerned. So, here's the favor," she pleaded. "Can you and Denver help out?"

Chapter 5

*P*arker's cell phone rang as he was leaving his office. He checked the caller ID. Sure enough, it was Luca. *Damn!* He knew he would have to answer it sooner or later. He couldn't put it off any longer.

"Hey, what the hell's going on? I've left some messages for you and didn't hear back. I've been expecting our last horse to arrive and it hasn't showed. Kept checking in with the barn manager and I'm kinda thinking something is wrong."

Parker could hear the tension in Luca's voice. "There's been a complication, and I'm working on it," Parker replied, pinching the bridge of his nose as he spoke. His head was beginning to throb.

"What kind of complication?"

"Seems like the horse went missing."

"What? How the hell did that happen?"

"Accident. Driver hit a deer. He unloaded the horse to wait for another rig and a huge semi flew by and spooked the horse. She broke loose and bolted into the woods...or I should say, the back side of a state forest."

"You gotta be kidding me," Luca growled. "Now what?"

"*Now* what, you ask? What the hell do you think I've been doing? That horse is my favorite mare and was supposed to come back to this farm after you got what you needed, and now I have no idea where the hell she is. What's more, I don't need your bull crap."

Luca tried to hide his anger. "Well, ya should'a let me know instead of keeping me in the dark, wondering where our package was."

Parker could feel a slow burn and knew he was going to say something he would regret. He held his anger back, knowing the ploy wouldn't work if he started cursing. No sense in getting Luca more riled up. "I'll get back to you as soon as I find out where my mare is. There's a lot of land between where she bolted and where she could be right now."

Luca wasn't about to let him go, and kept on talking. "So, how ya going to find her? Sounds like what you've been doing hasn't worked out."

Parker could hear the rage rising in Luca's voice. For a minuscule second, he paused, wondering how to calm Luca down without revealing too much about the missing mare. "That's my problem, not yours," he said through clenched teeth.

"Well, it sounds like it could become my problem. Ya know friendship only goes so far."

"You're not threatening me are you?" Parker was ready to take a swing at Luca. Good thing they weren't in the same room.

"No, no," Luca snorted. "Just find the damn horse so we can finish up our business, and I'll be out of your hair for good."

If Parker could have seen the smirk on Luca's lips, or read his thoughts, he would have been even angrier. He ended the call, his mind moving at warp speed. *This is going to be unpleasant*, he thought, massaging his temples and running his fingers through his hair. He expelled a deep breath, picked up his briefcase and walked quickly towards the elevator. Luca's snarky voice always made him ready to punch something. It was after hours and he was the only one entering the elevator. The doors closed and the elevator began to descend to the main lobby. He dropped his briefcase, leaned against the wall and took his cell phone out of his pocket. Tapping a number into the cell he mumbled, "Could things get any worse?"

The phone rang three times and a man with a gruff voice answered, "Hey!"

It was time for Parker's update on his latest contact with Luca, and it wasn't going to be pleasant.

Chapter 6

Little did Luca know, but Parker had already located his favorite mare. He'd scanned the internet for news where he thought the golden horse may have been sighted, and finally, *voilà*! A small-town newspaper ran an article and a photo of Magic. Now he was excited. But how should he get the horse back without ruining his operation and Luca's needed complicity? It was time to make a dramatic change in his plans. Luca was already antsy about the operation and he had to keep the sleazy guy on board with this last job. Six months was long enough to work the scam and it was getting too dicey to continue. Sure it had gone smoothly up to now, but Luca was no idiot and Parker's distrust for Luca was kicking in. So far, things had run perfectly, but this glitch had Luca on edge. Maybe Parker was being too wary, but if anyone had removed Magic's shoes and figured out what the numbers meant, he would have a lot of explaining to do. The dilemma was to get to the horse before Luca did something stupid, without putting his plan in jeopardy.

A flash of brilliance ran through his mind. He had to take the chance on bringing on an insider, and there was only one person he trusted for the job. This was not going to be easy, but he had no choice.

Bronwyn Dey had just nodded off to sleep when her cell phone rang. She immediately knew who it was without looking at the number. Only one person would phone her at this time of night—Parker. Her immediate reaction was both anger and curiosity. Of course curiosity won and she answered.

"Hello, Parker. Must be serious for you to call," she said with an edge to her voice.

"Please don't hang up, Bryn," he pleaded in a silky soft tone.

"Why would I do that even though I haven't heard from you in months?" she retorted. "For sure you must need something."

"Listen, I do need a huge favor, but it's not that I haven't been thinking about you all this time." He began pacing the floor trying to soothe the butterflies in his stomach just from hearing her voice.

"Yeah, sure you have," she answered with a yawn. "So, get to the point. What do you need?"

"I'm kind of in a jam."

"So, what's new? Explain." She was now wide-awake, sitting up on the edge of the bed. He had piqued her interest. It must be serious if he was calling her. After their last job, they had come close to becoming an official couple 'till they both chickened out. They were too much alike and too involved in their careers to take a chance on love muddying the waters. There was silence on his end. For a moment he was distracted picturing her in bed, auburn hair all messy, green eyes half asleep, and her quick wit testing him. Did she miss him as much as he missed her? He doubted it. If she did she would be with him and not in another state doing her own thing. For a moment he wondered if she was seeing someone else and if so, was he listening to their conversation. He should have asked if she was alone.

"Uh, are you alone?" he hesitantly asked.

"You don't think I'd be talking to you if I wasn't," she retorted. "Do you think I'm that stupid?"

"No, No. I don't, but I had to ask. After all, you have every right." Now the conversation was turning personal and he didn't want to go there. He needed her help, not her defensive posturing.

"Okay, skip the inquisition. Just what is it that you want from me?" Feeling her anger rising, she had to squelch the urge to hangup on him.

Parker knew from the sound of her voice he had asked the wrong question and he'd better get on with it before she hung up on him. "Well, I need your horse expertise," he quickly rattled out the words, "to help me retrieve my missing horse from a farm in a town next state over."

Chapter 7

*B*ronwyn rubbed her sleep-filled eyes. This was not what she needed, Parker back in her life just when she was moving on with Don. She lay back down and stared at the ceiling, ruminating on the conversation.

After Parker hung up, the snide remarks that slid from her lips bothered her, but at the time, she couldn't help herself. She hoped she didn't sound like a scorned woman. She had more pride than that. After all it was her decision, as well as his, to go their separate ways. What angered her most was the fact that he hadn't fought harder. Hearing his voice had incensed her and it took some time to finally listen to what he had to say without lashing out.

Forget falling back to sleep. She knew that wouldn't happen no matter how hard she tried. Parker's call had surprised her, and like it or not, just hearing his voice brought back memories she had closed the door on. When she finally stopped being a bitch and listened to the details of his latest job, and how the horse, vital to the scam, was missing, she was flabbergasted. What had seemed like a foolproof con was stalled and he was in a real quandary. He needed her help and he had thrown out the lure he knew she would take. Bryn's mind flashed back to her favorite horse on Parker's farm, a golden palomino named Magic. What were the odds that it was Magic that had gone missing? She was extremely upset that Parker had been that foolish to risk sending his prize mare to Florida, but when he explained why he had to she felt somewhat consoled. Now she couldn't say no to Parker. He had assured her that her only role in his grand scheme was to check out the farm where he believed Magic was.

She yawned and stretched again. Couldn't he have found someone else to do his bidding? More importantly, he had once again popped into her life and she was torn between anger and relief. Since their last time together, when they agreed to end their relationship, she wondered who the current woman was in his life. Bryn knew that he had his choice of sexy smart women and figured he would quickly move on. Why did she think about this now? She squeezed her eyes, trying to erase that thought from her brain. But there it was again, that old jealous feeling and she didn't like it.

What did she expect? She shook her head trying to erase the vision of Don's dark brown eyes, so trusting and loving. They had started dating not long after she broke up with Parker. Her friends called him her rebound, but she referred to him as her future husband. Don was everything that Parker was not. He was solid, dependable and more than that, in love with her. And he was easy on the eyes. He didn't have the rugged look that Parker had, but he was strong of character and devoted to her. She tried to block Parker's face from her thoughts, but she couldn't. It was the way he walked, the way he smelled and the amused smile he would give her when she said something funny. All of these things made her fall in love with him, and when he hugged her, he smelled of leather and horses and hay. Now that was a lethal combination for Bryn. She tried to erase Parker from her mind. "Stop!" she said aloud. "I don't want to even think about you. Damn you Parker! You are a distraction and a man I will never have. You are not worthy of me!" But even that didn't stop the rush of feelings that were propelling her right back to his arms, and once again she felt the magnetic draw he had on her. She pictured his face and how sad it looked when she told him that she saw no future with him. He tried to convince her to stay with him, but it wasn't enough. He didn't say the words she needed to hear. "I love you, and I can't live without you in my life." Was that too much to ask? She needed his assurance, not a marriage proposal. She waited for the words, but they never came. There was no, "I love you," instead he stopped, then choked out the words, "You know how much I love being with you and how important you are to me."

"That's it?" At first she was taken aback. She thought for sure he would beg her to stay. Then, the hot flame of anger rose from the tip of her toes to the top of her head. The snappy retort spit from her lips, "I am not just your some-time girlfriend. I want to be more than that and if I can't, it's time for me to walk away." Bryn had too much pride to stay with a man who could not love her the way she loved him. Once again he had hurt her and he didn't even realize it. To Bryn that was unforgivable.

She was proud that she had the strength to end their affair. It wasn't easy, but it was something she had to do. She didn't believe he was in love with her, and she doubted he would ever commit to a monogamous relationship. From the beginning, he had told her that marriage wasn't something he believed was in his future. Those words filled her with self-doubt. What if another woman came along and he left her? That was too painful to think about. She was never sure of him, and she was driven into a self-protective mode. This wasn't the first time she had made the decision to stop seeing him, and her biggest fear was that working with him again would compromise her resolve. Because of her own insecurities, she was apprehensive that he would be faithful to her. After all, he had never told her he loved her. And she had good reason to doubt him. When they worked their first job together, he nonchalantly told her he avoided commitment with any woman, and that he never saw himself as marriage material. Those words stuck. He blamed it on his life-style. She believed he used that as an excuse, and she would not allow her heart to be broken by a man who was unsure of commitment and what it meant. For once in her life, she thought with her brain rather than her heart. But still, that didn't stop the tingle in her stomach, the rapid heartbeat or the hot flush on her cheek, when she heard his voice.

Once again, she felt his strong attraction pulling at her, and she knew in her gut that he felt the same. She could hear it in his voice and knew he missed her. So, although she agreed to help him, she had insisted on the ground rules.

"Okay, I'll help you with this one job, but I do not want to meet with you ever!" She was adamant about that. They would only communicate via cell phone and if that wasn't enough she would drop out of the job and not help him. Parker was not pleased with her conditions, but he did agree. And although he needed her help, he had found a way of opening the door to the woman he could never completely walk away from.

Bryn thought back to the jobs they had worked on together. Their lives had been filled with intrigue and danger, throwing them into risky situations. This time, she would not muddy the waters with love. Besides, he had told her that this was a favor and one that would be simple and quick. Not like the intricate schemes they had been involved when they were a team.

Professionally and personally, she had moved on, or at least she had told herself she had. "Damn it! Now this! Why doesn't he stay the hell out of my life?" She never should have agreed to help him, although she did find his plan intriguing. A sudden surge of adrenaline welled up in her. It happened whenever she was on a new job and it was what made her feel alive. Taking chances and living on the edge. That's what propelled them together and that. was something she could understand. She consoled herself with the fact that their attraction to each other was brought on by working together on dangerous jobs. That made sense. "Deep breath," she told herself. "You know enough about love to understand the difference between comfort and challenge." Parker was all about gamble and conspiracy. That's what the attraction was, and she had deceived herself and labeled it as love. It was never love. It was all about risk. She felt better now that she had taken a hard look at their relationship and it was time to think about her next move. "What was Parker up to now?"

Bryn sat on the edge of the bed and moved her feet into her slippers.

Pug, her long-haired dachshund, padded over to her. He sensed her stirring and sat down next to her, waiting for her to get up. She reached down and stroked his head. "There you go, Pug. Good boy. I need a cup of coffee and more than that, I need to think about what I may have gotten myself into."

Chapter 8

*L*uca D'Angelo sat frozen on the chair staring ahead, his eyes glazed over in deep thought. The cords in his neck stood out, and he could feel his blood pressure rising. The call from Parker had blown him away, and he was not about to let this one go. First of all, he was fuming at the sudden turn of events and the missing horse story. And secondly, he was enraged that Parker hadn't told him immediately. After listening to Parker's shoddy explanation that their money horse had gone missing and he couldn't find her, well that was just too crazy. Most of all it looked like he wasn't even close to finding the quarter horse. Did he think he was that stupid? It didn't sound like he was searching very hard. Those horseshoes were worth more money than a thousand horses. Millions, to be exact! And how difficult could it be to find a horse running wild through some state forest? She had to come out somewhere.

That horse would've gone looking for another horse and

probably showed up in someone's backyard, he thought, rubbing his chin. His mind swirled with all the possibilities about why no one found the horse and not one hit the mark. Either the horse was dead or someone had found her and just kept her. She was a gorgeous animal, and who knows, maybe someone saw a prize fall into their lap and someone's loss was their gain. It's what he would have done.

Maybe Parker, his old buddy, was trying to pull a fast one on him. This last horse was going to end their six month partnership and then they were going their separate ways. Could it be that Parker decided to keep the last of the numbered accounts to himself and just lie about the missing horse? Or, if it's true, maybe he knows where the horse is and he isn't telling him. Luca's paranoia was beginning to get the best of him. He never trusted anyone and if it weren't for that chance meeting with Parker, his buddy from when they were kids, he wouldn't have taken on a partner. He always worked solo. But the pickings were too good to turn down. Easy money directly wired to an off-shore account. What could be better? He was ready to kick back and enjoy the fruits of his latest heist, and now this! It just didn't make sense.

Luca got up from the chair, walked to the fridge and took out a cold beer. He popped the tab and walked back, sat down and took in a deep slug, his mind still working on what Parker had told him. He could tell by Parker's voice that he didn't like the questions he had every right to ask. And then talking down to him, Luca D'Angelo, like he was an idiot, raised the hair on the back of his neck. When he questioned him more about where the accident occurred and the wooded area the mare ran in to, Parker wasn't as forthcoming as a partner should be. Then the next lie was that he had no idea how large the state forest was or how many towns and farms backed up to it.

"Big deal," he muttered. "I don't care what he says. The horse was bound to show up somewhere." For Luca everything was black and white and a solution was always at hand. He took in another swallow of beer and pondered more on the conversation. He didn't like it when he wasn't in control of a situation, and this fiasco was obviously one that Parker didn't want him involved in. Did Parker think he was a moron? What's he holding back? And exactly when did Parker learn the horse was missing? Why didn't he phone him right away? Something told him that Parker hadn't searched very hard, and he was pulling one on him. Again he thought about this being their last job. Just maybe Parker had kept the numbers to himself and never did set them into the shoes of his precious horse. And why did he decide to trailer his prize mare down to Florida when he had no plans to sell her? All the other horses had brought in top dollar at the prestigious American Quarter Horse auctions. Something wasn't adding up, and friendship aside, Luca didn't like the feeling of being conned. This last venture was the largest amount of money they had skimmed from the investment firm and he wasn't about to let it go.

"I guess I have to do the job myself," he said out loud as he drained the last drop of beer and tossed the can into a basket.

Luca may not have had a college education like Parker, but he was street smart and always one step ahead of the law. Short and built like a tank, he had a swarthy complexion and a large nose that showed signs of being broken from his many street fights. His thick arms, tattooed from shoulders to wrists, were strong and muscled and his short stocky bowlegs were deceiving in appearance. When he was a youngster, his olive skin complemented his white teeth but at forty, his dark small eyes had sunk into shadowed circles on his face. His face had a craggy look to it and his thick black hair twisted unmanageably on a head that seemed too large for his flattened nose and small lips. Interestingly, although his features were unappealing, somehow they melded into a somewhat attractive hard looking man. What he didn't have in looks he made up for in attire. He was a clothes hog and prided himself in his impeccable wardrobe. His pants, whether jeans or dress, were smartly creased and his trade-mark white shirts, opened at the collar, showed a well-muscled neck with a tattoo of a chain wrapping around the side of his collar bone running down onto his hairy chest. But for all of the fine clothes and the quick smile that showed a dimple on his left cheek, there was no doubt that Luca D'Angelo was a very dangerous man. He was wanted by the Feds for extortion and other criminal activity, but he had always slid from their hands just like jello from a spoon. Through just plain luck, or some of the best lawyers money could buy, Luca always got a free pass on his life of crime and never spent a day in prison. His ability to thrive in his life of crime made Luca an arrogant, overconfident conman who believed himself as untouchable. He deemed himself a Teflon Don and he had proved it more than once.

It was difficult to tell Luca's ethnicity, but he identified himself as Italian. Parker never believed it and thought Luca's single mother had changed her last name to give herself some respectability, but no one ever questioned Luca about his missing father or his lack of close relatives. Even as a kid, he wore a look that said "stay away."

Luca, clever in many ways, could have been a successful business man and legit if he had set his mind to it, but Parker credited Luca's DNA for his criminal career. Back in the day, he was Luca's only friend, their skimming addiction creating a strong bond and shaky respect for each other.

Luca loved living on the edge and conning was so ingrained in him that he fell into the path of crime and blackmail as easily as snow sliding off a hot metal roof. And he was no small potato in that field of expertise. He lived large, owned several homes, a fast speed boat, and was smitten with beautiful women. Gambling was his favorite sport and with a roll of the dice, he knew how to fix things to go his way. But by far, he believed that the job with his old pal Parker was the best skim yet. It was like taking candy from a baby. Most of Luca's illegal business dealings were complicated, and he had friends in places an honest person would never travel. It had been a long profitable journey, since he left the town that he and Parker grew up in, and he had made tons of money with some shady deals. This last sweet deal with Parker was one he was eager to complete and when it was over he vowed to find an island with gorgeous women and enjoy his new life.

Luca had an uncanny way of knowing how things worked, and he had several politicians in his pocket. And if they ever decided to double-cross him, he reminded them that he had a list with all of their names and all of their dirty business dealings coded with dates and contacts. The list was his personal life insurance policy. Lots of heads would roll and careers would be destroyed if they ever tried to two-time him. Flash drives made everything so convenient, and his saved list was hidden in a place no one would ever look. He was one clever dude, a pro, and he never made mistakes. Luca rubbed his forehead trying to clear his thinking. He ran his hand over his chin and thought about the grand scheme that he and Parker had worked on. Something told him that the missing horse spelled trouble. He had an uneasy feeling about this last huge play, but he wasn't about to give up the huge chunk of change he was due.

He got up from the chair and went to the kitchen to grab another beer. Popping the tab off, his mind ran through what his devious partner had told him.

Friend or not, Parker had better not put him in jeopardy of losing what was owed to him. Luca uttered a four-letter word and picked up the can of beer. Slugging down the cold brew, he knew it was time to take charge of the disaster. He set his half-filled can of beer on the counter and opened his laptop. It was time to do a Google search.

Chapter 9

Sam and Denver finished chores early so they would be ready for the delivery of the rescue horse. They had just put the dogs in the tack room and closed the door when they heard the sound of a diesel truck slowly winding its way up the long driveway. Denver left the barn and walked up the hill towards the house to give directions to the driver for unloading their new boarder. He watched as the pickup truck towing a black horse trailer expertly came to a stop next to the large turnaround. Denver walked to the pickup and spoke to the women behind the wheel, pointing towards the barn and paddock. She put her truck in gear and he headed back to wait with Sam.

Sam watched with admiration as Phoebe smoothly backed the pickup down the slight incline and stopped near the large turnout where the rescue horse would be unloaded. Sounds from the anxious horse, pawing at the floor of the trailer, began the minute the pickup came to a stop. The palomino stomped impatiently and whinnied, bringing return whinnies from the horses grazing in the field behind the barn.

The truck door opened and a pretty dark haired woman jumped down and held out her hand. "Hi, Sam, I'm Phoebe."

"Hi. I've heard so much about you from Jan." Sam smiled as she shook her hand. "This is my husband Denver."

Denver reached out his hand and with a big smile said, "Pleased to meet you, Phoebe."

"I'm so relieved that you're taking this girl," Phoebe said as she walked to the back of the trailer, Sam and Denver following. "She's one beautiful mare, and I can't believe I haven't heard anything from her owner. I'd be thrilled to keep her longer but just can't do it."

"I understand," Sam said. "It's a lot to take in a rescue, especially if you hadn't planned on extra feed and all that goes along with the care. Luckily, we brought in extra hay and have the room, so not to worry. She'll be fine here."

The yellow horse turned her head slightly and watched as Denver, Sam and Phoebe got ready to open the back doors of the trailer. She had quieted down, waiting for the next move.

Phoebe reached up, lifted the latch, swung open the back doors and stepped up and into the trailer.

Denver followed her. Yellow horse looked at Denver as if to say, "Let me out." Denver ran his hands over the side of the fine looking mare. "Hey there, girl. Aren't you a beauty! Sam, hand me the lead line, and I'll back her out."

Sam jumped up and into the trailer and gave Denver the lead. He clipped it to the mare's halter and backed her out of the trailer and down onto the ground.

The palomino looked around and gave another whinny to the horses standing on the hill. They had raced up from the pasture to see what the commotion was. She blew through her nose and pawed the dirt. They whinnied back, ran the fence line twice and then turned and loped back down the hill towards the lower field.

Denver ran his hand slowly down the mare's side and spoke quietly to her. "There you go, girl. How 'bout some hay and water?"

"What do you think?" Phoebe asked watching Denver with the mare.

"She's great," Denver said as he scratched the mare under her chin. "Real quiet and I can tell she has a good mindset. Someone has spent a lot of time working with this horse."

"She's been terrific at my farm. No problem. No vices and gets along with everyone. I hate to see her go, but for sure it will only be a matter of time before her owner shows up to claim her." Phoebe smiled, her eyes locked on the mare she had grown fond of. "To tell the truth, I didn't want to become too attached to her, and now you see why it would have been easy to do."

"I wonder what she's thinking," Sam said as she ran her hand down the mare's side. "She's stunning and her eyes are so soft and knowing. And look at her coat. It's beautiful! I love palominos and her coat is stunning. It glistens like gold. She has a magic look about her."

"Funny you should say that," Phoebe said. "I found the more I brushed her, the shinier her coat got."

Sam ran her hand over the mare's neck. "There is a breed, the Akhal-Teke, known for its gorgeous shimmery coat and I've seen a few quarter horses with a natural shine but this one is exceptional."

"I've never heard of that breed. Akhal-Teke, you say? Spell it for me and I'll look it up."

Sam carefully spelled out *Akhal-Teke* and Phoebe tapped it into her smart phone notes.

Denver studied the mare while the women talked. "My parents own a large quarter horse farm in Texas, and they have a sorrel mare with a coat that shines naturally. And all of her foals inherited the same type of coat. Dad gets big money for them and I'll tell you one thing, this mare here is a big money horse. Sam, hold the lead a minute."

Sam took the lead line and Denver walked around the mare, carefully examining her. He stopped at the mare's side, bent down, and picked up her back hoof. "Looks like she has a loose shoe. Our farrier is coming this afternoon and we'll have him take a look."

Phoebe walked over to Denver. "I noticed that, but thought her owner would show up by now. If I kept her any longer, I would have pulled her shoes. I will say, she gave me no problems. I would love to have taken her for a ride, but didn't want to chance it without the owner's okay. I had to keep reminding myself that she's not my horse."

"Don't blame you," Denver replied. "You don't want to ride a horse that's not your own. Why take any chances?"

"So, you're from Texas?" Phoebe asked remembering what Denver had said about his dad's farm. "I knew by your drawl you were a southern boy. I come from Virginia but graduated UMass, where I met my husband who also happens to be from Texas. We have friends and family in Dallas. So what's a Texas man doing in New England?"

"Now that's a long story. Let's just say I met someone who made it worth staying," he said as he shot a teasing glance at Sam.

Not to let it go by, Sam retorted, "Yup, and it took a New England girl to snag a Texas cowboy."

Phoebe laughed. "For sure we need to get together. My husband would love to meet another man who loves horses, and when I tell him you're from Texas, he'll have a million stories to tell you about how he worked on an oil rig one summer to earn money for college."

"Sounds like my kind of man," laughed Denver. "I'd like to talk to a guy who hails from the great state of Texas."

"Careful," Sam teased. "You're a New England guy now. He's even a Patriot's fan," she laughed

Denver winked at Phoebe. "Yup, but not when Dallas is playing."

Sam seized on the opportunity to tease him again. "I okayed that one. A man's got to do what a man's got to do. But if they're both playing at the same time, he watches in the other room, and I get all of the popcorn."

"Love it," Phoebe said closing the doors of the trailer. "Tell you what. I'll call Sam some time later in the week to see how the mare is doing and we can set up a time to get together. It will be fun."

"We'll for sure do that," Denver said. "But right now let's get this mare turned out. Sam, open the gate."

Sam walked to the gate and Denver led the yellow horse. Early that morning, they had prepared the turnout for the new boarder. A large blue trough was filled with fresh water and a pile of hay was set in one corner. Sam held the gate open and Denver led the mare in. He unclipped the lead line and the mare trotted to the hay pile. She pawed at the hay with her front hoof, moving it around on the ground.

The golden horse blew through her nose and then picked a strand of hay. Hay sticking out of her mouth, she surveyed the paddock, walked to the middle, pawed the ground again, and dropped down to roll.

"Looks like she feels at home already," Phoebe said, watching from the fence rail.

The big mare rolled to one side, grunted, rolled to the other side, then got up and shook herself off. She gave a kick and squeal and returned to the hay pile.

Denver stood back and studied the yellow horse. "She sure looks like she's ready to stay awhile."

Phoebe gazed at the mare she had become attached to. "Gosh, I hate to just drop her off and run, but I've got to get going. Kids to bring to soccer practice."

"No problem. And I'm looking forward to meeting your husband," Denver said, brushing the dirt from his jeans.

"Do you mind if I go in and say goodbye one more time?"

"Of course not. Go ahead." Sam understood Phoebe's urge. "Can't just drop off a horse without saying a last goodbye."

"I'll open the gate for you, Phoebe. Hold on." Denver opened the gate and Phoebe walked up to the yellow horse that had stolen her heart. She reached into her pocket and took out a horse cookie. Yellow horse gently took it from her outstretched hand. Phoebe kissed her on her soft velvety nose, and whispered a goodbye. Denver closed the gate after her. "By the way, Phoebe, before we forget," he said, draping his arm around Sam's shoulder. "Did you name her?"

"I named her Moxie. She needed a barn name."

"Moxie?" Sam repeated, grinning at the name. "What a great name. Let me guess why. She's dodged everything for some time and has shown a ton of courage. She's got a lot of moxie that's for sure."

"Good guess. The name came to me when I thought about how many near misses she must have dodged 'til she was found. It seemed fitting."

"So, Moxie it is," said Denver. "Kind of has a good ring to it."

Denver and Sam walked Phoebe to the truck and they were still chatting as she opened the door, climbed up onto the seat and turned the key to start the engine.

"Thanks for helping out and great meeting you both. I've heard so much about your farm and Curly horses from Jan."

Sam smiled. "Don't forget to call us when you and your husband can come by. You have my cell number. I know you said you contacted everyone about Moxie's move to our farm, and for sure, if I hear anything from the owner, I'll let you know."

"Thanks. That would be great. Hopefully, I'll see you soon," Phoebe said as she closed the truck door. She started the engine and headed up the hill towards the driveway.

Chapter 10

Sam and Denver waved to Phoebe as she drove down the driveway, then arm in arm, walked back to the paddock to see how their new rescue was doing.

"Gorgeous animal," Denver said, leaning on the rail scrutinizing the yellow horse. "I can see some excellent blood lines running through her veins. Always did like a solid quarter horse."

"She's a classy looking mare, but don't get too attached," Sam said. "It's only a matter of time before someone comes looking for her. To tell the truth, I find it interesting that no one has."

Denver draped his arm over Sam's shoulder and gave an affectionate squeeze. "I do too, but who knows, someone may be knocking on our door tomorrow and we'll learn more about her.

Dad would love this girl. She's everything a well-bred quarter horse should be."

"You Texans sure do love your quarter horses," she said as she tipped her head up and gave him a light kiss.

"Now that's the way to win a man's heart," he said as he kissed her back. "Tomorrow we need to have Don Shepherd pull her shoes. Looks like she has good feet so we'll probably leave her barefoot 'til her owner shows. I have a feeling if this horse could talk, she'd have quite the story to tell us," he laughed. "Imagine lost in the state forest, and then showing up on the highway. It's amazing that she's okay."

Sam bumped Den's arm with her elbow. "I told you she seems magical to me. Don't you wonder how she could have run loose for God knows how long, without getting hit by a car or truck? That alone astounds me and makes me wonder why the owner still hasn't claimed her. It just doesn't make sense," she said, heading to the barn to let the dogs out of the tack room.

"Seems crazy to me, too," replied Denver, walking beside her. "But I'm sure going to enjoy meeting the owner, whoever he or she is, and find out how this horse ended up there in the first place."

Denver opened the tack room door and was greeted by gregarious dogs running circles around him. He and Sam walked back to the paddock to take one last look at the mare, the dogs running helter-skelter between them.

Before they could stop him, Ranger made a beeline between the rails of the paddock and ran straight out to Moxie.

Denver whistled for him to come back, but too late. The dog was already sniffing the horse's nose. Moxie gently nudged the dog and then went back to eating her hay. That was enough for

Ranger. Curiosity filled, he returned to Denver and sat down beside him.

"Well, she's dog-friendly for sure. I like that." Sam bent down and patted Ranger's head, then leaned back on the rail to watch Moxie. "I wonder what her real name is. You know what? I think Moxie has a Curly horse disposition." Sam nudged Denver with her elbow. "Don't you think so?"

"Actually she does. But you compare every horse to a Curly. Good thing my good old horse Jet fits in."

"I'm only kidding, cowboy," she said playfully. "You know I love Jet. He's the best behaved, most lovable quarter horse I've ever been around."

Denver raised his eyebrows as he elbowed Sam. "And the best-mannered?"

"Of course," Sam knew where this was going

"And the most handsome?"

"For sure he is. But to be honest, you're better looking," she laughed

Denver felt a smile coming on but ignored it and kept on going "And aren't you lucky I'm willing to share my horse with you and allow your horses to be in the same field with him?" He was holding back a chuckle but his eyes said it all. He was enjoying this.

"Alright! I give."

"Okay, say it," he said turning her around, looking into her blue eyes. "Say it or I'll race you to the house, and if I win, you have to cook my favorite dinner every night for a week."

"Okay, okay. Every horse has its own special traits. I'm just addicted to Curly horses." In a mock movement of exasperation, she whipped her arms up in the air and then dropped them to her side. "I can't help myself. I'm addicted! I admit it. Darn it! I'm addicted to Curly horses."

"Good. It's a great thing to admit an addiction," Denver teased. "Don't you feel better now?" He was trying to hold back a laugh, but it was becoming nearly impossible.

"And why are you smiling when I admit I'm addicted to Curly horses?" She grabbed his arms and squeezed them as she looked into his crinkled eyes.

"Because I can't look at you without smiling," he said as he drew her into his arms. "You just make me smile."

Then she couldn't stop laughing. Taking in a breath, she wiped the tears from her eyes and said with determination, "But a Curly horse does get a few extra points in my book. No apologies there."

Denver rubbed his chin and frowned in fake exasperation. He gave an audible sigh. He couldn't help himself. The woman bedazzled him. Once on a roll, she always got in the last word. He had to give it to her. With just a smile she could lighten even their most serious conversation and that made her special. But most of all, it was her willingness to listen to what he had to say and make him think he was in charge, even when he wasn't, that made his heart melt. His Dad had taught him well. What to let go of and what to take a stand on. And as always, their back and forth teasing was what he loved most. "Alright, I'll give you that, but in my opinion, it's not just the horse pedigree that determines the behavior. It's the training and breeding program that count the most."

"Agree totally," she said amused

Darn, she did have the last word. Now there was nothing left to say, but he kind of liked that.

He turned his head towards the yellow horse and his eyes

wandered over her stocky body. There was nothing more he appreciated than a fine-looking horse.

"So what's your thought on this mare?" Sam asked.

"I think she's one great-looking horse, and if I were to cross a Curly horse with another breed, I would look at this line. Wonder if her owner has her sire?"

Sam smiled, jabbing her elbow into Denver's side. "Stop it. We have our Curly stallion and that's enough. And I bet the owner is heartbroken and must still be searching for the mare. The state forest is huge, and if she was trailered from another state, her farm could be a long distance from here."

Denver kicked the heel of his boot, thinking about the owner. "True enough. Maybe we need to put out more publicity on her."

"What's the matter with your boot?" she asked.

"Stone," he said leaning down and pulling a small pebble from the sole of his boot."

"Must have happened in the driveway," Sam said looking at the boot. "But back to publicity. Jan did tell us that her town newspaper put a photo and short article on the front page and that the local TV station did a small piece on her. But most of the hype happened right after she was found on the highway. Jan also posted it on Facebook and asked everyone to share it. I think I'll work on getting more information out and see if we can drum up more interest. Don't know what else to do, but if we're lucky, maybe the owner is searching on-line as we speak."

That afternoon, the farrier pulled Moxie's shoes, and shortly after, Sam phoned her Vermont friend Addie Andris. She told her the whole story about the rescue horse and explained how the mare had ended up at their farm. But, more importantly, Sam asked for her thoughts on the horseshoes that her farrier had pulled. She excitedly told Addie how, on closer examination of the unique shoes, they found numbers stamped in them. "Put your thinking cap on, Watson. Why do you think someone would stamp numbers into horseshoes? And, by the way, they are not like any shoes you or I have ever seen. Even our farrier Don said he'd never worked with shoes like that or knew anyone who stamped numbers in them."

Addie and Sam were long-time friends. Their friendship began when their children were youngsters, and they had become close confidants, bonding through their desire to introduce American Curly horses to the equine world. Three years ago, they had teamed up to uncover the purpose of a secret lab at a farm in Vermont. Solving the mystery, they now kiddingly called themselves Sherlock and Watson, and Sam knew if anyone could come up with an answer to this stumper, it would be Addie. They were two peas in a pod when it came to tackling mind-boggling situations. Their love of mystery novels and whodunit movies made them confident that in another life they would have been private detectives.

"Listen, Sherlock, I need to see the shoes myself, and then I'll be able to help."

Sam had to hold back a laugh. She knew she had hooked Addie into the mystery of the numbered horseshoes. "So, how soon can you be here, Watson?" Without a doubt, she knew her curious friend would bring her sound reasoning to help untangle the conundrum.

"Is tomorrow too soon?"

"Are you kidding? I can't wait." They talked a few minutes longer before Sam clicked off the phone and did a happy dance. Her next call was to Lyla to tell her that Addie was coming for a visit. Lyla, her friend and owner of a bakery and deli, insisted on providing lunch and dessert.

Chapter 11

True to her word, early the next morning, Lyla stopped by the farm and dropped off Addie's favorite chicken broccoli casserole, a bowl of salad made from her thriving garden, and a freshly baked strawberry rhubarb pie. It was Lyla's way of giving back to her friends who stood by her when she had confided to them that she had stolen a Mini horse, she believed she was saving from the mysterious Pine Hollow Farm.

Denver was away on a business trip and Sam busied herself with morning chores. She wanted to be ready for Addie's visit and a leisurely lunch. She was dead set on having all chores completed and nothing left to do but talk about the rescue horse and her strange horseshoes.

Luckily, Yellow Beast purred like a kitten and everything went smoothly. She threw hay in the corner of the corral and turned the mares and foals out. Next, she opened Rudy and Roger's pen so they could romp and play outside before she caught the little devils and closed them back in before Addie arrived. She left the stalls till last, turning the barn radio up so that she could sing along. The dogs followed close behind while she worked mucking stalls and getting the feed ready for the evening.

There was always something to do on the farm, and it was at these times, she missed Denver's help. Her last trip before returning to the house was to the chicken pen where she gathered eggs, reminding herself to give Addie a carton before her trip home. Within two hours, she had completed chores, penned the exuberant goats back up and headed to the house.

After a cold glass of water, she retired to the porch and sat down on the rocker. She put her feet up on the stool and leaned back. Her mind ran in a million directions, but there was nothing to do but wait for Addie.

It was difficult to quell her excitement and she was eager to show her the horseshoes, knowing she would not be coming this soon if she didn't have the same fire in *her* belly. They were a perfect team and she knew Addie was as curious as she was about the horseshoe riddle.

There was a missing piece to the puzzle and it was time to put their thinking caps on. Just as they had solved Lyla's whodunit, they *would* decipher this mystery. One thing for sure, she knew that Addie would have the same questions she did about the rescue horse and her numbered shoes.

The table was set and ready for lunch when the dogs alerted Sam to the crunch of tires on the gravel driveway approaching the farm. Before the vehicle came to a full stop, the three dogs were at the car, dancing in place, excited to greet their old friend. Addie stopped her car and waited for Sam to fetch the dogs so that she could park. Sam walked quickly towards the car and grabbed Jazz by the collar and gave the firm command, "Home!" The spirited dogs retreated from the driveway and returned to the house.

Addie backed into the parking place, turned off the engine and stepped out of the car. Both women hugged, excited to see each other.

Sam stepped back and looked at her longtime friend. "Oh my God, Addie. It's so great to see you. I'm so happy you're here and what's with the new do?"

Addie laughed. "Like it? Time for a new look. It's always been easier to have longer hair so I could tie it back and keep it off my face and I can still do that. But I got sick of the same old same old. Jace loves it and Eden says I look ten years younger." Addie ran her fingers through her hair, fluffing it out in an exaggerated shake of the head.

Jace was Addie's new man and Eden was her only daughter. Addie's shoulder length wavy dark hair was layered and highlighted and the light blue shirt she wore enhanced her olive complexion and dark brown eyes. One look at Addie, pretty and confident, was all it took to understand *who* she was. Her toned body and slightly muscled arms and legs, were the result of working every day at her farm.

Sam admired and respected Addie. It took dedication and resilience to bring up Eden and to run a large Therapeutic Riding Program. She was a self-made woman and nothing stopped her from reaching her goal when she set her mind to it. At her Vermont farm, she bred, trained and sold American Curly horses and ponies. A widow, her husband and love of her life had died when Eden was a baby; and although she had many offers for a long-term relationship, she preferred to live alone and take care of her daughter. Sam believed that Addie was the most amazing woman she knew and was thrilled when Addie had met Jace, the man who finally captured her heart. Jace was a perfect match for Addie and he made her happy. Of course, Addie who adored Denver, her gold standard for a husband, said Jace had to pass his approval before she moved on with the relationship.

Denver and Sam met Jace at Addie's farm and immediately saw how smitten they were with each other. Sam could hear wedding bells in the near future.

"I love it. Of course with your olive skin and brown eyes, anything would look good on you. Maybe I should try a new look. Wouldn't Denver be surprised? I've had this shoulder length blonde hair since I can remember. Maybe I'll color it red. I always did like auburn hair." She chuckled

Addie lifted her eyebrows in mock surprise. "Don't wreck a good thing. Your blonde hair is to die for, and besides, it would be a pain to grow out if you hated the color. If you're going to do anything, I saw on TV that pastel-colored hair is in. One woman had pink and the other some kind of blue. It looked kinda cool, so if you're going to go crazy, try one of those colors."

Sam rolled her eyes and raised her eyebrows. "Hmm. Let me think about it, and I promise, you'll be the first to know if I go pastel. But enough about us, although it's never really enough. How are Jace and Eden?"

"They're great and told me to give you a big hug. Jace is busy working on a new account and Eden is taking care of things until I get home. She can pretty much run things by herself and of course, Jace is there to help out. So, I'm all set for a relaxing couple of days. All kidding aside, Sherlock, it's good to be here.

I've missed you, not to mention Lyla's desserts. And as you reminded me more than once, it was my turn to visit. Besides how could I refuse to help solve another mystery? For sure you've piqued my interest with another one of your whodunits. By the way, where is my favorite cowboy?"

"Denver had to leave on a business trip, but he'll be home tomorrow. I invited Lyla for lunch but she couldn't get away. Of course she dropped off your favorite casserole and dessert before she opened her bakery. She said she'd stop by after closing and have coffee with us."

"It'll be great seeing Lyla. It's been a while. And at least I'll get to see Den before I go home. I miss my cowboy," Addie teased, reaching into the back seat of her car and grabbing her overnight bag.

"Of course you'll see him," Sam said. "And guess what? I heard from Chet. He's trailering horses up to Maine and he's stopping by later on today on his way home to Virginia."

Addie flashed a smile. "Now I'm in heaven. I haven't seen Chet in a couple of months. He usually stops at my farm if he trailers horses up my way. And if I sell one of my horses to someone in a state along his route going home, he trailers for me. It works out well for everyone and I get a chance to visit with him. I love that guy."

"For sure Chet has his fans, but we're his biggest. I remember the first day I met him how star struck I was. He was the spitting image of Willie Nelson and his voice even sounded like his. I still answer his calls with, 'Hi Willie' and he answers with 'Willie here.' Every time I play my Willie Nelson music I think of him. Do you think Willie has a twin and doesn't know it? Maybe I should ask Chet to check that out."

"I remember when you told me about Chet," Addie said. "I thought you were kidding until I met him."

Sam gave Addie a sideways look. "By the way, Watson, does it take another mystery to get you to come for a visit?"

Addie failed to suppress a grin as she opened the trunk of the car and took out a bucket filled with soil and the nub of a green plant. "Truthfully, Sherlock, it did help, but besides the fact that you piqued my curiosity, I've really missed you. And as a special gift to my best friend, I brought a start from that pink rose bush you admire every time you visit." Addie dropped the bucket on the ground and closed the trunk of the car. "It's been growing all spring and it's ready to be set in the ground."

Sam's smile went ear to ear as she bent down to examine the small plant. She was surprised Addie remembered how much she admired the pink rose bush. "Oh, Addie. Thank you *so* much. I love it. You're the best and I have just the spot for it. She laughed as she picked up the bucket and they walked arm and arm toward the house. "You know, Addie, I think we have really good instincts for solving mysteries."

Addie nodded her head in agreement. "What's more, we were almost right about Pine Hollow farm. Of course, the best thing that came out of that whole adventure is that Lyla's happy with her new bakery and her Mini horse, GiGi. So, tell me about your new brain-teaser and all about your newest boarder?"

Sam's face turned serious. "Honest, Addie, this is totally different." The words tumbled from her mouth. "No one has asked for my help, but it's something that has made me suspicious. I have an idea that something sinister is going on and I need your honest opinion to let me know if it's my overzealous mind or... just maybe... my instincts are right on." Sam took in a quick breath and waited for Addie's reply. They reached the porch and Sam pushed the screen door open with her shoulder and then held it open for Addie.

"I guess I need to know more before I can give you an honest answer. Have you told Denver about your hunch?" she asked as she dropped her shoulder bag on a chair.

"No, I didn't say anything yet. I wanted you as a backup before I tell him this feeling I have. You know how my mind works when something doesn't look or sound right? Call it my gut instinct but I can't help but think that something isn't right with this rescue horse." Sam's eyes narrowed and she put on her serious detective face. "Hey, wait a minute. Maybe that's my calling. Instead of writing pieces for magazines and teaching part-time, I should begin writing mystery novels."

"That's a thought," Addie chuckled. "I've always wanted to know someone famous and if you put your mind to becoming a renowned author, I could travel with you to all of your book signings and hold the page open for you to sign your name."

Sam raised her hands in an enthusiastic hurrah. "What an excellent idea! I need to stop working right now and write mystery novels." The idea sparked instant laughter.

"I can just picture it." Addie put on her best fake smile and pretended to pose for a photo. "Your name in lights, and of course me standing right beside you."

"Oh yeah, you mean peeking over my shoulder to get your face in the picture. A photo bomb! You have been known to do that more than once."

Addie was finding the whole idea hilarious." She couldn't stop laughing at the thought of the book signing events and her mind was running with the crazy notion.

"Oh my goodness! You are too funny! Stop it!" Sam wiped the tears from her eyes. "And who will take care of your farm while you're on the road with me holding the page open for me to sign?"

Addie thought a moment, wiping tears from her eyes. "Well, there's Jace and Eden, but with all of your notoriety and money, I could hire someone to run my farm. Wait a minute. Another thought. We'll have so much money from your best sellers we can have Den, Jace and Eden travel with us and the twins can meet us wherever your book signings take place. We can all travel the country on your dime."

Sam raised her eyebrows in mock wonder. "I get it. So, I'll do the writing of these best-selling novels, and because of my undying love for all of you I get to support everyone?" She smirked. "That sounds fair to me."

Addie wiped her eyes. "You got it, Sam, and best of all, I'll help with the plots. All you have to do is start writing, and I'll be your assistant." They were on a roll. The scheme to gain fame and fortune through Sam's career as a mystery writer grew larger and funnier each time they expanded on the crazy idea. As often happened, Addie and Sam were a comedy duo, each one playing off the other.

"Enough! I can't take it anymore." Sam was holding her sides which were hurting, from laughing so hard. "As much as I love the idea of *me* working and *you* all living off me, I have a better idea. We could work on getting Chet a gig as a Willie Nelson impersonator. That would open the door for us to be a part of something big."

Addie rolled her eyes. "No, it would never work and for one reason only. Remember, he *can't* sing."

The truth didn't stop Sam from continuing with the wild idea. "He could lip-sync. Wait! That wouldn't work. With our luck the recorder would die in the middle of a song. Guess it's up to you and me to make our fortune."

Addie nodded in agreement. "True, but right now we have another mystery to solve. Sherlock and Watson are on the case. We need to get working on what's staring us right in the face. Let's call it the horseshoe mystery."

"Hmm, I kinda like the ring to that name. I say we have a glass of wine and toast to our next mystery." Sam got up and headed to the refrigerator.

"A glass of wine works for any reason." Addie walked to the wine cabinet and took out two glasses while Sam uncorked a cooled bottle of Riesling.

Sam poured the wine into the glasses Addie had placed on the table. Raising her glass she said, "To Sherlock and Watson and our horseshoe mystery." She tapped her wine glass to Addie's and took a sip of the cool liquid.

"Oops! Another toast," Addie said. "To best friends." They clinked glasses again, took another sip of wine then placed their wine glasses back on the table.

Addie began filling the salad bowls while Sam went to the oven to retrieve Addie's favorite casserole. "No one can make a casserole like Lyla," Addie said, giving an exaggerated sniff towards the oven.

The conversation turned to Lyla, her bakery, and her new life. She, and her Mini horse GiGi, became the topic of discussion. They were both so proud of what she had accomplished and were happy they had a big part in it. After a leisurely lunch, Sam leaned back in her chair. "I am so stuffed but my mouth is watering just thinking about Lyla's pie. Let me get it," she said, pushing her chair from the table.

"I think I can squeeze in a small piece." Addie picked up the Christmas napkin, carefully examining it before she wiped her mouth. It wouldn't be summer without Christmas napkins on Sam's table. "I see you still have leftover Christmas napkins. Maybe you shouldn't buy so many for your Christmas Eve party."

Sam was rummaging through the drawer looking for the pie server. "Oh, I got those on sale after Christmas. I couldn't resist the red cardinals. I was going to put them away until Christmas Eve but what's wrong with using them now? Just a little snow on the branches is nothing. Buy one get one free, so I loaded up. I have some with snowmen, but I'm trying to save them."

"Always looking for a bargain aren't you? I need to remember to do that."

Finding the pie server, Sam carefully carried the pie to the table and set it down.

Addie leaned over and took in a whiff of the pie. "Wow! This looks so delicious, but to tell the truth, I'm too stuffed to appreciate it. I have an idea. I really want to see those horseshoes and the rescue horse you've been oohing and aahing over. Let's wait for dessert and coffee till we come back from the barn."

"Okay, Watson, let's go. Sherlock and Watson are on the case." Sam placed a mesh food cover over the pie, and drained the last of her wine. "We're off to solve another mystery. Now all we have to do is put our heads together to figure out what the numbers on the shoes mean and list all of the possible reasons that the owner of this fabulous mare hasn't shown up to claim her. Easy peasy!"

Chapter 12

Sam and Addie ambled toward the barn, chatting along the way. They had a lot of catching up to do and there was no pause in their conversation, which covered everything from horses to kids. Every now and then, they stopped to admire some of Sam's flowers. The beds were exceptionally beautiful this summer, and Sam offered to cut a bouquet for Addie to bring home. They often exchanged perennials from their gardens and the last time Sam was at Addie's farm she had given her a root from her rhubarb plant, the largest rhubarb Sam had ever seen. It was now thriving in her garden and she had made several strawberry rhubarb pies with the large stalks. She had given Lyla a piece of the root, and she planted it in her garden. Lyla's root grew into a huge plant with giant stalks, and her rhubarb custard pies were a specialty at her bakery.

The barn doors were closed to keep out the heat of the day, and as Sam slid them open, all of the cats came running to greet them, except for Mia who was lying high on a tall stack of shavings.

"Wow, you have a happy group here," Addie said as she bent down to pet the gray cat rubbing her leg.

Hearing the barn doors slide open, a mare enjoying a siesta pulled herself up from her bed of shavings and briskly shook her body. She nickered, waiting for a cookie treat from Sam.

Addie walked to the first stall, reached in and ran her hand over the mare's velvety nose. "Hi, Tama, and who is this beauty next to you?" Addie reached down and touched the head of the foal beside his mom.

The colt next to the striking black mare was enjoying Sam scratching under his chin. "Isn't he a beauty?" She ran her hand under the colt's thick curly mane. "His name is Angeni, which means spirit in Native American language."

"So, I know you will never sell Kai, Tama's first black filly, but is this colt for sale? He looks like once he sheds his baby dark coat, he'll be solid black. He's very good-looking."

"Well, that's true, I'll never sell Kai. After the coyote attack, I kept Kai with her mom longer than any of my weanlings, but I knew she needed more time to heal. And I didn't breed Tama back, so Angeni is only her second foal. He's every bit as beautiful as his sister, but I can't keep every horse born on my farm. What's the point of breeding if you're not selling?"

"I agree," Addie said, her eyes analyzing the handsome colt.

Sam drew in a quick breath before continuing. "My friend Diane told me about a breeder who never could part with any of her weanlings or yearlings and it got out of hand. She ended up with too many horses to care for. If I ever stop selling, I'll stop breeding. I don't believe in breeding horses and have them end up at auctions. That's just too horrible."

Addie knew better than to interrupt Sam when she talked about the senseless breeding of horses, and she listened intently while she scratched the back of the black colt. "Okay, I get it and I agree. There are lots of rescues out there, so we don't need to produce more horses unless we are sure there's a market. But before you say anything more, I'm very interested in buying Angeni."

"Really? You have so many gorgeous Curlies on your farm."

"True, but I love this colt. Remember how you fell in love with Kahasi when you came to my farm? That's the way I feel about this handsome guy."

"Gosh, Addie! I'm taking this as a huge compliment for my breeding program. You are so far ahead of me with your program, and I can't tell you how happy this makes me. Without a doubt, you are first on my list, and I only say that because I want you to think about it. You may change your mind."

Addie snickered. "Now, when have I ever changed my mind about a horse? A man, yes. But a horse? Never."

Sam found just the opening to tease Addie and she raised her eyebrows in mock disbelief. "Oh, I think you've found the man you haven't changed your mind about, and his name is Jace Andrew."

Addie's face beamed. "Well, maybe you're right. He does fit into my life the way no other man ever has."

"So, does this mean I'm going to be *your* wedding planner? Remember how you took over my life and set my wedding date and planned *my* wedding? I think this is going to be a fun night, and I am going to take out my calendar and set your wedding date for next year."

Addie laughed. "I guess when they say payback is hell, I now know just what they mean. Sam, I'm not ready for marriage yet. Jace and I are taking it one step at a time. First I want a ring on my finger, but now that you've cornered me I need to tell you something exciting. Jace has hinted he has a special birthday gift for me and I think it's the diamond ring we looked at last month."

Sam's eyes almost bulged out of her head. "You looked at rings? And just when were you going to tell me this?"

"I was waiting till later to break the news." Addie couldn't hold back her excitement. She had wanted to surprise Sam, but the words tumbled from her mouth. "I'm truly in love with Jace and he is with me. I never thought I'd find a man to love as much as I loved Andy, but Jace is one great guy, and I'm *crazy* about him. Eden is so excited and I promised her I would tell you. To be truthful, I was going to wait until I had the ring on my finger and then invite you and Denver to the farm to celebrate."

Sam did a little happy dance, then hugged Addie, and in a flash, they were both doing the happy dance.

Once the happy dance ended, Addie stepped back and said, "Enough, already! Where are the horseshoes? I want to see them and I can't wait a minute longer."

"Thought you'd never ask. Come with me, and after that, I'll show you the rescue mare." Sam walked briskly to the tack room to fetch the shoes.

Addie's attention turned to the cats, one circling her and the other rubbing her leg and purring. She bent down and ran her hands over the gray cat. The cat lifted her back in pleasure, begging for more. The sister cat rubbed against her leg, eager for her turn, each one vying for Addie's attention. After petting each of the cats, Addie followed Sam to the tack room, reaching it just as Sam walked out carrying two horseshoes.

"Here they are," she said handing one of the shoes to Addie.

Addie turned the shoe over to examine it. "Wow! These are classy-looking shoes, and for sure they are not the sort that most people use for their horses." She held the shoe up to the light, turning it over again. "I bet they were specifically made for whoever owns the horse. They look very expensive. And I see what you mean by the numbers. Someone knew what they were doing. That's for sure. Now I understand your curiosity."

"Let's take them outside and have a better look," Sam said

"Agree. I really want to examine them both up close."

They strode quickly to the front of the barn and out into the sunlight. Sam pulled the barn doors closed. "I have an idea. It's really hot out here. Let's go look at the yellow horse and then bring the shoes back to the house. We can have something cold to drink and examine them on the porch."

"I like that idea. Let's check out the mare that has you so excited. She must be very special to wear these shoes."

Sam lifted her sunglasses from off her head and put them on. "It all shouts money, doesn't it? This is why we can't figure out why we still have the mare and the owner hasn't come forward. Something isn't right, but now that I have the sharp wits of Watson to help, I'm sure you'll find some clue we missed."

Addie removed her sunglasses from her shirt pocket and put them on. "Lead the way, Sherlock."

Chapter 13

Sam and Addie took a quick look at the yellow rescue horse and then returned to the house. It was too hot to linger for very long, but Addie had the same opinion that Sam and Denver had. Moxie was not an average horse and was probably worth a lot of money. Addie was as puzzled as they were. Why hadn't anyone claimed the beautiful mare?

The sun was blistering hot and they were both dripping with sweat by the time they got back to the house. It was a pleasant relief to enter the air-conditioning. This time, the dogs didn't get up to greet them, preferring to stay lying on the cool tile. The heat had done a job on Addie's new look and loose curls hung near her face. She lifted the back of her hair to cool her neck.

Sam undid her hair tie, and then slicked back her hair and tied it again. She tore two large pieces of paper towel from the holder, ran them under cold water and handed one to Addie. They both wiped their faces and Sam wiped the back of her neck. Addie wiped the sides of her face and then then followed suit. After washing their hands under the cold water, Sam reached up and removed two large glasses from the cabinet. She handed them to Addie while she went to the fridge and removed a tall glass pitcher of ice tea. Addie carried the glasses to the fridge, placing one at a time under the ice maker. After filling the glasses with crushed ice, she set them on the kitchen island next to the horseshoes. Sam poured the ice tea into the glasses and neither said a word until they had each taken a deep gulp of the cold liquid.

Quenching their thirst, and filling their glasses a second time, Sam picked up one of the shoes to examine it more closely. Although she had done so several times before Addie's visit, she thought maybe she had missed something.

Turning the horseshoe every which way, she ran her fingers over the numbers. Addie studied the shoe she was holding, carefully inspecting the stamped numbers, no detail escaping her eagle eyes.

"You know something *is* strange about these shoes. They look too out of character for normal riding and look at the gold flecks in them." Addie held the shoes directly under the overhead light. "I know the mare is fabulous enough to wear queen-like shoes, but something about them seems off. And I don't think for one minute that she's *not* very important to someone. I think what your gut is telling you is right, and if I were a betting woman, I would say the person knows where she is and is waiting to claim her, but the million dollar question is why?"

Sam nudged her in the arm, kiddingly. "I told you the mare was special, and you're right—the shoes are unique. It's as if they were never meant for riding, but who would do that? Why put shoes like that on a horse in the first place? I mean, they were strong enough to last while she was lost in the state forest, but I don't think they were meant for normal wear and neither did my farrier, Don."

"I agree." Addie was still turning the shoes over, carefully looking for any clue to their origin. "One thing for sure. It looks like they are new and hardly worn, and you said only one was loose when you got the mare? But, to tell the truth, Sherlock, I think you are on to something. Who would go to the trouble to stamp numbers on a horseshoe and what the heck do the numbers mean? Is it just a way that the farm keeps track of their horses?"

Sam drained her glass of cold tea and picked out a small piece of ice to chew. "Let me get my laptop and see if we can find anything about numbered horseshoes."

"Good idea. Let's see if there's something important that we may have missed." Addie put the shoes on the counter and drained her glass of ice tea.

They spent the next half hour Googling horseshoes of all types and materials, but found nothing of significance. The only information about stamps or numbers on horseshoes was mentioned in a research paper on ancient Greece. On excavation of Greek battle grounds, horseshoes worn by war horses were found with some markings but none of their research provided clues to any type of numbers. Sam closed the laptop and suggested they take a break and have some of Lyla's pie, and Addie thought that was a delicious idea.

They carried their mugs of coffee and plates of strawberry

rhubarb pie onto the porch. The dogs did not attempt to follow, choosing to stay in the air-conditioned house. Despite the heat, the porch was a pleasant refuge, and with the large ceiling fan whirling above, quite comfortable. Addie placed her plate and mug on the small table next to the porch swing and Sam placed hers on the table next to her favorite rocker. Neither said a word as they sat down. They were both quiet as they settled into a moment of contemplation and relaxation. Addie picked up her coffee mug and took in a sip of the dark liquid. "Ahh, this is great," she said slipping off her shoes. "What a beautiful day. And look at your flower beds. They are gorgeous. I wish I had your green thumb." Addie had oohed over Sam's flower beds all the way to the house. "Where do you think you'll plant the rose bush I brought you?"

Sam had just taken a mouthful of the pie. "This is *so* delicious! How does she make her pies taste so good? And her crust is so light and flaky." She put her fork down and took a sip of coffee as she glanced around her back yard, filled with flowers of all shapes, colors and heights. "I think I'll plant it along the stone wall where the other rose bushes are. It will complement the color of the other roses."

"That's a great idea. Maybe I'll try that along the small pond that I've dug out."

Sam pointed to the rock wall. "I've decided to only plant roses along that wall. "You can see I have a large variety and they bloom at different times. The only thing I hate is the deadheading. It takes time but in the long run it's worth it because I always have some color."

Addie wiped her mouth with the Christmas napkin and smiled. "Between the taste of this pie and the smell of the roses near the porch, I feel drunk with pleasure. Honestly, I am so relaxed and so happy to be here. I needed this."

"And I'm glad you took the time to visit, even if I had to entice you with another mystery," Sam teased. "Those are sea roses that you smell. They are the most fragrant rose I have, but loaded with prickers and not for cutting. The upside is their beautiful scent fills the air all around the porch. The downside is that they spread like wildfire, but if you want, I can give you one of the shoots that have sprouted near the mother bush. Just remind me to dig it up before you go home."

"That would be great. I think I'll plant it by the pond. And I don't mind them spreading. I think a hedge of rose bushes along the edge of the pond would look beautiful. Tell you what, I'll help you plant the bush I brought and then we can dig up the sprout along the porch and dump it in my bucket. I really love the fragrance of these roses."

"I do, too, and I think you can use the petals as a fragrance in the house. I'm a big fan of spring and summer, even if those seasons are the most work. I love the flowers and the greenery and I try to stop each day and savor the moment. Minnie always reminds me to take the time to look at sunsets, the birds and the flowers. She says life moves too quickly, and you need to stop or it will leave you in its dust."

"I love that woman. She is the wisest, most eccentric lady I know. Next time I visit, I want you to be sure she is here."

"I promise," Sam chuckled. "But I won't tell her that. She'll be nagging me to have you back next week." Sam finished the last bite of pie and pulled a small stool over to put her feet on. "Honestly, Addie, I am so full. I think just a salad and whatever you'd like would be all I can eat for dinner."

Addie placed her empty pie plate back on the table. "That was delicious," she smiled pushing the swing with her feet. "But I think we'll have to plan on more than a salad for dinner. You forgot about our buddy. Remember Chet? You said he'd be stopping by on his way home to Virginia and Lyla will be here after she closes her bakery shop."

"You're right. How could I forget that? I can't wait to see him. I wonder if we can talk him into staying over for the night. Den will be home tomorrow morning and I know he'd love to see him. Since Lyla's stopping by, maybe I'll call her and see what leftovers she has from her luncheon menu. No, wait! On second thought, I have sauce in the freezer and we can have pasta and salad and the rest of the pie for dessert."

"Spaghetti?" Addie sat up from the swing. "Don't bother Lyla. I haven't had your pasta and sauce for some time and that sounds perfect to me. Just have her bring dinner rolls, another thing that she bakes so perfect and yummy. I absolutely love her cheese rolls."

"Okay, Watson. I'll call her. But right now we have to think, and think hard, about the horseshoes. Any brilliant ideas since lunch?"

"Hmm, not yet but when you go in to call Lyla, bring out the rest of the bottle of wine and a pad of paper so we can write down our ideas. We did that last time when we were investigating the farm where Lyla's Mini was born and it helped."

"Good idea." Sam got up from the rocker and headed towards the kitchen. It was time for Sherlock and Watson to get to work.

Chapter 14

Chet arrived around four in the afternoon. Sam, Addie and Lyla were sitting on the porch enjoying a glass of raspberry tea. The pasta was simmering on the stove and the salad was prepared. Lyla had brought two loaves of fresh cheese bread from her bakery, and to be sure they had enough dessert, a chocolate cream pie.

It was a little after four when they heard the pickup truck grinding up the driveway, pulling its long horse trailer.

Sam had already put the dogs in their crates so they wouldn't get in the way of the truck when Chet backed into the turnaround, and wouldn't trample him when he got out.

"That sounds like Chet," Addie said getting up from her chair and walking towards the door.

"Go ahead and greet him. I'll let you get your hug first," Sam laughed. "Lyla and I will wait here." Sam knew the special friendship Addie and Chet had and she also knew that if they lived closer they would have been a couple a long time ago. Not to say that she didn't think Addie's love for Jace wasn't genuine, but Addie and Chet had a special connection. They spoke the same language and you could see it in their eyes and mannerisms when they were together. Chet had a serious girlfriend down in Virginia and Addie was genuinely happy for him, and he had promised to bring her to Addie's farm next time he was running Vermont. Lyla had met Chet when he, Sam and Denver stopped in for lunch at her shop, the last time he had stopped on his way home to Virginia. Chet owned a large farm and bred Curly horses and as a side job, he, trailered horses up and down the east coast.

Sam and Lyla could hear Chet and Addie talking non-stop as they opened the porch door. Sam got up to greet him, reaching her arms out to Chet. "How's my cowboy?" she asked as she gave him a big hug.

Chet's face creased with a huge smile. "Better now that I'm with my favorite women," he laughed.

Lyla was still in awe by the striking resemblance he had to Willie Nelson, Sam's favorite country singer. Sam had told her the story about first meeting Chet when he trailered her colt up from Virginia. She related how stunned she was and at a total loss for words when he jumped down from the seat of his pickup truck. He was a Willie Nelson look-alike and she had to suppress the urge to laugh. When Lyla was introduced to him, she could see exactly why Sam had been taken aback.

Chet was wearing jeans, brown boots, blue shirt and an old black western hat. His blue eyes, crinkled around the edges, were set on a rugged face darkened by sun, and his bristled dark haired goatee was sprinkled with gray. A short braid, tied with a leather string, hung down the back of his neck and the corners of his mouth were creviced with lines. He looked exactly like a younger version of the famous musician.

Lyla stood up ready to shake Chet's hand, her eyes doing a quick appraisal of the cowboy. The Willie look-alike walked over to her. "Forget the handshake and give me a hug, pretty lady." She blushed as Chet wrapped his arms around her in a big hug. She was still shy with people she didn't know very well, but that didn't stop Chet. He stepped back and grinned, "So, what kind of dessert did you bring today?"

"Chocolate cream pie," she beamed. "Hope you like it."

"My favorite," he said walking to the stove. He lifted the top of the pan and took in an exaggerated whiff of the sauce simmering in the pan. "Okay, now you ladies have me feeling like I'm starving. Before I walked in the door I was only a little hungry, but now that's changed big time."

"The table's set and everything is ready to serve. How about a cold beer before we sit down?" Sam asked walking to the refrigerator. "You look like you've had a long drive and could use a cold one. Will it be your usual?"

"And it will give us time to finish our tea," Addie said

"Go ahead and twist my arm," he said in his slow southern drawl." He removed his hat and set it on one of the chairs. "It's been a hot day and I can use a cold one. Trip was long, and I had a little problem loading one of the horses up in Maine." Sam handed him the frosty bottle of beer and he took a long drink before setting it on the table. "Where's my man Denver?"

Sam went back to the stove and stirred the sauce. "He's on a trip but will be home early tomorrow morning. Do you think you could stay overnight and get to visit with him? He said to try and talk you into it. Won't that be fun and we can catch up. It's been too long since we've *all* been together."

"Well I'll have to check with the little lady waiting for me at home," he chuckled. "Other than that, I don't have anything pressing to get to."

Addie chimed in. "Don't let Audrey hear that. I bet she misses you."

Lyla sat and sipped her tea, watching the three friends tease each other. She loved listening to Chet's singsong voice. It was different from Denver's Texan twang, but pleasing to the ear.

"Just tell her that you want to see Denver, and that's the truth. Besides, you've had a long trip and you need to rest. I'm sure she'll understand," Sam said.

The banter went back and forth while Addie, Sam and Lyla busied with the dinner. Lyla sliced the bread and Addie carried the salad to the table. Sam poured the sauce into a large bowl and Lyla went back to the counter for the plate of pasta. A small bowl filled with grated cheese and a pitcher of ice water was placed in the middle of the table. Chet watched the scurry of activity while he sat drinking his beer. Although he asked several times if he could help, the attention was all on him and he loved it. The table set and the dinner ready, he excused himself and went to the bathroom to wash up. It had been a long hot ride and he was famished. He had talked to Audrey about his plan to stop and see the ladies and he would phone her after dinner. It was a change in plans to stay overnight, but he wanted to see Denver and he knew that Audrey would be happy he wasn't driving straight home. She worried about him driving too many hours without rest. He dried his hands with a towel and headed back to enjoy the great food and the company of good friends.

Chapter 15

By the time they finished dinner, it was after 7p.m. Sam took a phone call from Denver, who asked if Chet would be staying overnight. He repeated how much he would enjoy seeing him, and hoped he could.

Chet was on the phone with Audrey when Denver called. Sam, still holding the phone, walked into the room where he was in deep conversation. "Hold on a minute, hon," he said.

"Den's on the phone and wants to know if you'll be here in the morning. He has one early meeting and then he'll be on his way home."

Chet removed the phone from his ear. "For sure I will. Audrey doesn't want me driving this evening and said she was really appreciative that you asked me to stay overnight and to thank you for your hospitality. She worries when I drive all night."

"Great. Tell her your friends agree with her. You need some rest before going on the road again. And tell her we hope to see her soon."

Sam returned to talking to Denver. "Chet says he'll be here when you get home. Addie will be heading home later in the afternoon. You can show Chet our new rescue. I was just about to tell him about her when the phone rang."

"Sounds like we have a plan and I'll see everyone late morning. Love you, Sam."

"Drive safe. Love you too."

Sam returned to the kitchen and carried the leftover strawberry rhubarb pie to the table and then returned with the chocolate cream pie. Lyla and Addie were deep in conversation.

"Time for coffee and dessert," she said, placing the pie on the table. "Addie would you please get the dessert plates and coffee mugs?"

"I'll help," Lyla said getting up from her chair just as Chet returned to the kitchen.

"And I'll fix the coffee, Chet said walking to the coffee maker. "What'll it be ladies?" he asked spinning the K-cup carousel to view the flavors.

"Anything strong," Lyla said.

"Same here," Sam replied as she set the pitcher filled with cream and the sugar bowl on the table.

Addie was at the counter where the mugs were sitting. "Make mine a light blend, Chet. And do you want the bird mugs or Sam's Christmas mugs to go along with her Christmas napkins? Never mind. I choose the bird mugs. Christmas napkins are one thing, but I'm still into summer, so *forget* it, Sam."

One by one, Chet carried the bird decorated mugs filled with steaming coffee to the table and set them down. Addie asked which piece of pie he wanted but he couldn't decide so he opted for a slice of each. He quickly devoured both, and wiping his mouth with the napkin said, "Honest, Lyla, they're both so delicious, I can't decide which one is my favorite, so I need another slice of each. Cut me another two slices, Addie," he said, holding out his plate.

By the end of the dinner, they each complained they were so full they could not eat another bite of anything. Sam wrapped the leftover pie for Denver to have the next day, and she promised to bake Chet's favorite sticky buns for breakfast and said she would make extra to bring home to Audrey. Lyla reminded everyone that she had also brought a box of Sam's favorite ginger cookies, which brought on groans of laughter. Addie said that she would need to go on a diet if she ate like that every day and she was glad that she didn't live close to Lyla, since she knew she could easily turn into a junk food addict.

With exaggerated rumblings about eating too much food, they cleared the table of dishes and stacked them in the dishwasher. Carrying refilled coffee mugs, they settled in the living room. Sam had not mentioned the horseshoes all evening but it was the perfect time to bring them out. She and Addie wanted Chet's thoughts about the shoes and the stamped numbers. Sam and Addie had their own ideas, but Chet could add a new perspective on what it could mean. Maybe he had seen horseshoes like them before and would give them a suggestion on how to proceed.

Addie leaned back in the chair and filled Chet in on the rescue horse while Sam went to retrieve the shoes. Chet listened intently to the story and asked several questions. He said he was eager to take a look at the yellow horse in the morning, and he, too, was intrigued by the rescue horse and her shoes. He was as puzzled as they were. Whey hadn't someone claimed what appeared to be a very expensive horse? Chet laughed when Addie said Sherlock and Watson were on hunt for answers and his expertise would either help them solve the mystery or leave them even more befuddled.

Chet was leaning forward in the chair totally absorbed in Addie's recount of the story and Lyla was listening intently trying to sort out all of the facts when Sam walked into the room carrying the horseshoes. She handed one to Chet and one to Lyla.

"Here they are. What say you, Chet, our *old* sage?" Sam winked at Addie.

Chet made a fake gasp. "Come on now…don't mind the sage part, but *old*? Never! What is it that Minnie says? Older *but* never old!"

Addie laughed. "I agree with Chet and Minnie and I have a question. Do you have to be old to be a sage?"

That brought on more laughter and a silly discussion between Lyla, Addie and Sam about what makes a person a sage.

Chet listened with one ear as he turned the horseshoe over and examined it. He was quiet and pensive as he ran his fingers over the raised numbers and studied the shoes' composition.

The women stopped talking and all eyes were on Chet as they watched with bated breath for his assessment.

He broke the silence. "Remarkable," he murmured. "I've only seen this type of shoe one time. Very expensive and usually only on show horses. Special material used to make these," he said holding one up. "As far as the numbers, I can honestly say I've never seen horseshoes stamped with numbers like this. Must mean something special to the owner, but I can't even guess what they represent. Maybe he keeps track of his horses this way, but I doubt it."

"I knew it!" Sam stood up and raised her arms. She did a little dance and then sat down. "Tell him, Addie, I mean, *Watson*, what we think it all means."

"A conspiracy of some sort!" Addie got up and did the same dance.

Chet turned serious. "Calm down ladies. It doesn't mean that the numbers on the horseshoe are something illegal. By the way Sam, what does Den make of all of this?"

Sam failed to suppress a grin. It all made sense to her. "He's as much in the dark as we are, but of course his mind doesn't go to the same place mine does. He's much more logical than I am, but I'll tell you this. He's as mystified as we are and admits it's odd. But Chet, until the owner shows up and tells us what the numbers mean, we have nothing to go on."

Lyla chimed in, "I think you and Addie should go with your hunch about the rescue horse and find out more about the numbered horseshoes. You were dead-on with my Mini horse, and if you think something's not making sense you need to dig deeper."

Addie moved to the edge of her chair and nodded her head in agreement. Her voice became serious. "I agree with Lyla. So, what's our next move, Sherlock?"

Chapter 16

Immediately after picking his luggage up from the airport baggage claim area, Luca headed to the car rental terminal. The flight, first class as always, was on time and had been uneventful.

While sipping a gin and tonic, he had used the quiet time on the plane to run through his plan of action for finding the million dollar horseshoes. Stealing the horse was out of the question. That might alert the law and this deal was too rich to chance that. And trying to prove he was the owner of the mare made things too dicey. What if Parker had already contacted the farm? That alone would open up an investigation and he couldn't trust his old buddy to not give him up. He had thought of every angle and possible scenario, but the only plausible way to the numbered account was to get his hands on the horseshoes by whatever means necessary.

Luca felt a surge of adrenaline as he walked briskly to the car pickup area. He stopped to check in with the attendant then headed to the spot where a black Cadillac SUV was parked. Luca threw his luggage onto the back seat, opened the driver's door and slid in. "Cool. Maybe this will be my next wheels." He half-smiled as he pushed the button to start the engine. He tapped the directions for the hotel into the GPS, and the automated smooth voice of a woman with a British accent said, "Turn right and then go straight on for 2.5 miles."

Luca couldn't help but grin. *Now that was sweet,* he thought. *Efficient sounding, while at the same time, the automated voice had a sexy ring to it.* Wouldn't he love to have a live variation of her in the passenger seat next to him?

He pushed the black leather seat button to move into a comfortable position and moved his shoulders up and down. He had a lot of planning to do but now he needed to concentrate on driving. Next stop, his hotel. He needed a drink.

Driving the highway, he was lost in thought. At times, his musings were interrupted by another direction change. 'Stay to the left of the motorway.' He loved that. Motorway? Any American knows that it's called a highway, but he imagined a pert blonde Brit sitting at a computer directing him as he pressed the button to activate Cruise Control. One thing for sure, he didn't want to be stopped for speeding and it gave him the freedom to think about his internet search for anything posted about a missing horse.

"Yeah, Parker. Like you couldn't have done the same thing? Who you trying to kid?" he mumbled

And it hadn't taken long to find a hit on his Google search. All he had to do was focus on the towns where the accident took place, and there it was. A small town newspaper had an article on the front page about a horse running along the highway near the state forest. The article even had a photo of the horse and it sure looked just like Parker's favorite mare, Magic.

"Well, Miss Magic. Come to daddy," he said aloud sneering as he steered the Caddy into the passing lane.

As soon as he passed the tractor trailer, he pulled the SUV back into the right lane and followed a fast moving gray Lexus. "Damn, wouldn't Parker love to know that his favorite horse was now labeled a rescue horse? Humph!" Luca found it so amusing he laughed out loud. His old buddy Parker, who thought he was so important and bred blue ribbon show horses, had his prize mare now called a rescue horse.

Luca chewed the inside of his mouth. The whole debacle left him with a sour taste and his gut was sending up red flags. It was time to make his final move before Parker made his.

He checked his speed and moved back into cruise control, realizing he was following a car tearing along at 85 miles an hour. Not good. The speeding Lexus pulled away from him. Another time he would have kept up and even passed the driver, but for now he had more important things on his mind. He remembered the thrill he felt when he googled the name of the farm listed in the article and voila! It brought him to a Facebook page. The page was filled with photos of American Curly horses, which he had never heard of, and there were a ton of postings asking for help to find the owner of a palomino quarter horse found running free near the state forest.

"Sweet!" Now all he had to do was outfox his so-called partner.

Luca snarled as he mimicked Parker's voice, "'I don't know where the mare is. I can't find her, and she could be anywhere. I'm working on it.'" Luca raised his voice and spoke as if Parker was listening. "Lucky for you, my loser friend, that you don't find her, and if you do, you'd better hope that we don't cross paths at the same time. It won't be a pretty picture."

Luca's paranoia kicked in. He had a feeling that Parker already knew where his horse was, but he was holding back because he had plans to double cross him. Well, he would beat him to the punch. He would get the horseshoes himself and play along with Parker's game of, "I don't know where the horse is."

"My God! That man must think I'm stupid."

Although they were sometime buddies in their younger years, he, Luca D'Angelo, didn't get where he was by being stupid. Smart ass Parker, that arrogant so called educated man! He could feel the anger rising and he pounded the wheel of the Caddy. Did he really think he didn't see the set-up? His mind was racing. Maybe the whole lost horse story was a smoke screen and Parker planned to keep the final pot of gold for himself. Feeding him the lost horse story just gave him time to move in on their last deal.

Luca swerved to avoid a driver who didn't yield to the merge sign as he came up the ramp. He laid on the horn, and shook his hand at the driver. "What the hell is wrong with these New England drivers?" he yelled

He lifted his left hand and unconsciously massaged the back of his neck to relieve the tension, then moved his jaw back and forth to unclench his teeth. Damn, he needed a drink and this time it would be Scotch. He rubbed his forehead trying to clear the cobwebs, and his lips pressed together in a thin line. He let out a few expletives and felt better. "You rat, Parker! Why'd you have to go and try and pull a fast one on me?" And then a smirk came over his lips. What Parker didn't know was that *he* had already thought about backstabbing him before the horse went missing. He was always one step ahead of his know-it-all buddy and he had already planned to send the last horseshoe numbers to his own personal account. After all, Parker wasn't *that* good a friend. Did Parker sense he was going to double-cross him and come up with this stupid lie?

His mind ran over their first meeting and how they laid out their grand scheme to become overnight multimillionaires. One night when he was slugging down a few bourbons, he had spotted Parker sitting at the end of the bar at an old watering hole he frequented. Parker didn't see him, but Luca always took a quick scan of people sitting at the bar and it was happenstance that they were in the same bar at the same time. He watched him for a while before he decided to say hello. Parker had told him he was in town on business and that he had just left a tedious meeting with some meatheads from another firm. He needed a drink to quell his desire to smack one of them and was surprised to see Luca in the same bar. They hadn't seen each other in years and spent an hour laughing about the scams they had pulled off when they were kids. After downing several drinks, Parker had asked him if he wanted in on an iron clad skim operation he was planning at the investment firm where he worked. It would take two men and Luca was the only person he could trust. Who was Luca to refuse such a sweet deal? It was perfect and they had skimmed millions from Parker's accounts. This transfer of untraceable currency was to have been their last big move working together and it was the frosting on the cake. It was more money than all of the other transfers put together and until this debacle, it was supposed to be *all* his! Parker would *never* see a penny of the last transfer and wouldn't be the wiser until it was too late and he was gone. He snorted as he thought about how he would have the last laugh on his uppity partner.

Luca's concentration was interrupted by the voice of the GPS. "Take the next exit, then turn right." Luca steered the Caddy into the right lane. He could taste the Scotch and feel the heat of the smooth liquid flowing down his throat, and he was eager to get on with this final business. Tomorrow would be the day. He wanted to have the horseshoes in hand before his old pal Parker pulled a fast one on him. He would show him. For a brief moment he envisioned soaking up the sun on his private island, a gorgeous redhead lying next to him and a tall glass of Tequila in his hand. Luca squeezed the bridge of his nose and then rubbed his chin. Parker would never see this coming.

His lip curled up ever so slightly as his mind scrambled to try and make some sense out of everything Parker had told him. Luca was not a man to laugh easily, but he had a sudden impulse to do just that. He was an all-out gangster and laughter didn't come easily. The only time he felt upbeat was when he was with his cronies and he was bragging about some scam he had just pulled off.

Luca could feel fatigue slowly creeping through his body and he yawned and blinked his eyes. All this overthinking was exhausting, but he couldn't stop analyzing every angle of the situation. "Come on, Luca. Think, and think hard about your buddy Parker. What's he up to?" His eyes narrowed and he felt raw anger welling up in him. He smacked the steering wheel with his hand. "Parker's holding back something. I can feel it." Luca's mind was racing. "And if what I think is true, I'll deal with him when the time is right. No one ever gets away with two-timing Luca D'Angelo. When someone double-crosses me they better be ready for the consequences."

Luca's brows furrowed and he took in a quick breath. "Damn!" A disturbing thought flashed through his mind. *What if someone in the quarter horse world recognizes Magic?*

He'd better move fast on this. Those farm people have no idea how valuable Magic is. The thought of it made him chuckle. He loved it.

Chapter 17

The hotel lobby was luxuriously decorated. The polished, gray marble floor was adorned with large groupings of potted trees and topiaries. Over-sized, gray pots of flowers intermingled with beautiful antique chairs covered in pale pink velvet. A rich oriental carpet led to a beautifully appointed lobby desk covered in decorator glass blocks.

Luca was greeted by an attractive blonde desk clerk with a melodic silky voice. She efficiently looked up his information and slid his credit card through her computer while he carefully eyed her up and down. Sensing his hard eyes moving over her body, she stiffened as she turned to face him and handed his card back. "Is there anything else I can help you with, Mr. D'Angelo?" she asked, looking him straight in the eye. Maybe it was his thin smile or his piercing dark eyes, but she sensed he was a dangerous man.

"Not at the moment," he said in a low voice while placing his credit card back in his wallet. The desk clerk slid a plastic key card over the counter and his eyes met hers for a moment too long. "Almost forgot. I need a wakeup call at 6 a.m." He could have set his cell phone alarm, but he was paying top dollar for a room at this upscale hotel. 'First class everywhere' was his mantra, and he never flinched at asking for the amenities he was entitled to.

"Yes, sir," she replied as she tapped the keys of the computer for the wake up time. Putting on her best fake smile, she said, "You're all set for the call and enjoy your stay at our hotel."

"I'm sure I will," he said as he turned to walk away. And then to himself, he said, "But it would be much more enjoyable if you spent the stay with me."

Luca dropped his bags off in his hotel room and after a quick bathroom break headed to the lounge. Entering the lounge, it took a minute for his eyes to adjust to the dimly lit room. At the far end of a long mahogany bar, several patrons sat talking with the bartender. He walked to the empty end of the bar and pulled out a stool and sat down. Satisfied after scanning the bar for anyone suspicious, he motioned to the bartender. A young, dark-haired guy wearing a white shirt with rolled-up sleeves came right over and asked, "What'll it be?"

"I'll start with a shot of Jack Daniels, and do you have a bar menu?"

"Sure do," smiled the bartender with the name tag 'Dennie' pinned to his shirt. Dennie reached for a menu from under the bar, slid it to Luca and walked briskly away to fill the grim man's order. *I have a feeling this guy is not one to be messed with*, he thought as he poured the whiskey.

Dennie returned with the shot of Daniels and without looking up from the menu, Luca tossed down the shot. "Another," he demanded. "And bring me a chaser of Coors," he muttered, still studying the menu.

By the time Dennie returned with his second shot and the ice-cold glass of beer, Luca was ready to order. Dennie knew this man was not one to make idle conversation, so he took the order without comment. He'd quickly glanced at the dark-faced man when he placed the shot and beer on the bar in front of him. It was his bartender game. Study the patron, come to a conclusion of who he or she was, and then through idle chitchat, see if he was correct in his initial appraisal. He could tell by the end of the evening if the patron would be a good tipper or a lousy one. More often than not he was right, and the game made the long evening bartending more interesting. Scrutinizing the man from the corner of his eye, he knew without a doubt that he was short with words but good on tipping. The tip would be large, but he would need to treat Mr. Gloom like he was his only customer. Dennie was a skilled bartender, and he earned more in tips than of any of the wait staff. He knew how to read people, and at the end of the night his servitude to the man would be all worth it.

Luca swiveled slightly on his bar stool, his eyes scanning the other patrons sitting at the far end of the bar. It was an old habit and one that kept him safe, but on-guard, at all times. Muddled conversations from several couples sitting at tables mingled with the background music of Frank Sinatra. Seeing no one that made the hairs on the back of his neck stand up, he took another gulp of beer. His natural paranoia was an ingrained part of his persona and kept him one step ahead of trouble with the mob and out off the radar with the feds. That thought made him chuckle. He knew the feds were continually sniffing around trying to make a case against him and more than once they had almost succeeded. Luca could feel his lip pull into a sneer. Let them go at it. He was cleverer than any of them and it would be a cold day in hell when they would ever nail him for anything. His hand unconsciously rubbed his chin, and he squeezed his eyes shut for a second. He was ready for another shot of Daniels, and he signaled the bartender, Dennie, or whatever his name was. Smart bartender. All he had to do was signal, and Dennie was right there with his drink. *This* bartender had it right.

Luca wiped his mouth with the back of his hand. *What the hell*, he thought. *I'm here for the night and ready to knock a few down.*

Dennie, waiting on other customers, but with one eye always on Darth Vader, saw the slight motion of Luca's hand and was quick to return with another shot of Daniels. The glass didn't even have time to hit the bar when Luca lifted it to his lips, tossed the whiskey down, and then took a long swig of beer. The hot rush of heat from the whiskey surrendered to the stream of ice-cold beer, and Luca felt himself gradually being pulled into a state of relaxation as the alcohol coursed through his body.

It wasn't long before Dennie returned with his order. The steak and shrimp dinner lessened the sting of too many shots of whiskey, and Luca was beginning to feel a slight buzz in his head.

That buzz to Luca meant a big STOP! He was a man who could drink any of his buddies under the table, but tonight, although tempted to keep on drinking, he shut himself off. This was not the time to let his guard down. Drink enough to relax, but not enough to become dead drunk, was the thought that ran through his mind. He didn't want to get up with a hangover. He needed a clear head to pull this one off.

Dennie was always at the ready with either a shot of Jack or another cold beer, but finally Luca had quenched his thirst and his desire to drink. He could feel his eyes becoming small slits as they gave into the exhaustion that was snaking up his body. After he dropped a large tip on the bar and a little extra for good service, Luca left the lounge and headed towards his room. He pressed the button to the elevator and was relieved when the doors opened that there was no one else on it. The elevator stopped on the 12th floor and he exited and walked down the richly carpeted hallway. Finding the numbered door to his room, he staggered slightly as he slid his key card into the lock.

Entering the room, Luca emptied his pockets and placed the contents on the bureau. He could feel the heavy weight of fatigue seeping through his body. Sitting on the edge of the bed, he grimaced as he pulled his socks and shoes off. It had been a long day. After undressing, he carefully placed his tailored pants and silk shirt on a fancy gray side chair and flopped down onto the bed. Tomorrow would come soon enough and he was glad he'd thought to ask for the wakeup call from the hotel desk. That was his last thought as he dragged the covers over his inebriated body and fell into a deep snoring sleep.

At 6 a.m., Luca, dead to the world, was awakened by the loud shrill of the telephone sitting on the bed stand next to him. He groaned and leaned over and answered it with, "Ya", then placed the telephone back on the hook and rubbed his blood shot eyes. "I need a hot shower and a strong coffee," he mumbled as he rolled out of bed and stumbled to the bathroom.

As the hot water from the shower poured over his half-awake body, he rehashed every detail of his plan. Before leaving Florida he had contacted Samantha Steele at the farm where he believed

Magic had ended up. "Rescue, my ass," he snickered as he poured shampoo on his head and rubbed it into his thick black hair. He still found it humorous that Parker's valuable horse was now considered a rescue. Before they ended their last phone call, they agreed there was no need to talk again until the horse was located, and then they would figure out what to do next.

But he, brilliant Luca, would have the last laugh. Parker had no idea that he had found the horse, contacted the owners of the farm, and he was in Massachusetts, ready to pick up the horseshoes. And best of all, he had a perfect cover story for going to the farm. Parker should remember that *he*, Luca D'Angelo, was always one step ahead of him.

Luca felt more human and less tired after the long shower and he took his time to shave and dress. He had made the appointment to meet the owners of the farm for 1p.m. That gave him plenty of time to have breakfast and drive to the farm, feeling refreshed and on game. He had booked his room for three days and his flight was all set for the return trip to Florida. He would have the numbers of the account in hand and for a moment he almost felt giddy. It was time to put his plan in motion.

Feeling like a new man, Luca headed down to the dining room and ordered a large breakfast of bacon, eggs, toast and coffee. He skimmed through the local paper, paying attention to the sports page, and then returned to his room, carrying a fresh mug of coffee. He sat down at the desk and opened his laptop. To be on his best game, he needed to refresh himself with *all* of the facts. He had researched the American Curly horse and now believed he was packed full of vital information. It was his way of opening a dialogue with this Samantha Steele woman. Make her feel comfortable and give them something to talk about. Next, he studied the towns near hers. He was going to keep to the story that he, his wife and daughter were moving to Massachusetts. He owned a computer software company and decided to return to New England because he wanted his daughter in a private school. Fortunately, in his research, he had found an academy for girls, and he was going to say that he was here for a tour. He would tell the Steele woman that he had lived in New England some years ago and thought the schools were a better fit for his daughter than the ones in Florida. Luckily, several years back he *had* lived in Boston so that was no stretch.

In his type of work there was always some truth in the lie. The con would continue about his wife and daughter. He would say that his daughter loved horses and he was a horseman himself. Luca knew that bringing a daughter into the story would be a great hook. Of course the Steele woman would have questions and his half-baked story about searching for a home near the school was a clever one. But the best ploy was that he had promised his thirteen-year-old daughter Margareta, that she could have a horse. Margareta had read an article in one of her Equine magazines about the American Curly and had made him promise to buy her one if they moved. There was no denying his daughter's wishes and although he was in town for the tour of the academy he had some spare time, so he thought he would look at Curly horses.

Luca smirked as he thought how brilliant his plan was. He would even take photos to send to his pretend daughter to show her the horses and the farm. He leaned back in the chair and crossed his arms behind his head. *I'll have to smile a lot and act very professional and friendly. A piece of cake*, he thought. *I can be anyone I want to be. Look at Parker, the*

friendly handsome guy, and he's the biggest scam artist ever.
His lips curled into a sneer as he thought about his partner.
"Got no respect for that guy," he mumbled as he returned to
the laptop and typed in another Google question. "Yep, do
your homework and get it right the first time." His first trip to
the farm was to meet the owner and case out the place. He
needed to see it all, the layout of the farm and the simplest
way in and out. "Of course, I'll ease my way in to get a look at
the so-called rescue horse, and I'll make it all the Steele
woman's idea. Maybe I'll put some money down on one of her
sale horses. That should do it. I'll play that one by ear but
everything is on the table. It all depends on how it goes and
how much access I'll have to the horseshoes.

A sudden thought flashed through his mind, *What if she*
replaced her shoes?

Chapter 18

Bryn's white Lexus slowly wound its way up the dark gray traprock driveway to Sam's farm. The long drive had given her plenty of time to think about how Parker had once again dragged her into another one of his hair-brained schemes. Not only did he want her to validate that it was indeed Magic, he wanted her assurance that the horseshoes were there. Luca D'Angelo had come up in their conversation and he had warned her about his cunning ways and emphasized she was only there as a scout and should not try to take him on. He was a dangerous man if cornered, and could pose a threat to her and the owners of the farm. Her job was to find out if he had phoned about the missing horse or had already been at the farm. If either of these scenarios had occurred, it would complicate the already dicey situation and could compromise everything.

How could she accomplish gathering all of this information

without raising the suspicion of the woman she'd spoken to on the phone? Her story had to ring true, but it would be tricky. She would have to improvise as she went along, but she was confident that once she met the woman, Samantha Steele, she would know how to proceed. Bryn knew she would have to wing it, and hope she could pull off the phony story line.

First, she needed a tour of the farm. That was simple. Next, she had to verify that the rescue horse was indeed Magic and confirm that the special horseshoes were still on her. But the crucial question was had anyone else inquired about the horse. If D'Angelo was in the picture, all bets were off and the whole plan would demand urgent action. For now, she had to make the Steele woman believe it was *her* idea to show her the rescue horse. All information gleaned would then be relayed to Parker as soon as she left the farm. Bryn took in a deep breath. She was ready to begin.

Fieldstone walls bordered the graded road as it meandered up the slight hill. She had made the appointment for 11 a.m. and it was just about ten minutes past that. The top of the driveway opened into a sprawling farm with numerous out buildings and white painted fences. Bryn carefully pulled into a large open space she assumed was for parking and turned the engine off. Before she could even open the car door three boisterous dogs, tails wagging, came running up and circled her vehicle.

"Jazz! Ranger! Sally! Come!" The dogs quickly turned away from Bryn's car and made a mad dash to the small framed woman walking towards her. Bryn watched in amazement as the woman in one quick motion raised her hand and they obediently sat down. "Stay!" Bryn heard her say.

Bryn opened the car door and stepped out just as Sam reached her. Smiling, Bryn held out her hand. "Hi. I'm Bronwyn Dey, but my friends call me Bryn. I must say how I admire your control over your dogs. Wish I could get my dog to behave like that."

"And I'm Samantha Steele, but my friends call me Sam," the pretty blonde haired woman with a sprinkle of freckles on her nose said warmly as she shook Bryn's hand. "Don't let those three fool you. They each have their moments that drive me crazy," she laughed.

A quick look at the woman standing in front of her made her glad that she had dressed casually in jeans, blue shirt and boots. She quickly appraised the friendly woman wearing jeans, tall black riding boots and a pink shirt. Large sunglasses covered her eyes, but Bryn bet they were blue. Sam's hair was pulled back in a loose ponytail and her voice had a slight southern lilt to it. Maybe it was her training or maybe it was what they had in common but it took only a second to recognize a fellow horsewoman.

"Too funny, isn't it?" Bryn said laughing. "We both have nicknames and give our full names when we meet someone new. "I should just say my name is Bryn and not bother with the rest of it."

"Me too," Sam chuckled. "I wonder why we don't just do that? No one except my mother calls me Samantha."

"And hardly anyone but my mother calls me Bronwyn. I was named after my aunt and one Bronwyn in the family is enough." Bryn reached back in the car for her sunglasses sitting on the center council and then closed the door. The sun was bright and she hated squinting. She slipped them on and turned back to Sam. "Thanks for taking the time to see me today. I know it was short notice."

"No problem. I have nothing special planned and always love

to meet another woman who loves horses." Sam looked back at the dogs, still waiting for the command to release them.

Bryn was amazed. "Your dogs are so well-behaved. I have only one, and I can't picture him being this obedient. I did take him to dog class when he was younger, but it's not his fault that I didn't take the time to keep up with the training. So, unfortunately, he only knows the commands 'sit' and 'down'. I am a lazy dog owner."

Sam gave a bemused smile. "It takes a lot of patience and persistence, believe me. If I didn't have lots of guests at the farm, I probably wouldn't worry as much or have worked as hard at teaching them to behave. But, in the long run, it pays off. What kind of dog do you have?"

"A long-haired dachshund. I love him to pieces but I'm afraid I've spoiled him too much. His name is Pug."

"I love dachshunds." Sam pointed to the dogs still waiting for her signal. "Sally's a yellow lab, Ranger is a labradoodle and Jazz is a mixed breed. My best-trained dog is Ranger. He's very smart but a little unruly. It's crazy hot today, isn't it?"

"It sure is. I didn't notice as much in the car with the air on. Looks like it's supposed to be this way all week." Bryn could feel droplets of water beading on her forehead and her long sleeved shirt was beginning to feel sticky. Although her hair, like Sam's, was pulled back and tied up off her shoulder, it didn't do much to keep her neck cool and she suddenly felt very thirsty.

As if reading her mind, Sam turned towards the house. "Let's get out of this sun and go into the house where it's cooler. We can get a glass of something cold and sit on the porch. Do you like lemonade?"

"Love it," Bryn said as she turned to follow Sam.

"Don't worry about the dogs. They're very friendly. I'll bring them in the house with us and put them in the back room where they'll be cooler and out of the way."

They walked to where the dogs were sitting and Bryn asked, "Can I pet them?"

"Sure, feel free. They love the attention."

Bryn leaned over and pet Sally's head. "Aren't you the pretty one," she said. Sally's tail wagged furiously, eager for more.

"Okay, let's go." Sam gave the okay and the dogs followed them to the house. They made their way onto the porch and stepped into the kitchen. Once again the dogs sat and waited for her next command while she took a pitcher of lemonade from the refrigerator and poured the cold liquid into two glasses.

"Thank you. I needed that." Bryn took a long drink of the ice cold lemonade and Sam was quick with a refill.

"I'll be right back," Sam said. "I want to put the dogs in the back room." She beckoned to the dogs with the command, "Come!" The dogs got up and followed her down a long hallway to the back of the house. Bryn was in awe of the amount of training that it must have taken to get the dogs to obey each command. She would have to be more diligent with Pug's training.

As soon as Sam was out of sight, Bryn's whole manner went into auto-mode. She quickly scanned the layout of the antique farmhouse. Glass in hand, she took another sip of lemonade and looked around. She was in a large country kitchen, surrounded by windows. In the middle of the richly aged wood plank floor was a kitchen island covered with a heavy butcher-block counter top. She set her glass down and looked up at a long wrought iron rack where stainless steel pans of different sizes and colors were hanging. Next to the pans was an assortment of utensils, perfect for any type of cooking. The display of cookware indicated a woman who enjoyed being in the kitchen.

Bryn had a gift for analyzing and observing behavior and one thing she had learned was that you can tell a lot about a woman by being in her kitchen. She had the eye of a professional and was always fascinated by the homes people lived in, as well as their body language. She was acutely aware of the difference between the words that people spoke and what they were really saying through their non-verbal communication. Parker admired her innate ability to engage people in dialogue even in the most risky circumstances and she was the perfect ally for the jobs they had worked on together.

An antique pewter fixture provided light over the island, and several jars of spices and seasonings sat beside a wooden recipe box. Next to the recipe box, a blueberry pie still warm from the oven made her mouth water. Its sweet smell wafted through the air and she thought how good it would taste with a cup of hot coffee. Next to the pie were two yellow dessert plates and matching mugs. *This woman loves to cook, and I hope one of those plates is for me*, she thought as she glanced at the pie and plates. Long counters wrapped around the kitchen and white Shaker-style cabinets stretched across the length of the quartz white and black counter tops. The kitchen was a pleasing blend of old and new making the space inviting and workable. An aged Hoosier cupboard stood against one of the pale yellow walls and what looked to be a dozen Depression glass mixers topped with red handled beaters made a beautiful statement. Bryn, an antique connoisseur wannabe, recognized them immediately.

A cozy breakfast nook surrounded by windows was punched out of one side of the kitchen. Bryn imagined having coffee and croissants for breakfast in the inviting sunlit recess. Built into the nook was a square wooden table with four white chairs decorated with red pads. Over the sink, a fabulous garden window opened into the back yard. Bryn walked to the window and looked out onto a collage of various colored flowers planted in numerous places along the white fenced yard. To the side of the fence there was a gate that opened into a dog yard. A huge white painted dog house was set off to the side and several yellow balls were scattered here and there. An assortment of colorful birdhouses standing on tall poles caught her eye and she wondered how many species of birds visited them.

The view from the window was exceptionally beautiful and her immediate thought was that she was looking at a picture in a garden magazine. For a moment she forgot why she was there. She could only wish she was this talented and could repurpose her small dreary yard into something this lovely.

Bryn turned when she heard Sam's footsteps in the hallway, and her mind instantly reverted back to the reason she was there and what was expected from her. For a moment she felt guilty that she was deceiving Sam. The gracious woman wouldn't have been so inviting, if she had an inkling why she was there.

"Your home is beautiful. A mix of everything," Bryn said to Sam who had picked up her glass of lemonade as she walked by the counter.

"Yes, we've been slowly remodeling this old house. I was married last year, and since Denver moved in, he has been slowly rehabbing many of the rooms. An old house takes a lot of work and upkeep."

"Oh, I agree. I don't have an older home, but I've just finished painting my bedroom and it has a whole different look.

By the way, I love your backyard and flowers," Bryn said with genuine appreciation.

"Don't laugh, but my flower beds are scattered all over the property, and there's no rhyme or reason to any of it. A bad habit I have. I buy plants that appeal to me when they're blooming, plant them in different places and then forget where I set them. In the spring and summer I'm constantly surprised to see what comes up. I call them my pop-up flowers. See those yellow straw flowers in the corner?" Sam pointed out the window and into the garden. "I bought a pot of them last year at the garden show in town, and for the life of me couldn't remember where I planted them until this week when they bloomed."

Bryn could relate. It was just the sort of thing she would do.

"My friends and family say I'm addicted to flowers." Sam said chuckling.

"Well, sounds like it's an addiction I wish I had. There are worse things. My obsession is double-stuffed Oreo cookies. Your addiction is healthy, but mine means calories."

"I guess we all have our guilty pleasures, but you look so fit that I bet if you ate a *whole* package of Oreos it wouldn't matter." Sam said as she scrutinized Bryn. "I bet you're a runner."

Bryn suddenly had a feeling that Sam was analyzing her a little too much. Maybe it was her own paranoia, but she quickly changed the subject. "I run a few times a week, but I'm not a fanatic about it. Back to your gorgeous flower beds. I wish I had your magic touch. Unfortunately, I don't have a green thumb like you, and I kill all of my plants. Maybe you can give me some tips?"

"I'd be happy to, but for now, let's relax in the family room and finish our drinks before we look at the horses. You can tell me all about your interest in American Curlies, and then I can show you some of my favorites."

Bryn took in a deep breath. She was ready to tell Sam the story she had rehearsed for days, but out of the blue she was slammed with sudden remorse, and she had to remind herself that this was just a job, as she picked up her glass and followed Sam into the family room.

A huge, distressed wooden beam spanning the length of the ceiling separated the kitchen and family room, creating an open but inviting space. Colorful area rugs were scattered over wide oak floorboards and on the far wall a wood stove insert filled the opening of a massive stone fireplace. A heavy wooden mantel spanning the length of the fireplace was set with tall pewter candle holders and large pewter charger plates. An empty tall iron log holder stood at the side of the fireplace and next to it stood an assortment of fireplace tools. Hanging on the wall above the mantel shelf, a painting of a herd of running horses caught Bryn's attention.

Sam walked over to an over-sized brown leather sofa decorated with brass hardware and set her glass on a small table. Sitting next to the sofa, were two leather recliners and two overstuffed floral chairs.

Bryn sat on one of the plush chairs and Sam sat on the leather sofa. "How old is this house," she asked as she placed her glass on a railroad industrial cart repurposed into the coffee table.

"It was built in the 1800's and owned by the same family who farmed the land. Back then it was a cow farm. The original house was much smaller, but at different times it was updated and several rooms were added on." Sam nodded towards the kitchen. "We opened the kitchen wall and added this family room."

"How many acres do you have?" Bryn asked, eyeing the coffee table she had placed her glass on.

"We own sixty acres. It's more than enough to take care of. Most of the land is pasture for our horses and the rest is hayfields."

"I know how much work that can be. I had a sometime boyfriend who has a horse farm up in New Hampshire. I loved his farm. I was in horse heaven."

"What kind of horses does he have?"

"He owns and shows quarter horses, and we did a lot of riding back then. Sometimes I wonder what I miss most. The horses or him," Bryn laughed

"So, I take it you're not together anymore?"

"No, it was a relationship that we tried several times to hold together, but unfortunately, I loved him more than he loved me, and I vowed to *never* let that happen again. My mother's philosophy is to find a man who loves you more 'cause that's the only way you can keep him close to you, and what I used to find funny, I now tend to agree with."

Now it was Sam's turn to laugh. "Oh my gosh! Your mother sounds like my grandmother. Minnie always says things like that to me. I don't think they should ever meet. Between the two of them, we wouldn't stand a chance. Luckily, Minnie loves Denver and was pushing me towards him since the day she met him." Sam took another sip of her lemonade. "Can I refill your glass?"

"I'll be floating, that's for sure, but yes that would be great." She needed a moment to think. Parker's face flashed through her mind. She rubbed the front of her neck, a habit she had when thinking. Letting her guard down was not a part of the plan and she knew she was sharing her real life too much.

What's wrong with you, Bryn? she thought. She never mixed

business with pleasure, but this wasn't like any of the other jobs she and Parker had worked on. She was doing him a favor, and other than that she wasn't involved with his latest caper. All he asked from her was to meet the owner of the farm and find out what she could about his missing mare and her horseshoes. It was such a simple assignment that she was almost lulled into a feeling that she wasn't there to do a job.

Sam returned with the pitcher of lemonade and poured some into Bryn's glass, handing her a new napkin.

The pause while Sam went to the kitchen gave Bryn a chance to set her mind to the job at hand. "Where did you find this fabulous piece?" she asked, running her hand over the top of the coffee table.

"The Brimfield Flea Market. Den and I never miss it. I had been looking for quite some time for a big chunky coffee table. We found this railroad cart last year and he refinished the top. I love the grain in the wood and the heavy wheels on the bottom. Have you ever been to the Brimfield Flea Market?"

"No, but for sure I'm going to put it on my list. I love antique shows."

"Maybe this fall you can join me for a day at Brimfield. If you're interested in antiques, it's the place to go."

Bryn felt her heart skip a beat. She would love to do just that, but understood that once her job was done she would probably not return. She quickly changed the subject and pointed to the painting over the mantle. "I absolutely love that painting. Is it an original?"

"Yes it is. I fell in love with it when Denver and I were in Texas visiting his parents, and they gave it to us for our wedding. I'm totally enthralled with it and never miss a chance to walk over and look at it. Maybe it's the colors or the wildness of it, but it always draws me."

Bryn got up and walked to the fireplace to get a closer look. "It's magnificent. Who is the artist?"

"She's not well-known in the art world, at least not yet. Her name is Jill Martin."

"I'm going to put her on my list of artists to follow. It looks like we have the same taste in art work."

"Perhaps we do. I love southwest artists and always pick up some turquoise pieces of jewelry when we visit Den's family in Texas."

"Is that where your husband is from? Kind of a long way from home, isn't it?"

"Yes, and I'm so lucky that he decided to relocate here. He does miss Texas, but we try and visit as much as possible."

Bryn placed her glass back on the table and walked to the bay window overlooking a fenced in yard filled with tall yellow and purple flowers. "Is that where you cut the flowers I see in vases spattered around your kitchen and family room?"

"Yes, I love fresh flowers but didn't have much luck growing them because of my two troublesome goats, Rudy and Roger. They eat anything that looks like food, so I found a place inside the fence to plant a bed of flowers for cutting."

"Goats? You have goats? Oh, that's right you did mention that. Do you use them for milk?"

"Heavens, no!" Sam laughed. "I don't have time for that. They're a couple of rascals that I ended up with. When I'm doing chores I give them free range but I have to watch them. They're quite the characters."

"The flowers are so beautiful right outside the window. I

wouldn't have thought of doing that." Bryn was fascinated with Sam's menagerie of animals and her green thumb. "So, you mentioned that you also have chickens?"

"Sure do. Nothing like fresh eggs, and once you've eaten one, it's hard to go back to store-bought. On the way to the barn, I'll show you the coop and introduce you to Rudy and Roger. Hopefully when we're done checking out the horses, you'll come back to the house and we can have blueberry pie and a cup of coffee."

"Thought you'd never ask. It smells delicious," Bryn said. "I'm ready to see the horses whenever you are."

"Okay, let's go," Sam said putting her empty glass on the table. "Oh, and by the way. I just thought of something. You said your friend has quarter horses. Maybe you can take a look at a rescue I have and see if you can tell me something about her?"

Bryn couldn't believe her good luck. Now she was glad that she had mentioned dating someone who had quarter horses. "I'd be glad to," she said as she followed Sam out of the house. This was turning out better than planned.

Chapter 19

On the way to the barn, Sam stopped and introduced Bryn to Rudy and Roger. She opened the gate and the small black and white goats tumbled over each other in their eagerness to greet the women.

"What the heck! They are so cute. What kind of goats are they?" Bryn was captivated by the friendliness of the goats.

"Pygmy goats, and most of the time they *are* fun to be around. I've taught them some important commands and that helps." Sam bent down and scratched Roger's side.

"I didn't know you could train goats." Bryn was on her knees running her hand over Rudy's head.

"Goats are very smart and can be trained. Some people even use them to pull small wagons. I give treats to teach them to respond to commands."

"What kind of commands do they know?"

"Go home, No, and Come! If they want to stay out of their pen, they need to come when I call them. I can't have them running off the property causing trouble. It was easier to keep an eye on them when the twins were home. Denver helps when he's out working around the barns, but they require a lot of watching when their running loose."

"I can see why you have them, even though you say they look for things to get into. They *are* adorable." Bryn got up and brushed the dirt from her jeans.

"Well, you're only seeing their good side today. They're kissing up to us, hoping to be let out of their pen. I can't tell you how many times they've run up behind me and butted me in the back of the legs. Not hard of course, just playful knocks. But there have been times when they've caught me off guard and I've almost pitched over. My twins Kristy and Justin love the little munchkins."

"What do you do when they misbehave?" Bryn had never been around goats and was very interested in the delightful Rudy and Roger, who were chasing after each other, jumping up and down on an old picnic table.

"They get a time out," Sam laughed

"Too funny. A time out for goats. I've tried that with Pug but it never works."

"Doesn't seem to work as well with my dogs either, but Rudy and Roger hate being penned and know when they do something wrong, that's *exactly* where they're going."

"Enough! Both of you!" Sam scolded the playful goats. "We're here to see horses, not play with goats."

Sam and Bryn headed toward the barn, passing by the chicken coop. The bleating cries from Rudy and Roger called after them and Bryn had the impulse to return to their pen. "Will they keep calling until you let them out of the pen?" she asked

"No, they'll stop once we're out of sight." Sam said, leading Bryn down the hill to the lower barn.

Along the way they talked about the goats and dogs, and Sam knew that, like herself, Bryn was an animal lover. Anyone listening to their chatter would have thought they were long-time friends rather than strangers who had only just met.

Entering the barn, they were greeted by a parcel of cats and the low nicker of a horse.

"Wow! How many cats do you have?" Bryn asked, bending down to stroke a friendly gray and white cat rubbing against her leg.

"Last count, eight." Sam chuckled, picking up a small yellow cat. "One of the females missed my trip to the vet to get spayed, and she had five kittens. I gave three away and kept this yellow tabby and the one you are petting. I need cats in the barn to keep down the rodents, but enough is enough. My daughter Kristie loves cats. She was home from college when they were born and begged me to keep the two kittens. I couldn't say no and two more barn cats don't matter that much. Did your friend in New Hampshire have barn cats?"

"Yes, he had several, but not this many. What about the predators? Do they go after your cats? I know Par..., she almost said his name, always worried about the coyotes." Bryn had picked up the gray and white cat, now purring in her ear.

"We have coyotes, but Fisher cats are the worse predators for small animals. Once in a while one of the cats ventures out at night, but most of them are smarter than that. And they're all here every evening for feeding." Sam was petting a solid black cat that had been sitting on a high rafter overhead. "We also have other barns and some of the cats stay there at night."

"And who do we have here?" Bryn asked reaching over to pet the black cat.

"This is Mia, my favorite cat, and we call her The Trickster. She has an uncanny knack of climbing straight up a beam or a tree so fast you almost miss it. There's no other barn cat that can match her skills. She likes sitting high on the beams but she always comes down when she hears my voice. She's very smart and our oldest cat." Sam picked a piece of loose hay off her shirt. "Enough with the cats. I brought you to the barn to show you something special. Follow me."

Bryn gently dropped the cat on the floor. She knew there was a horse in the barn; she had heard it when they entered. The stalls at the front of the barn were empty, but the nicker had come from a stall at the back of the barn. Maybe it was Magic, but she didn't want to seem too eager. "I knew you had at least one horse in here and for a moment, I wondered about it, but as you can see I was too busy with your cats. They are so darn cute."

"All of our horses are turned out into the pastures or smaller corrals. The horse you heard is one of our mares who foaled last night. She had a beautiful filly."

Bryn felt a moment of disappointment, but it passed quickly when they walked to the stall.

Standing at the stall door was a beautiful brown pinto Curly mare, and beside her stood a foal that looked just like her dam. "How exciting *that* must have been. And look at the curly coat and the ringlet mane! I can see why you love your Curly horses." Bryn was enamored with the foal. "She's so precious," she said smiling ear to ear.

Sam unlatched the door of the stall. "Do you want to come in?"

"Can I?" Bryn was fascinated. "The mother won't mind?"

"No," Sam laughed. "My horses are used to being around people from the time they are born and I encourage the interaction."

Bryn was a little nervous but couldn't resist. She said hello to the mare first, rubbing her side and then moved her hand slowly down to touch the soft coat of the foal. She murmured to the foal. "Hello, precious. Aren't you the pretty one?" Her hand gently touched the short curly mane. "Have you named her yet?"

"Yes, we named her Namid." Sam turned her attention to the foal.

"And her mom's name?" Bryn was fascinated with the gentleness of the mare and the friendliness of the foal.

"Tiva. Isn't she a sweetheart?"

"She really is. Do their names have meanings?"

"Tiva is the Hopi name for Dancer, and Namid is the Cheyenne name for Stardancer. I use Native American names for my foals. It seems fitting since Curly horses were the favored mounts of the Native Americans." Sam patted the rump of Tiva, then bent down and ran her hands over the foal. She gently rubbed her all over in small circular movements, the foal not moving away but standing at her mother's side. She bent down and picked up each small hoof and then gently placed it back down.

"Wow, this foal seems so gentle. Did you imprint her?"

"Yes, and now I'll continue to work a little with her every day."

Bryn kept her eyes on the mare picking at her hay. "My friend in New Hampshire imprints his foals. You know, Sam, I'm really impressed with this mare and foal. I told you on the phone that I had researched the Curly breed, and, honestly, I am so happy that you said yes to a visit from me. Thank you again for taking the time to show me around your farm." Another lie flowed from her lips. Yes, she did research the American Curly horse, but that wasn't why she was here.

Sam turned to face Bryn. Her smile was ear to ear. "Can't you tell how much I enjoy showing them to you? It's really *my* pleasure."

Bryn was in horse heaven. She loved being in the stall snuggling the horses. The dark eyes and curled eyelashes of the foal mesmerized her, and she was lost in the moment. Nothing else mattered except the sweetness of the foal and the smell of the barn. The aroma of leather, horses and hay filled the air, and she breathed in deep, letting it all settle in. She truly missed being at Parker's farm, and inhaling the earthy scent of horses was just another sad reminder.

One question after another spilled from her lips. She wasn't lying about her interest in the unique horse, and now that she had seen them first hand, she wanted to learn more. For Sam, conversation about her Curly horses was something she enjoyed since most people weren't familiar with the breed. Small tidbits of information about them were shared with Bryn, eager to hear Sam explain how she became interested in the breed. Bryn listened to every detail, every now and then nodding her head. Sam's discourse was interrupted by the distant whinny of a horse from a lower pasture behind the barn.

"It's getting late and I know you came to look for a riding horse, but I couldn't resist showing you our new baby," Sam said as she closed the stall gate and bolted it.

"Are you kidding? I can't thank you enough for showing me your new foal. I absolutely love her," Bryn replied as she followed Sam out of the barn and to a paddock where two geldings were eating from a pile of hay.

"The only horses I have for sale are the two you're looking at," Sam said pointing to the horses in the corral, a brown pinto and stocky bay. "I mostly breed, and sell my foals as weanlings or yearlings. We bought these guys from a Curly breeder in Texas. They're great riding horses. Every now and then I have someone looking for a well-broke horse, so when we find one, Denver and I don't hesitate to buy. They were trailered here a few months ago, and I've already had a lot of people calling for appointments to see them. I'm sure they'll sell quickly, so if you have any interest, you need to move on it."

Bryn leaned against the rail and watched the horses. She had a sudden desire to ride, and a faint smile crossed her lips. Bryn's eyes said it all. "I really like them. Both are gorgeous and either one looks like he would be great under saddle." The last time she had ridden was when she was at Parker's farm. "I know you don't have time today, but would you mind if I came back, of course at your convenience, and rode one? You mentioned that you had a ton of trails behind your pastures."

"Sure. I'd love to take you out on some of our trails. And I would never sell without the buyer riding a sale horse. Why don't we plan on the day after tomorrow, say Thursday? You can check your calendar and see if that's good for you."

"Okay, I'll do that. As I said, I'm in town this week looking for a house to rent in Osterville. I can't keep a horse on any of the properties I've looked at so far, and my job requires travel so I would have to board if I bought. Do you board here?"

"Not routinely. Although we have stalls and plenty of pasture, Denver and I are pretty busy with our own horses. The only boarder I would even consider would be an adult. I can't be responsible for children running through the property. Some people just don't keep an eye on their kids. A few of my friends had problems with boarders because of that. But anything's possible. You could probably find a barn closer to where you settle. Osterville isn't that far and they have a lot of riding stables."

Bryn had no intentions of buying a horse and she wasn't interested in moving to Osterville, but the lie continued. "Well, I'm not ready to buy just yet, but I would love to go riding with you. I haven't been on a horse since last year and I'm itching to ride after looking at these geldings."

"I'm always ready to go riding. I'll tell you what; we can plan on doing just that over coffee and pie and you can ride whichever one of the two you are interested in. Oops, I almost forgot. Follow me. I want to show you the quarter horse I mentioned. Maybe you can see something that I've missed, since your friend raises quarter horses. Or as you called him, your former friend," Sam teased.

Bryn's heart skipped a beat. It was the perfect opportunity to see if the rescue horse *was* really Magic. Although Parker was 99% sure, her job was to verify, and more importantly be sure she still had on the numbered horseshoes. "Sure, I'll take a look." She didn't want to appear anxious. She followed Sam to a small fenced pasture.

Two horses, a beautiful black Curly and a golden palomino, were nibbling grass. They leaned over the rail and Sam whistled. The black Curly lifted its head and immediately began trotting towards her. The palomino turned to see where her pasture-mate was going and quickly followed. The black Curly came to the fence, reached her head over and nuzzled Sam's hand.

"Hi there, girl. How's my beauty today?"

"She's exquisite! I love her solid black color. And her thick, crimped mane and wavy tale look like nothing I've ever seen." Bryn stretched her hand over the rail and scratched the mare's neck. "Her coat is so shiny and wavy. It looks like crushed velvet," she said as she ran her hand down the friendly mare's side. "Oh, my gosh! What's that scar running down her side?"

"When she was a foal she was attacked by a coyote. She almost didn't make it, but thanks to our vet and friend Doc Mike, she's healthy and strong. I'll tell you the whole story next time you come by."

"Now you have my interest. Is she for sale?"

"Never," Sam smiled. "She's my forever horse, aren't you Kai?" Sam leaned in and gave the mare a horse cookie and then kissed her on her nose.

The palomino had trotted up and stopped next to the black mare nudging Bryn's arm for attention. She gave a low nicker. Although she expected the yellow horse to be Magic, she was shocked to see her.

Oh, my God! It is *Magic!* She was so excited, she almost blurted out her name. Magic nuzzled her hand, looking for the cookie Bryn always carried in her pocket. Bryn scratched the yellow mare under her chin.

"Wow, she sure has taken an immediate liking to you," Sam remarked watching the yellow horse and Bryn interact. "It's almost as if she knows you."

Bryn knew immediately that Magic remembered her. She

quickly stepped back from the fence, ignoring Sam's words. "So, this is the rescue you were telling me about?"

"Yes, and as you can see, she's not only beautiful but friendly." Sam rubbed the mare's head and scratched the side of her neck. "I don't know that much about quarter horses, but this one is fabulous. Wonderful confirmation and the color of spun gold. Something about this girl is special. I felt it the minute I watched her unload from the trailer."

"I agree." Bryn took in a deep breath and stepped further back from the rail. She had butterflies in her stomach. It was the golden mare she had fallen in love with and a rush of joy came over her. She hadn't been this happy in a long time, and she felt a tug at her heart as she looked into the dark brown eyes of the golden mare. She had to stop herself from being over enthusiastic. Her face turned serious and the tone of her voice changed. "She *is* very friendly. Has anyone else asked about her?" Bryn wanted to go under the fence and wrap her arms around Magic's neck and tell her everything was going to be okay. But she had to hold herself back. The golden horse watched her every move and nickered again, trying to get her attention.

Sam chuckled at the mare's obvious attraction to Bryn. "This is too funny. She *really* likes you, and if I didn't know better, I would think this mare is calling your name."

Chapter 20

Bryn's eyes swept over Magic and then down the front legs of the mare. She was glad she had her sunglasses on so Sam couldn't see her staring at Magic's front hooves.

"So, what do you think of her?" Sam asked, brushing a strand of loose hair from her eyes.

Bryn was focused on Magic's front hooves, and she almost didn't hear Sam's question. *Oh, no! Where are her shoes?* She took off her sunglasses to get a better look at the yellow horse. It was a good reason to slowly evaluate the mare without risking attention; after all it was Sam who had asked for her opinion. She walked closer to the rail, but not near enough for Magic to appear too friendly towards her. Bryn studied the mare, curbing her impulse to show any excitement. "She's a beauty. That's for sure. Looks sound, and I believe you're right when you say she's a big-money quarter horse."

Magic gazed back at her curiously, waiting for her to come closer.

"I find it hard to believe that no one has contacted you after all this time. She doesn't have any cuts or scratches on her, and she looks good, considering what she went through. By the way, what do you call her?"

"Phoebe, the woman who rescued her, named her Moxie. Said this girl has a lot of Moxie to make it this far on her own. I kind of like it, so we've kept that name. I'm sure she has an elegant name, and as soon as her owner claims her, that's the first question I'll ask."

"Moxie, that seems fitting," Bryn said, still gazing at the yellow mare. Parker's face flashed through her mind and she had to stop herself from laughing out loud, imagining what he would say when she told him Magic's new name. "I see she's barefoot. Did she lose her shoes?"

"No, her back shoe was loose, so my farrier pulled them all."

Damn. Now what? Bryn thought. Without skipping a beat she said, "A horse with shoes on. That must be different for you. I remember reading where most Curly horses are kept barefoot."

"True, we keep them barefoot and only trim, although, I did have an older Curly who had an injury to his front hoof so I kept him shod. But you're right; Moxie is the only horse that came with shoes. Our farrier said for now she doesn't need them, so we're keeping her barefoot until her owner shows up."

Bryn's heart skipped a beat. Sam didn't know it, but she had stumbled on a vital piece of information. Magic didn't need shoes, except for traveling to Florida. Not only was the mare worth a great deal of money, but the signature horseshoes were even more valuable. How to begin the next question ran through her mind.

Bryn began adlibbing as she tried to find out what Sam did with Magic's horseshoes. "Funny how everyone thinks differently about keeping horses barefoot or shod. I know many owners are going with the barefoot idea, but others not so much. Maybe the owner of this mare was riding on hard surfaces so he kept her shod." She paused and began again. "So, did your farrier take away the shoes? I know some people save them, for whatever reason."

Sam felt a sudden unease with Bryn's question, but she couldn't put her finger on why. She turned and looked at Bryn who had her sunglasses back on. "You're right. I don't have my horses shod, but guess what? My farm is a collection site for used horseshoes."

"What? Now that's too funny. A collection site? Why?" Bryn was puzzled

"Let me explain," Sam laughed. "I know it sounds a bit crazy." They were both leaning on the rail watching the horses that had meandered back to munching grass. "My friend runs a therapeutic riding program, and her daughter has a girls' club, aptly named Angels Club. The girls collect the shoes and decorate them."

"What on earth for?" Bryn asked

"They sell them at their annual fund-raising event for the riding program. Some of the profits from the sale go to the riding program and the rest stays in their club to help people in need. They are a wonderful group of girls. I'll show you a few I've bought from them. They do a beautiful job and I have them hanging on several doors in my house."

Bryn was startled. Her eyes narrowed at this sudden change in events. "So, that's where you send the discarded horseshoes?"

"Uh-huh. And other horse owners support the girls by dropping off their shoes at my farm. Problem is, what started out as a few local farms donating shoes has gotten bigger and bigger." Sam shrugged. "Den said it's getting out of control and I'm beginning to agree. Now, I'm getting shipments of discards from farms out of state."

"That's amazing!" Bryn was trying to comprehend what Sam was telling her and how to move forward. "I'm intrigued by the whole idea." She drew in a quick breath. She needed to be careful with her questioning. "So, where do you store *all* the shoes that are dropped off?"

"Come with me and I'll show you. They're kept in one of our back barns. Follow me."

Bryn followed Sam to a small dirt road that ran along a large pasture. *I can't believe this. What next?* Her brain moved into high gear and her heart quickened.

Parker was an expert farrier and his horseshoes were special orders. The blank shoes came to him, and he stamped the numbers on the inside ridge for Luca to retrieve. It was a simple task. Magic's shoes had a black edge around the top and a slight gold fleck in the iron. She was sure that Sam's farrier would have mentioned the numbers. And it wasn't as if she could ask her. Either Sam wasn't disclosing that piece of information, or she never thought more about it. It didn't make sense. Sam was one smart lady, and she must have wondered what the numbers meant.

The dirt road meandered along the side of the pasture, continued down a slight slope, and stopped behind a small barn. The barn doors were open and the sun rays cast shadows on the floor. Bryn expected more barn cats, but evidently, they were staying in the large barn. Although eager to see the pile of horseshoes, she was beginning to feel wilted from the heat and was ready to return to the house. She removed her sunglasses, and looked around. "This is a great barn. What do you use it for?"

"It's mainly used for storage, or for new horses that need to be quarantined when they arrive at the farm." Sam took off her sunglasses as well and put them on top of her head.

"I can see that. It's so clean. For sure no horses are here right now, but really a charming old barn." Bryn peeked into each of the stalls as she walked by. "I count only four stalls, but they're really large. If I ever build a barn I would probably build one this size."

"You're right. It's perfect for a couple of horses, and better yet, it's situated on this small rise so storage is underneath, large enough for unloading hay or shavings. That's where we keep the shoes for pickup."

Bryn tried not to appear impatient. "So, how was this barn used when the property was first settled? It's different. Usually a barn has a loft but you say storage is below?"

Sam described how back in the day cows were kept below and the stall area, where they were now standing, was used for storage.

Bryn listened intently as she scrutinized the space, envisioning how it must have looked years ago. She absolutely loved the quaint barn and could picture herself enjoying the seclusion while sitting on a rocking chair with a cup of coffee and a good read. Rustic and cozy, it was perfect. Set back from the rest of the farm, the delicious aroma of hay and horses still lingered in the air. For a moment she was lost in thought. She inhaled deeply taking it all in. "You say you store the discarded shoes below?"

"Yes, they're out of the way, but there's easy access for pickup. Follow me, and I'll show you."

They left the upper part of the barn and walked down the slope behind it. The barn reminded Bryn of a house with a walk in basement. Huge sliding doors opened to a sizable storage area. Tall stacked bags of shavings were piled along one side of a wall, and in a back corner Bryn could see a large wooden crate.

Sam flicked on a light. "I try to keep everything in order, so I had Den set up this corner for holding the horseshoes. Deliveries are dropped off here and then picked up by my friends."

Bryn walked to the crate and looked in at a small pile of discarded horseshoes. She expected to see a lot more. "How long have these been here and when do they get picked up? Seems like a lot of work, but fun," she said, making casual conversation.

"Oh, this is the latest haul. Last week they picked up a load about three times this size. I don't like to let the pile get too big before pickup." Sam leaned down and selected a shoe and showed it to Bryn. "Looks like this one will require a little cleaning before they decorate it," she laughed tossing it back onto the mound of discards. "The only work on my part is setting the time for delivery and pickups, but I'm happy to do this for my friend's daughter and her club. They're a great group of girls and work so hard, but you can imagine how many shoes can accumulate when you're the drop-off center."

"How did you manage to become the recycler of horseshoes? I understand why you do it for the girls, but how do other farms know that you're the drop-off center?" Bryn quickly scanned the pile of shoes looking for any sign of Magic's.

Before Sam could answer, a sudden thought flashed through her mind. If they took a load out last week, Magic was already here and her shoes may be gone. She tried to take a little more time to scan the discards, but she was certain Magic's shoes were not in the pile.

"Ready to go back to the house?" Sam asked "I don't know about you, but I'm thirsty and sweaty."

"Me too! I *am* melting, and I think I've seen enough. I must say I'm duly impressed." Bryn smiled as she turned to follow Sam back to the house.

Walking back to the house gave Bryn time to think about her next move. Sam didn't reveal anything about Magic's, aka Moxie's, shoes and Bryn was totally perplexed. Bryn was at a loss. More importantly, how could she come up with a reason for going back to the barn so she could rummage through the pile without raising suspicion? She wiped the perspiration from her forehead with her hand, and asked herself why *she* should worry about it. She had done her job and verified that Magic was at the farm, but now there was a major setback. Parker would not want to hear that Magic's shoes were missing. And the encounter with the mare had been a close call. She knew without a doubt that Magic remembered her. At Parker's farm, she had spent countless hours grooming Magic and she had been her favorite horse. Darn! She would have to remember to use her new name Moxie. She almost slipped a few times and called her Magic.

Chapter 21

The house was pleasantly cool and Sam immediately headed to the coffee maker and filled two mugs. Bryn carried the steaming mugs to the table and Sam carried the pie. Sam turned an eagle eye to Bryn as she reached for her mug of coffee and took a sip of the hot beverage. Something didn't ring true about the meeting between the yellow horse and Bryn. Horses have good memories, and if they had a preference for a trainer or rider it was expressed even after a lengthy separation. But why would Bryn lie? *It's just my mind working overtime*, she thought. She liked the woman sitting across from her and if she knew the mare, wouldn't she have said something? *Too crazy.*

Bryn caught the quizzical look in Sam's eyes and knew it was one of curiosity. She broke the mood quickly. "This pie is delicious. Baking is something I've never learned how to do. Too busy I guess, and living alone doesn't help."

"Thanks. I love to bake but I'm not half as good as my friend Lyla who owns her own deli and bakery." She sensed that Bryn had a busy, unsettled life. To look at the pretty woman one would think she had everything, but Sam sensed loneliness in demeanor.

Bryn felt a twinge of envy as she sat eating pie and drinking coffee with a woman who was content with her life. Bryn wasn't a very good cook, never mind a baker. It's *not* that she wasn't interested; it was because she never had the time to devote to learning how. Her career kept her busy and she traveled a lot. Living alone was not conducive to preparing fabulous dishes. Most of her meals were take-out, but once she settled down and had a family she vowed to learn more about cooking and baking. She had planned on marriage and children, but it didn't look like it was in the foreseeable future. Since turning thirty-two in May, she feared that time was running out and that she was not destined for motherhood. After watching a special on TV, extolling the benefits of freezing a woman's eggs, Bryn had the urge to phone her gynecologist and set an appointment to learn more.

Maybe it was listening to Sam talk about her twins and her husband, but she suddenly felt empty. For the first time, she believed she had spent too much time on her career and not enough time on herself. She had become addicted to the heart pumping rush of adrenaline that coursed through her body each time she was on a job, but the instant kick wasn't as appealing as it used to be. Is this what her mother meant when she said that time changes everything and someday she would find that her career wasn't enough? Not that her mother knew the true nature of her occupation, because if she did she would have been in a constant state of anxiety. The sudden realization that she wanted more than this type of work made her shudder. It was time to make major moves and without a doubt, this would be her last job with Parker or anyone else. She made up her mind, that after this operation she would change careers.

Sam and Bryn spent the next hour chatting as they leisurely dined on delicious pie, accompanied with refilled mugs of coffee. Their banter moved from horses to kids and then jobs. Bryn had told Sam that she worked for a large corporation that required a fair amount of travel, and Sam had shared her life as a journalist and part-time instructor at a local college. But most of their conversation centered on horses, their love of barns and how much pleasure they found in farm life. For Bryn, it was easy to keep the small talk pointed in that direction. She had a lot in common with the woman sitting across the table from her and if she wasn't there on a false pretense, she knew there was a strong possibility they could become friends.

"I've taken up enough of your time," Bryn said, wiping her mouth with a brightly decorated poinsettia napkin. Sam had already explained why holiday napkins and paper plates decorated with snowmen were still in use. The longer she and Sam talked, the more she enjoyed her company. Sam had made her feel comfortable and treated her like she had known her forever. It didn't take long for Bryn to understand why Sam had solid friendships and a richly filled life. It was clear. She had not taken the time to build friendships, and she suddenly realized what she was missing. Her job had been her priority in life but she had given up everything for it. Now she understood why she chose the men in her life. Like it or not, she chose men who could never commit to intimacy or a plan a future with her. In her line of work the two could never coexist.

At this moment in time, she was reminded that something was missing in her life. It was the feeling of easiness and the sheer enjoyment of laughing with a girlfriend. She needed real friends, not just acquaintances. A pang of guilt shot through her. She genuinely liked Sam and wished she could tell her the true purpose of her visit. But revealing it could put Sam in a dangerous situation. For now, everything would have to remain a mix of both truth and lies. Bryn got up from the table and picked up her sunglasses lying next to her plate. She took her leather handbag from the back of the chair and carried the plates to the kitchen counter, draining the last of her coffee as she walked.

"You don't have to do that," Sam said

"Nonsense. Of course I do. You've been a great host and I've taken way too much of your time. The least I can do is clean up my mess. I wish we could go riding tomorrow now that I have the itch. Thursday seems too far away," Bryn said.

"I do too," Sam said, dropping the napkins into the wastepaper bin. "But this fellow who called was insistent on seeing the farm and horses tomorrow. He said he was only here for a few days and it's the only time he can fit into his schedule."

The hairs on the back of Bryn's neck stood up. Every instinct sounded an alarm. For some reason she assumed that the person coming tomorrow was a woman. She took in a deep breath to compose herself, her hand tightening around the coffee mug. "Do you get many men looking for horses? I find that most of the time it's women looking for themselves or their daughters. I know men ride, but women shop." Bryn tried to joke about it, but this was no laughing matter.

Sam placed her empty mug on the counter. "True, it's mostly women looking for a horse. But this man said he was looking for his daughter. He and his wife are relocating and he promised his young girl a horse to help ease the move."

"Really? Sounds like a nice dad. Where are they moving from?"

"Florida. He said they were originally from New England and wanted to move back here."

Bryn gulped. This didn't sound right. Could Luca be trying to blindside Parker? Had he found the farm on his own, and was trying to double-cross him? Now what? Luca was a snake and would stop at nothing to get what he wanted.

Should she ask Sam if she could come by tomorrow after the potential buyer left, then show up earlier to check him out? No, he may recognize her. She had never met him, and she wasn't sure how much he knew about her and Parker. If he had been to Parker's farm there may still be photos of them. Well, at least there used to be. She felt a pang of regret when she thought of Parker and for a moment she forgot where she was in the conversation.

"Hey, what're you thinking? You look so sad," Sam said

"Oh, for a moment I thought of my last visit with the man I thought I loved." The truth came easy.

"Why don't you call him? Maybe he misses you. What do you have to lose?"

Bryn paused. She carefully calculated her words. "Maybe I will, but getting back to tomorrow and this interested buyer. Will your husband be here when he comes? I know I don't like strangers dropping by when I'm by myself." She needed more information about this man and if it was Luca who made the appointment, she shuddered at the thought of Sam being alone with him.

"Oh, no. I wouldn't have a man I just talked to over the phone come by without Denver here. Usually, the people looking for a horse are referred to me by someone I know, or a friend of a friend. There are too many loose cannons out there. I have the dogs but what good would they be *against* a gun?"

Sam was only half-kidding. She knew enough to be careful with strangers. Minnie had taught her to be aware of her surroundings and to listen to her gut. Living alone, Sam had always been cautious and it wasn't often that someone made an appointment to see a horse without a reference. But, she did sell horses and every now and then she made an exception to her referral rule.

"That makes me feel better," Bryn said. "A woman can't be too careful, and I'm not trying to make you paranoid. Is he giving you any red flags?"

Sam looked at Bryn, her eyebrows raised in a questioning manner. "I'm surprised that you are concerned about someone that I only mentioned. Are you a private detective or something?" she asked kiddingly.

Bryn laughed. "No, not quite, but let's say that I've learned to listen to my instincts. Like most women, we usually toss red flags aside and make excuses for what doesn't seem right." She was trying to lighten the conversation. "For example, I'm very intuitive about the people I've just met." Smiling, she said, "I knew the minute I met you, I would have chosen you as a friend if we lived closer."

"You know, you're right. I knew when we exchanged the shortened version of our names we were kindred spirits. Maybe it's horses that we have in common or maybe we laugh at the same things, but it does feel like we've always known each other."

Both women went silent. Sam was amazed at how Bryn had picked up on her feelings about the caller who was coming tomorrow, and Bryn was thinking about how to find out if it was Luca who was nosing around. Bryn needed to speak with Parker about this turn of events. It was all too coincidental. *Follow your own advice, Bryn. If it smells like a rat, it is a rat.* It was essential to have more information about this man. "What if I call you tomorrow and if this buyer, you didn't tell me his name, leaves early we can go on a short ride?"

"That might work. He's coming around ten, and if he's gone by noon, we can have lunch. Denver has an appointment in the afternoon and you can meet him before he heads out. You know, Bryn, I could be way off about this guy. Sometimes I carry on a lot about nothing. Crazy thing is I find humor in a lot of things most people wouldn't. But for some reason this guy's voice reminded me of an actor. He was slow and deliberate as if reading a script and it almost made me laugh."

"Have you ever had someone come to the farm that you were uneasy about? You do live sort of off the beaten track."

"No, not really. Before I met Denver, I was on my own raising my twins, and my first concern was always for my safety and theirs."

Bryn nodded in agreement. "Well, I think it's a good idea to always think of your own safety. You don't have to apologize to me. I feel the same way. I live alone and I'm always careful. Tell you what. Call me when he leaves. You have my cell number. It'll be fun to go on a short ride and it's not supposed to be as hot tomorrow. And I insist on bringing something if it's lunch time."

"Thanks, but don't bother. Lyla will be stopping by and she drops off desserts for us at least once a week. Hey, just thought of something. Maybe we'll ride the horses to her deli for lunch. You will love the trail that takes us to her place, and wait 'til you see how convenient it is for horses and riders."

"That sounds like fun. I can't wait."

Sam walked Bryn to her car.

Bryn slid in, turned the ignition on and rolled down her window. "So, I'll see you tomorrow or the next day. Just let me know when. I am so excited to go riding again."

"Me too. It will be fun. Oh, and not that it matters, I just remembered the guy's last name that's coming tomorrow. It's D'Angelo. He's short on words, so I doubt he'll stay very long. Some people are like that. Just show the horses, and if there's interest, they put down a deposit and that's it. But one thing for sure, if I don't like him, I won't sell him a horse. I did Google his name and address. I'm fussy about where my horses go. He said his daughter wanted a Curly horse and he found our farm on the internet."

Bryn was stunned. Her eyes widened. She was right. She drew in a short breath and kept calm, showing no surprise. Without hesitating, she said, "D'Angelo. That does have a nice ring to it." Bryn's mind was racing.

Of course he would give his real name. He knew Sam would run a check on him, and Luca's real business lived in the shadows. He had no police record, and therefore, on the surface, he was a model citizen. To most people he was a successful business man, but to the FBI he was a well-known criminal and on their radar. For sure, Luca would tell Sam he lived in Florida. Bryn knew his tricks. Just like her, he told a little truth and packaged it with lies. Luca coming tomorrow? This was not a good thing. He was up to something. And to add to the quagmire, she had no idea where Magic's shoes were and she was still deliberating on how she could get Sam to offer up that piece of information without raising her suspicions. How would Luca manage that? What were his plans? For sure she had to stay one step ahead of him.

Bryn put her car in drive, promising to return after the potential buyer left, and Sam walked back to the house. The minute she was at the bottom of the driveway, Bryn phoned Parker. The phone rang several times, but there was no answer. She was forced to leave a message and she spoke rapidly. "Parker, call me as soon as possible. I have something urgent to tell you and it is *not* good news."

Chapter 22

*L*uca was out of bed, showered, shaved and dressed by six in the morning. His appointment with the rescue horse woman, Samantha Steele, was at ten. It was about an hour drive to her farm and he had plenty of time for coffee and a large breakfast of eggs, bacon, and home fries at the hotel dining room. He left his briefcase in the room and closed the door, hesitating a moment and looking both ways down the long carpeted hallway. There was no one waiting for the elevator, and that was a good sign. He could not shake off the uneasy feeling that Parker was watching him and his eyes darted back and forth looking for any sign of his old friend. His usual guardedness was in high gear. The elevator came to a stop with a ding and he stepped in, pressed the button to the second floor, and leaned against the elevator wall as it dropped from the 15th floor without stopping. With a ding, the doors opened and he stepped out.

He walked past the usual business people filling their mouths with food or drinking coffee and talking about their latest deals. Luca's dining preference was a booth or table against a wall so that, without being obvious, he had a clear view of anyone entering or leaving the dining area. He carefully scanned the room and, seeing an empty table, walked briskly to it. His natural mistrust had paid off more than once and since he was trying to blindside Parker, nothing could be taken for granted. He hadn't heard from his old buddy since his last call telling him the sad tale of how Magic had bolted into a state forest and was nowhere to be found.

There were no diners seated next to him and that suited him just fine. He was in no mood to listen to loud voices from anyone seated next to him. One of the perks from staying at the upscale hotel was the lack of diners early in the morning. Luca wasn't a morning person, and idle talk rattled his nerves. One look from his piercing dark eyes was usually all it took for people to understand his annoyance, and hushed voices immediately replaced loud ones. Luca had brought along the newspaper that was left on the carpet outside his room and he placed it on the table next to his plate, glancing around as he did so.

As if on cue a slender waitress, who looked to be about fiftyish, approached his table.

Luca barely nodded to her, but his eyes had done a quick assessment of the woman standing next to him. Lolly, the pin on her shirt said, wore her dark brown hair pulled back and off her shoulder. She was dressed in hotel style, black pants, white shirt and black apron.

"Hello, my name is Lolly," she said in a sing song voice "And I'll be your server this morning." She nimbly turned the glass up and poured water from a pitcher into it while at the same time asking what he would like to drink.

"Coffee, hot and black," he grunted, hardly glancing up from the newspaper he had opened. "And I'm ready to order."

Luca drained the cup of coffee before breakfast arrived and gestured to Lolly for a refill.

When Lolly returned to the table with the coffee pot in hand, Luca studied her for a long moment. Too long for her comfort. "Your breakfast will be here shortly," she said in a crisp, cool tone to the man whose dark, piercing eyes finally returned to the newspaper. A chill ran down Lolly's spine. *I've known men like this,* she thought as she walked away. *I'd better check and make sure his order is ready to serve. I've a feeling this man doesn't compromise on anything, never mind a cold breakfast.* She headed to the kitchen knowing that the man was watching her, feeling his eyes boring into her while checking her every move.

Luca's eyes never wavered as he stared at Lolly walking swiftly towards the kitchen. "Nice," he murmured as his eyes fixated on the small framed woman as she entered the kitchen. He took another swallow of coffee, and then returned to reading the sports page. Lolly arrived with his order just as Luca had folded the paper and placed it on a chair next to him. "More coffee," he mumbled as he opened the napkin and placed it on his lap.

"Yes, sir," Lolly replied filling his cup with fresh coffee. "Can I get you anything else, sir?"

"No, that'll do it."

Lolly turned and headed to a table where two women dressed in business suits had just sat down. She could still feel the eyes of the dark man watching her every move.

Luca eyeballed her as she smiled and made small talk with the women. "Hmm, I'm here for a few days and maybe I can charm her into a drink after her shift. Don't see a ring on her finger and I could use the company." His lip turned into a small twist. "Lolly," he whispered. "Now that has a pleasing ring." After a prolonged breakfast, and consuming more cups of coffee than he could count, Luca asked Lolly to bring him his check. He handed her his room card for billing. His narrow eyes never left Lolly as she walked away with the card and then returned to the table. "Thank you," he said with his best friendly smile.

Lolly couldn't wait to get away from the man with the strong odor of after-shave cologne. "You're welcome, sir," she said, forcing a cursory smile.

Luca pushed his chair back and dropped a large tip on the table. "Now that should sweeten her up."

He made his way through the dining room towards the elevator. His mind was in high gear as he thought about Magic and how he would get his hands on the horseshoes.

Luca returned to his room and packed up his laptop and other essential items, including a small gun that one of his shady contacts had delivered to the front desk. It had been packed in a gift box with a *Happy Birthday* card placed on the top. He smirked at the cleverness of it all and almost laughed out loud when the desk clerk said "'Happy Birthday'" to him when he retrieved the package. Luca had significant resources and had set everything in motion before he left Florida, and when the job was completed the gun would disappear. He was hoping he would not have to use it, but Luca was not a man to go on a job without a firearm at his side.

It was going to be an interesting day, and one that he knew would keep him a step ahead of Parker.

Chapter 23

*L*uca pulled the Caddy onto the highway and turned on the air. He gave a relaxing sigh. *Nothing to do now but drive*, he thought. The display on the GPS said the trip would take about an hour and that gave him plenty of time to review his plan to coax the Steele woman into showing him Magic, while making it all her idea. He settled into the plush leather seat, reached over and picked up the carafe of hot coffee sitting in the console cup holder. Luca was a man of habit and a mug of steaming coffee was better than lighting up a cigarette. He had kicked that habit a few years ago and replaced it with coffee, which according to news reports, was a healthier habit. Luca smirked as he thought about living a healthy lifestyle. For sure his line of work didn't promote good health, so why worry about smoking or drinking. "Oh yeah coffee and bourbon." Those were his healthy habits. He remembered the day he had thrown away his last pack of cigarettes. Watching his father slowly die with an oxygen tube stuck up his nose had changed that habit pretty quick. He didn't mind dying by a bullet, but to suffer like his old man had? Now *that* was a different story.

The coffee was still steaming as he put the mug to his lips and took in a short sip. He placed the mug back in the cup holder, cranked the air up high and concentrated on the directions coming from the tantalizing voice on the GPS.

An hour later, the GPS announced, "You have reached your destination," and Luca slowed the Caddy to take a right turn onto a dirt driveway.

"What the hell kind of place is this?" he mumbled. The temperature on the dashboard read 85 degrees, too hot for this time of year. He was glad he had dressed lightly wearing jeans, a short sleeve white shirt and brown loafers. He wanted to get in and out fast and after glancing at the temperature he knew he wasn't going to hang around any longer than necessary. He was a man of few words and his face usually showed no expression, but today he knew that he would need to lay on the charm and ask a lot of stupid questions. Hopefully, he could dazzle the woman with his toothy white smile and friendly manner. He didn't notice that he was almost at the end of the long drive when Parker flashed through his mind and he lost it. He smacked the steering wheel in exasperation and anger. What a disaster! If he was going to beat Parker at his own game and transfer the money to his own Cayman account he would have to move fast.

Luca heard dogs barking as he pulled into a parking place at the top of the winding driveway. He turned the car off and released his seat belt. Before he could step out of the car, a man was at the door to greet him, and Luca was immediately agitated.

He was prepared to meet a woman. Who the hell was this guy? He never thought of a husband since he had only spoken with the owner of the farm, at least he thought she was the owner. Was this all for nothing?

Luca pulled himself together, turned on a quick smile and got out of the car. He reached his hand out and said, "Hi, Luca D'Angelo."

The tall man grinned as he gave a firm handshake. "Denver Maxwell. Sure is a hot one today. Bet you'll be glad to get back in the car with the air on."

Luca recognized his slow pattern of speech. *He's a southern boy*, he thought. "Yeah, just glanced at the temp on the dash and it said **85**, but standing here, it feels more like 100." Luca could feel small beads of perspiration forming on his forehead.

Denver smiled and nodded in agreement. "Can I get you something cold to drink before we head to the barn?"

"No thanks. I'm all set. Rather get going and take a look at your horses. I can always have a cold drink later."

"My wife will join us as soon as she finishes dinner preparations," Denver said. "We have some friends coming by later."

"Oh, I won't hold you up too long. I spoke with her on the phone. She told you why I'm here?"

"Yup. You're looking for a horse for your daughter. We have two Curly geldings for sale and one of them may work out for you. Follow me to the barn. We brought them in earlier so they'd be out of the heat and you could look at them in a cool place. It's way too hot to be walking the field to look at horses. "

"Appreciate that." Luca raised his eyebrows. *What? Change of plans?* Now he was really concerned. How would he get to check out the palomino if she wasn't in the barn? Luca followed Denver to the barn, all the while scoping the place out. His mind was racing. He had hotel reservations for three days, time enough to finish up this job, but he could feel himself becoming more and more agitated over this sudden turn of events. This wasn't how he had planned it all out. How could he bring up the subject of a yellow quarter horse when this was a Curly horse farm and this dude looked like he wasn't one to fall for any kind of feigned interest in other horses? Women he could bamboozle, but this man seemed too savvy to believe an outright lie. He couldn't risk trouble with him or with the law. *Now what?* They entered the coolness of the barn and Denver flipped on the light. Luca heard the nicker of horses at the far end. *Well, this sucks. All the stalls are empty except for the horses at the back of the barn.*

Several cats ran up to him as he followed Denver down the aisle. One brushed against his leg, and he almost kicked it with his foot. He uttered a curse under his breath, hating the thought of cat hair on his pants.

Denver stopped at a stall door at the end of the aisle. "This here is Tex," he said picking up a halter hanging on a hook by the door. He slid the stall door open and stepped inside. Luca looked on as Denver deftly placed the halter over the horse's head, clipped a lead line to it and walked the gelding into the aisle.

"He's a fine-looking animal," Luca said as he made his way around Tex, his hand moving over and down the side of the horse. And that was no lie. The striking bay boasted a gorgeous thick black curly mane, a long wavy black tail, and his soft dark brown eyes were set off by long curled eyelashes. Luca had never seen a Curly horse and he was impressed by what he saw. Tex stood patiently waiting for the next command while Luca made small talk. "Handsome guy, real stocky and well-behaved. He looks to be about 15 hands."

"That's what he was when I last measured him." Denver scrutinized the man as he examined the horse. Something about the man with small dark eyes made him uncomfortable. What was it? Was it his eyes, his phony smile or just his body language, but he seemed artificial. One thing for sure, he was certain he would never leave Sam alone with him. Maybe it was a male thing, but he felt an increasing unease as he studied Luca's behavior. For a man who never mentioned he had been around horses and was only here because of his daughter, his mannerisms spoke loud and clear he *was* a horse person. Funny, Sam didn't mention that. Then again, maybe she forgot to add that piece of information. Denver pushed his feelings about the man away and concentrated on the horse. The man was here looking to buy a horse for his daughter, he reasoned. It was that simple. Why read anything more into it?

"Too big for my daughter," Luca said, interrupting Denver's thoughts. "I need something smaller. How many hands is the other one?" he asked pointing to the next stall.

"He's about the same size. Do you still want to take a look?"

"Sure, bring him out."

There it was again. The man's voice had a demanding quality to it. *I hate selling horses to strangers*, Denver thought as he led Tex back into the stall and took his halter off. He hung the halter back on hook and walked across the aisle to Arrow's stall. "This gelding is a safe horse for a young girl. Is your daughter a good rider or is she a beginner?"

Luca leaned against the stall gate and rubbed his chin. "She's been taking lessons for a while and she seems pretty good at it."

He hated the useless questions. Forget the horses in the barn. Where the hell was the yellow horse?

Denver led Arrow out of his stall for Luca to inspect him more closely. Luca's keen eyes studied the gelding. Arrow was a gorgeous brown pinto with beautiful markings. A wavy white forelock almost covered his eyes and his bushy mane was thick with curls. Luca walked around Arrow, running his hand down the gelding's right side, then moved to the other side sliding his hand over his broad back and down his back legs. The gelding dropped his head, and Denver rubbed him between his ears, all the while watching Luca.

Luca mumbled something indiscernible and picked up the gelding's hoof for closer inspection. He didn't need to look any further. He knew a good horse when he saw one. This horse was solid and well put together, and if he were interested in buying, this flashy gelding would be his choice. The stocky animal was striking, boasting great bone and a lot of substance. Arrow looked like he had draft horse in him, but Luca didn't want to seem too knowledgeable in front of Denver so he didn't ask.

Luca scratched Arrow under his thick mane. "Great looking horse," his face broke into an amused grin. "Can I ask you something?" Without waiting for Denver to answer he continued, "I can tell you're not from New England. I'd recognize a Texan accent anywhere, but I could be wrong. What's a southern boy doing in Massachusetts?"

Denver gave Luca a half smile. "You got that right. I am from Texas. I have family there, but fell in love with New England, and more importantly the woman I'm proud to call my wife. You know the old saying; home is where the heart is."

Eager to continue the conversation, Luca said, "I know that

feeling. Lolly, my wife, is the best thing that ever happened to me, and of course my daughter Margareta is the apple of my eye." Luca had practiced saying the name of his non-existent daughter, over and over. Margareta was the name of his sister's daughter, and he decided to use her name so he didn't screw up his bluff. Luca knew it was easy to get lost in too many lies, and the name of the perky waitress was an easy one to remember.

"So, been around horses much?" Denver wanted to clear that one right up, but he already knew the answer. If this fellow standing next to him said no, he would shake his hand and say goodbye. It seemed odd that he never offered this piece of information when they first met. Most people begin sharing their horse history if they're looking to buy. It lets the seller know that the buyer is knowledgeable about horses and won't be snookered into a bad deal.

"Matter of fact I have. I used to work at a stable when I was a kid. I had a friend whose family had horses so I got to know a lot about them. We used to ride together. I haven't had the place or time for horses, but now my daughter has the horse itch. That's all she talks about. You know what I mean. Once a girl falls in love with a horse, it's all over. You either have to send her for lessons or buy one. She's been taking lessons to prove that it's not just a passing fancy, and now that we're relocating I thought it was a good time to buy one for her. And besides, it'll keep her busy and away from the boys."

Denver smiled. "I agree that's a smart thing to do. Sounds like she's ready for her own horse."

Luca took a handkerchief out of his pocket and mopped his forehead. "Whew! Getting warm in here." It was always difficult to make casual conversation whether truth or lies, but so far he believed he had made his lies become the truth. Why, he almost believed them himself.

"It sure is. Feels like it's getting hotter as the day's moving on. Let me put Arrow back in his stall and we can go to the house and grab a cold drink."

Luca chewed the inside of his lip. He had to think of a way to stall. He couldn't leave without seeing the yellow mare. "Sounds good, but how 'bout I take a picture of Arrow with my cell before we do that. I'll send it to my wife and daughter so they can take a look at Arrow."

"Good idea. Let's walk outside for a minute so you can get a good shot of him."

Denver led Arrow out of the barn and into the blazing hot sun. Luca took several photos of the gelding, all the while thinking about his next move. Just when he thought he had stalled for as long as he could, a pretty woman came into view. She was walking towards them and waving.

"Oh, here comes my wife." Denver waved and smiled at the slightly built blonde haired woman heading towards them. Luca, who always had an eye for a pretty woman, gave her the once over before she even shook his hand.

Denver leaned down and gave her a quick kiss. Sam turned toward Luca and held out her hand to shake his. "Hi, I'm Samantha," she smiled. "Looks like you picked the hottest day of the year to look at horses."

Luca held the hand of the woman with the lightly freckled nose a little too long for Denver's taste but then again something about this man agitated him and he felt himself move into a defensive mode.

Denver was still holding Arrow's lead line, but he decided to wait a moment longer and watch the man's body language with his wife before he led the horse back to his stall.

"Nice to meet you, Samantha." Luca forced his biggest smile. "You're right. I think I did pick the hottest day to look at the horses you have for sale. But I'm on a schedule and this was the only day I could fit in the time. Your husband's been showing me the two Curly geldings you have for sale. They're really good looking animals. Arrow's the one I would choose for my daughter, and I just took some pictures to send to my wife and her. I'm thinking he's a little too big for our daughter, but he seems like a great horse so I'll let her mother decide. Margareta is very tiny and only thirteen, but I'll see what they think about the size of Arrow. The girl has her heart set on owning a Curly horse and although I've never seen one before, I'm impressed."

"Well, Arrow's a beauty." Sam said as she scratched the horse under his chin. "And I would say he's a great horse for a beginner rider. He's got no bad habits, you can catch him in the field, he stands while being saddled, and he's good for the farrier and loads easily. You couldn't pick a finer horse and I want you to know that we wouldn't sell this horse to a young girl if I wasn't sure of him. Do you want us to saddle him up and you can ride him in the round pen?"

Luca paused as if mulling it over. "Naw, don't have time today, but if my daughter and wife say yes, I'll come back again and see how he handles."

Denver was ready to end the whole conversation. He didn't want to waste any more time if the man wasn't interested in buying. "Look, we've taken him on the trails and our neighbor's daughter has been on him several times so if you're at all interested, you need to let us know by tomorrow."

Luca nodded. "Oh, you can be sure I'll get back to you as soon as I talk to the wife and daughter."

Denver's patience was running thin. "Let me put Arrow back in his stall and we can go back to the house and get out of the heat." He turned and walked Arrow into the barn.

Perfect, thought Luca. "So, Samantha, you have a beautiful farm here. How many horses do you have?

"Oh about ten, including our stallion we use for breeding." She crossed her arms tightly and stood back, keeping enough space between herself and the man with the hard eyes. Bryn had warned her to be careful with strangers and maybe that's what made her uncomfortable around this man. Funny how Bryn had it right and she was glad that Denver was with her. This guy looked too slick and something about him didn't ring true. And another thing, his smile didn't seem natural, more like he was forcing it. Sam was a good judge of people, and a lot of it came from being in the horse business.

Luca kept his voice smooth and friendly. "I'm looking for a farm like this. Where are your fields and your other horses?"

"We have pastures and run-in sheds for all of our horses. Most of our fields are over the ridge," she said pointing west. "Our larger hayfields are below our horse pastures." Her unease about the man diminished a little as she and Luca talked farms and horses. Luca and Sam continued chatting until Denver returned. "Den, I didn't know Luca was a horse person until now."

Luca grinned. "I was telling your husband about my experience with horses when I was a kid before you came to the barn. I have to say, I didn't know anything about this breed but I'm impressed with your geldings."

Denver walked over to Sam and wrapped his arm around her

shoulder. "Yeah, it seems that Luca rode horses when he was a kid." Now that Sam was more at ease with this Luca fellow, he thought that he may have misjudged him. On the surface, he appeared like a devoted father looking for a horse for his young daughter and that went a long way in Denver's book.

Luca shook his head in agreement, all the while taking stock of the situation. A brilliant idea flashed through his mind and his brain flew into high gear. He needed to throw a little sweetener into the pot and this was the perfect opportunity. "Do you think you and Sam could show me around before I leave so I can take a look at your setup and think more about what I'll need to keep a horse for my daughter at our own place? You seem to have the perfect operation here. And besides, if we buy her a horse I'll probably have to buy another for me to ride, and then of course my wife will want one too. You know how that goes, and after looking at your horses I'm thinking it'll be Curly horses for everyone."

That drew Denver's interest. "Sure, we have some time before you leave, as long as you don't mind the heat," Denver said, his southern hospitality kicking in. A request to see the farm was something he couldn't turn down.

At last things were going Luca's way and now that he was on a roll he felt a lot better. "Hey, I'm from Florida, and this is nothing as far as hot summer days go. Where do we begin?"

Chapter 24

*L*uca followed Sam and Den to the top of a small ridge. A steamy summer breeze drifted through the trees and the smell of rain was in the air. For a moment Sam's mind traveled back to the day when a destructive tornado swirled through her town. Just as today, the heat was oppressive and foreboding. A slight shudder ran through her body. Saturday evening's forecast predicted that a sudden drop in temperature would cause severe thunderstorms and a deluge of rain. Everyone was assured that there was no sign of a tornado in the forecast, and the summer storm would finally end the oppressive heat wave.

The weather throughout the country was changing. The freezing, snowy winter in New England had ended abruptly and the hot humid spring began early. She didn't want to dwell on the weekend forecast but it was on everyone's mind. Memories of the rare tornado sent another ominous chill through her body. As far as she was concerned, climate change was happening and she wondered why the naysayers were still in denial.

Sam brushed a strand of loose hair behind her ear and wiped a bead of sweat from her forehead. As they reached the top of a gentle rise, Luca stopped to take in the view, giving Sam and Denver a moment alone. She whispered to Denver, "Let's keep this short. It's too hot for me out here." Sam looked back at Luca and could see the sweat forming on his white shirt and guessed he wouldn't want to stay much longer. He didn't appear to be a patient man, although he certainly showed a keen interest in their farm.

Having paused as long as he could, Luca walked up to the rise and stood next to Denver.

Denver pointed to the fences separating each of the fields. "You can see clear down into most of the fields from here."

Luca was amazed at the richness of the landscape. His eyes followed the fence lines as he looked from one distant field to another. The clear blue sky loomed above the green sloping pastures and far below he could see horses grazing. The view overlooking the grassy fields was magnificent and for a brief second he was captivated by the rolling mountain side.

Sam stood next to Denver, enjoying her favorite spot on the farm. This was the place where she took a break while driving, Yellow Beast, her fickle tractor. Denver had welded a small metal carrier to the crooked instrument panel to hold her thermos of hot coffee, a water bottle, and a snack. Many times she caught sight of deer grazing beside her horses and there was always a hawk or two gliding over the fields looking for small rodents.

When Denver and Sam married, they decided that her farm was where they would live and he brought along a lot of his farm equipment. Sam was thrilled to have his John Deere at what was now considered *their* farm. Ever since she had met Denver, she had gushed over his shiny tractor and dreamed of someday owning a Deere. Although they didn't need two tractors, especially one as finicky as Sam's, they decided to keep Yellow Beast as a backup for small chores. But a funny thing happened once the Deere came to the farm. Yellow Beast gave her a lot less trouble, and except for a little stubbornness starting, it ran like a charm. Sam insisted the Beast couldn't take the competition of the Deere and they both had many laughs about it.

"Look." Sam pointed to the sky. "That could be the hawks that have been checking out our chickens." Denver's eyes latched onto the predator birds, following their every move.

Luca shielded his eyes and looked up to watch the low flying hawks glide over the fields. "Bet they keep your mice population down. There must be a lot of fox if you have mice in your fields."

One of the powerful birds dove down into the field and came up with a small prey hanging from its razor sharp talons. "Hey that looks like a rabbit," Sam said. "I *hate* that. Why can't they stick to mice or snakes? You're right, Luca. We do have fox and I love watching them, especially when they have kits. It's the coyotes that I have a hard time living with. They seem to become more brazen every year."

"I'm not a fan of coyotes either. You can never be sure of them." Luca's eyes settled on two mares standing under a large oak tree taking refuge from the hot noon day sun. Lying on the ground, and barely visible, their foals slept contentedly. The fields stretched down, sloping slightly as they meandered towards a long fence line and Den and Sam pointed out several bands of horses to Luca. His eyes took it all in as he surveyed the property, keenly looking for any sign of the yellow horse. "So, your hayfields are beyond there?"

"Uh huh," Denver said. There are gates at each end of the fields and if you look to the left you'll see our haying machinery."

"So, you must take in a lot of hay. Those fields look pretty large." Fidgety thoughts darted through his mind and he was still trying to make small talk. Where was Magic? He still saw no sign of her.

"Yup, in a good season we can bring in a couple thousand bales and we have enough left to sell, which helps with the upkeep of the farm." Denver was in his element showing Luca the farm and didn't seem to mind the heat one bit.

"Well, I don't know about you, but I need a glass of cold water. I am as dry as the desert, "Sam said. "Let's walk back towards the house. Have you seen enough, Luca?"

"Fine with me," he replied, once again wiping his brow. He could feel his lower lip twitching as he thought about his next move.

"Okay, darlin'. You look like you're ready. Hot sun always melts sweet sugar," Den teased. Sam could feel the flush on her face and it wasn't from the sun. Denver had a way with words that made her blush. She didn't look at him and kept her head turned away so he wouldn't see the slight smile on her lips.

They left the ridge and wound their way around the barn, taking a different path back to the house.

Along the way, Luca saw another barn and several paddocks. "This is a part of the farm we didn't pass before," he said to Denver, his eyes keenly giving everything the once over as he looked for any sign of Magic.

"No, we didn't. These paddocks are for mares and new foals or weanlings." Denver gestured to a large paddock. "First day out of the barn for that mom and her baby."

A tall pile of hay had been dropped in a far corner, and perched on top of the mound; a black Curly foal was stretched out. Even Luca was amused by the sight. The mare was pulling hay from each side of the pile, ignoring her foal's choice of bedding.

"Now, *that's* a pretty picture," Sam said as she pulled out her iPhone and snapped a photo.

Denver chuckled. "Wonder what'll happen when the foal's left with no bedding? That baby's in line for a rude awakening."

Even Luca found something to smile about, but his mind was moving at lightning speed. Still, *no* Magic!

Sam had offered Luca a cold drink when they finished the tour of the property and he had accepted the invitation to buy time. He had to admit their farm was a good-looking setup. He was impressed with the layout, and it took a lot to impress Luca.

The sun was becoming stronger as noon approached and the humidity made the day stifling. The heavy air enveloped Luca and it reminded him of a steamy summer day in Florida. Not a good day to tour the farm he thought.

Sam remembered she had told Bryn that they could go riding if the buyer left early, but it was too hot for the horses to venture out on the trails. As soon as D'Angelo left she would reschedule the ride with Bryn.

Luca was out of patience. Sam was still babbling about coyotes and asked if he had ever had problems with them in Florida. He hesitated, his eyebrows furrowed trying to remember what she had asked and mumbled, "No," as he wiped his forehead with his handkerchief and listened to Denver explain something about the farm. He was past paying attention to either of them. Hot and tired, he was ready to leave as soon as he could figure out how to bring up the question of the rescue horse.

Luca had dropped behind, purposely slowing his pace to buy time to search the farm for a horse that wasn't a Curly.

Sam was puzzled by his short answer of, "No," but quickly realized Luca wasn't paying any attention to them. She squeezed Denver's arm and gestured to Luca who was looking off towards the field they had first passed.

Denver raised his eyebrows knowingly. He mouthed, "He's hot and ready to go."

"Good," Sam mouthed back. She had enough of this tour and was eager to go back into the coolness of the house.

"What the hell," Luca muttered. He stopped dead in his tracks and removed his sunglasses. Holding his hand to shield his eyes, he squinted in the direction of a field they had passed on their way to the ridge. He hadn't seen horses in that field, but he quickly realized they must have been in the run-in shed. That's why he had missed them. Sam and Denver hadn't mentioned any horses turned out in that particular field; they were too intent on showing him the pastures over the ridge. Luca counted two horses and from the distance and he was sure one was a palomino. He knew his quarter horses and *for sure* the yellow one was not a Curly.

Sam and Denver looked back to see why Luca had stopped.

"What's up?" Denver hollered.

Luca pointed to the horses. "I didn't see those horses when we walked by that field on the way to the ridge."

Denver waited for Luca to catch up to him and Sam. "That's because they're smart. Too hot for them today, so they stayed in their sheds. They probably left the shed to get some water. Want a closer look?"

"Sure would." Luca placed his sunglasses back on and walked beside Denver to the gate of the field.

Sam began to follow but changed her mind. She motioned to Denver. "You two can finish the tour. I'm ready for a break. I also need to make a phone call to cancel riding today. It's too hot to take horses out."

"Okay, darlin, we won't be long," he said as he squeezed her hand.

Luca never turned his head or noticed the exchange of words between Sam and Denver. He was all eyes on the palomino. Both horses were a distance away and he tried to control his eagerness to get closer. There she was, all shiny and perfect standing next to what looked like a black Curly.

"Now that yellow horse doesn't look like a Curly horse," he said trying to restrain his enthusiasm. "I'd bet that's a quarter horse. How'd that come about? Is that one yours?"

"You've got a good eye for quarter horses. Just like my dad. That one isn't mine although I kinda wish she was. She's a rescue and we're holding her here hoping the owner will show up."

"Really, how'd that come about?" Luca's eyebrows furrowed with insincere interest as he removed his sunglasses to get a better look at the yellow horse.

"Long story, but the shorter version is that a friend of Sam's was called about a horse running loose on the side of the road at the edge of the Brimfield forest. She trailered her to her farm, thinking the owner would show up pretty quick but that didn't happen. So she asked us if we'd keep the mare until the owner claimed her."

Luca's eyes studied the mare. "Seems odd that the owner still hasn't collected the horse. So no one has even called about her?"

Denver shook his head. "Not yet. For sure, if I were the owner, I would have been searching until I found her. It seems crazy to me, but who knows, maybe the owner is out of commission or something."

For a moment neither man said anything. Denver interrupted the silence with, "Do you want to see her up closer?"

Luca couldn't believe his good luck. This was going to be his day after all. "Sure, are we going to go in the field?"

"No need to do that." Denver whistled loudly and both horses turned their heads toward the sound and quickly trotted to the call that meant a treat. Just as Denver pulled the horse cookie from his pocket, they were at the fence.

The black Curly nuzzled his hand as she took her treat, and the yellow horse reached her head down to take a cookie from his other hand.

"There you go, girls. Hot enough for you today?" Denver ran his hand down the side of the black Curly and then did the same to the palomino. They were warm but not sweating.

Luca was stunned when the yellow mare trotted to the fence for the horse treat. There was *no* doubt about it. It *was* Magic. He removed his sunglasses to get a better look at the mare. His eyes swept over the mare and then down onto her front hooves. Without thinking he muttered, "What the hell! She's *barefoot!*"

Denver looked over at Luca when he heard him muttering. "What's that?"

Luca tried to hide his annoyance. "Oh nothing, I was just mumbling about what a fine-looking mare this is. Well-muscled and strong looking hooves. I notice all your horses, including this one are barefoot. That's a strong selling point." He turned to his usual bag of tricks of compliments to weasel more information out of the cowboy. Proud of his ingenious way of improvising he snickered and thought, *Now that's how it's done. Damn, I'm good.*

Denver caught Luca's snicker and went silent. Something wasn't right about this guy, but he couldn't figure out what it was. And he was talking to himself. The man had only spoken a few words during the whole tour of the farm and now he's asking about horseshoes? "We try and keep our horses barefoot. It's not for all horses, but it works for ours."

That was the perfect opening for Luca. "Well I guess the owner of this mare felt the same way and left her barefoot. Looks like good feet to me."

"To be truthful, she came shod but our farrier didn't think she needed her shoes replaced, so he pulled them and just gave her a trim. Why replace shoes on a horse that may be leaving soon?"

Luca drew in a short breath. "Yeah, I would have done the same. So, did your farrier save the shoes for the owner?" He couldn't think quick enough to beat around the bush any longer. He had to know.

"Naw, he left them here. I don't think Sam saved them for the owner. If I know her, she sent them along with the other horseshoes for her friend's daughter and her club."

"And what the heck do they do with used horseshoes?" Luca was flabbergasted. Talk about throwing a wrench in the whole mess. He took in another breath. It was all he could do to hold back screaming.

Denver felt his fingers clench together as he heard the snarl in Luca's voice. Why did this guy care so much about the horseshoes? It was none of his business. "Well, the girls decorate the shoes and sell them at a fundraiser for a therapeutic riding program."

The sun was directly overhead and beating down on the two men and the horses. Bored, when no more treats were offered, they trotted back to the shade of their run-in shed. Denver was tired and the heat was getting to him. Not only was he suddenly dripping with perspiration but the man standing next to him was making his blood pressure rise. He reached his hand up to wipe the sweat from his brow and glanced at the man standing next to him. He knew by Luca's body language and tone that he wasn't interested in girls doing charity work. The man was more interested in the rescue horse and the missing shoes, but why?

Chapter 25

*L*uca arrived back at the hotel with a million questions running through his head. And the number one was, what did the Steele woman do with the horseshoes? He deftly steered the Caddy into the hotel parking garage and eased into a spot next to the elevator. He turned off the ignition and leaned back, moving his head from one side to the other and his shoulders back and forth.

He hadn't realized how tightly he had clenched his teeth and now his jaw pained and his neck was stiff and achy. He opened the door and stepped out. He let out a loud grunt as he grabbed his laptop from the back seat. "This last job is killing me. I need a drink and a massage," he mumbled as he opened the hotel door, walked to the elevator and pushed the button for the lobby.

"Think, Luca. Where the hell are the shoes?" He cursed again. "Are they in the house, or the tack room, or in the pile of discards in the back barn?" His mind was racing. "How can I search the place without getting caught? What a hell of a spot to be stuck in." He knew they were at the farm, but where? And how much time did he have before Parker showed up? A shot of bourbon would help him concentrate and ease the pain of his sore muscles. That's what he needed. Timing was imperative. He had to find the missing shoes before Parker claimed his horse, and he was sure it would be very soon. It didn't take a rocket scientist to figure out that Sam and Denver would have saved the shoes for the owner of the horse. Without a doubt, Parker was ready to pounce and claim his horse, but he, Luca the great, was one step ahead of him. He had the Steele woman and her husband eating out of his hands. They were honest people and he was sure they had noticed the numbers stamped into the shoes, but they would never suspect that they were account numbers. Any horse person or farrier would realize just by looking at the shoes that they were expensive and not for normal every day wear. They probably thought they were show shoes, and specially made for a blue ribbon horse. Luca's mouth moved into a half grin and he almost laughed out loud. What they didn't know was that the numbers would sweeten his bank account in the Cayman Islands.

The Steele woman had slipped right into his snare when they were drinking the cold lemonade and chatting in her kitchen. It seemed that he, Luca D'Angelo, had made the couple feel at ease talking about horses and it didn't hurt that he showed a strong interest in buying one or two of them. For good measure, and to sweeten the pot, he left a cash down payment on one of the geldings. "Yeah, cash rules," he smirked.

After listening to the Steele woman talk about how they saved discarded horseshoes for some kids who decorated them to sell, he knew for sure she wouldn't have ditched the special ones that Magic came with. Imagine that? Horseshoes worth millions and some kids were going to sell them for a few bucks. If the thought didn't anger him so much, he might have found it humorous. Instead, his lip twisted into a sneer. The only thing that stopped him from slamming the wall was his own genius at casual conversation which drew out the information he was looking for. For sure it was not his forte, but it had worked today. At least now he had an answer to one piece of the puzzle, but there were still so many unknowns and questions about the whole screw up.

His first stop, before going to his room, would be at the concierge desk to book an appointment for a massage. A large tip for the guy, what's his name Art, would ensure the masseuse was an attractive female with silky hands. He could feel his muscles relaxing just thinking about it.

The elevator dinged and stopped, and the doors slid open to the spacious main lobby. To his irritation it was crowded with business people standing in line at the long counters. Some were checking in and others were waiting for bellhops to carry luggage to their room. He had forgotten that there was some kind of conference going on for two days and he was angry and irritated. His brain was frazzled and his senses were wracked by the cacophony of voices, shuffle of bags and people screaming into their cell phones. His mouth drew down at the corners. "Why do people shout into their cell phones? Do they really think we give a rat's ass about their importance?" He had to stop himself from walking up to the lobby microphone and telling everyone to shut the hell up. They were rattling his brain and his patience. For a moment, he thought he should go to his room and phone for the massage appointment instead of working his way around the

crowded lobby to the desk. He quickly checked out the line and
saw that the concierge was just finishing up with an older white
haired man dressed in shorts and a summer shirt, toting a laptop.
Luca strode quickly to the desk to get there before anyone else
had the same idea. He hated lines but thought he had lucked out
with only one person ahead of him. But, just as he reached the
desk, the elderly man hesitated and said something to the
concierge.

Come on, he thought. *Stop the damn jibber jabber.* He was in
no mood to stand in line and wait his turn. Nothing was going
right and his trip to the farm had revealed nothing but disaster.
Sure the horse was there, but for whatever reason neither Sam nor
her husband mentioned the damn shoes and he couldn't figure out
how to ask about them without sounding an alarm.

Luca stood behind the elderly man and waited, trying to keep
his temper in check. He squeezed the bridge of his nose trying to
control the urge to swear and he could feel his hands begin to
twitch. The elderly man began to step away, and then paused.
"Thank you, sir, that helps a lot. And you say you'll call a cab
when I'm ready?"

"Yes, sir," the concierge smiled. "Just phone the desk. Someone
will assist you. You have a great stay. There are lots of interesting
places to visit in our city when you are not at meetings, and we're
here to assist you and to make your stay with us as pleasant as
possible."

Cut the crap, Luca thought. *You might think the old guy had a
million dollars invested in this hotel. They couldn't pay me
enough to put up with that bullshit.* He felt his mouth twitch into
a sneer but quickly pulled it together when the man finally
walked away. Luca put on his best fake smile and said, "How are

you, Art?" It was his practice to call staff by their first name. They always had a name tag pinned to their shirt or suit and Luca thought he got better service by using it when he wanted something.

The concierge remembered him. "I'm fine, Mr. D'Angelo. How may I help you today?"

Luca made an appointment for a massage and Art assured him he would book an attractive woman to soothe his sore muscles. At least one thing was working to his satisfaction. He slipped Art a twenty and headed to his room.

It had been a long hot day and an even longer drive back to the hotel. He had promised to get back to the Steele woman as soon as he spoke to his wife. But what was his next big idea? He was in a bind and his only move left would be to return with the balance of the money for the gelding. If being accommodating didn't work, he would try and coerce the Steele woman into telling him where she put the horseshoes. At first he would be pleasant about it, but if she didn't cooperate then that would be another story.

After showering and dressing he felt like a new man and he had plenty of time to spend at the lounge before his massage. His mind shifted to the hot little waitress Lolly. He had his mind set on getting to know her better, and now that he had used her name for his fake wife, he felt they had a more personal connection. Wouldn't she love to hear that he had used her name in a scam? It was brilliant and he was more determined than ever to convince the pretty waitress to spend some personal time with him.

The lounge was almost empty and there were only a few customers sitting at the bar talking to the bartender. As his eyes adjusted to the dim lighting he nonchalantly turned his head towards the other end of the bar to check the place out. A man dressed in casual clothes and drinking a beer glanced over at him. Luca nodded, and the man tipped his glass towards him in a gesture of acknowledgment. Before he left, he would pass him an envelope filled with cash for dropping off the package wrapped in birthday paper. Seeing him enter the lounge, the bartender Dennie immediately came to take his order. Luca desperately needed a drink and he suddenly realized how hungry he was.

"Into the same libation this evening Mr. D'Angelo?" Dennie asked.

"Make it a double Johnny Walker straight up," Luca said leaning into the bar. "And I'll have a large shrimp cocktail to go with it." A double shot would do the trick. Running his fingers through his hair, he scrunched his eyes to relieve a dull headache that was just beginning. His fingers squeezed the bridge of his nose and he inhaled a deep exhausted breath.

Dennie scurried to pour his drink and sent the order for the shrimp cocktail to the kitchen. He walked briskly back to the man with the growl in his voice and placed the drink in front of him. Without looking up or at him, D'Angelo tossed the drink down and said, "Another." The hot fire of the whiskey swooshed down his throat giving him the rush he needed.

Dennie returned with another refill and sat it down in front of Luca. "Your shrimp will be here in a minute, Mr. D'Angelo."

Luca grunted something and Dennie went to the kitchen to see if the shrimp cocktail was ready. It was, and he delivered a large stainless steel cocktail glass filled with shrimp nestled in ice. Next to the appetizer, he set a napkin and fork, a side bowl of cocktail sauce and a small dish with lemon slices. "Will that be it for now, Mr. D'Angelo?"

Luca held his hand up signaling "yes," and Dennie returned to another customer who had just idled up to the bar. He would keep an eye on the swarthy man, waiting for the motion to refill his drink. Dennie had been a bartender long enough to know that D'Angelo was not the type of man to be put off, and he would never want to get on his bad side. Besides, the guy was a great tipper and he would keep the drinks coming as long as D'Angelo was sitting on the stool.

Joe, Dennie's fellow bartender, had warned him about the man. Joe had advised him to keep tabs on the swarthy man. "Keep the drinks flowing and don't try and make conversation." They talked after work, over a cold beer, about the strange man. D'Angelo reminded them of a movie gangster. "He could play the part without even trying," Joe chuckled.

Dennie laughed. "Yeah, like a mobster in an old black and white. I think he's been watching too many of them."

Chapter 26

An hour later, Luca was back in his room, sitting at the desk and making his phone call to Sam. He had carried a glass of JB back to his room and took a sip as he waited for her to answer. She picked up on the fourth ring and putting on his most pleasant voice, he told her his wife agreed with him about the horse he chose for his daughter. She loved Arrow and was thrilled with the photos sent from his iPhone. Sam asked about his daughter and he said that Margareta was very excited and told him it was her "dream come true." Margareta had thanked him so many times he had to stop her. She couldn't wait to see Arrow and give him a big hug.

Sam gushed when he told her what his daughter had said and she replied how pleased she was to be a part of making his daughter happy. Hearing Sam ask about Margareta, he knew he was on the right track with the wife and daughter ploy. He smirked again as he listened to Sam say how much Margareta would love Arrow. *Everyone loves kids and horses*, he thought. It almost made him wish he had a kid. Making up a fake family, and talking about them as if they were an authentic part of his life almost made him believe it himself, and he found himself caring about a daughter and wife that didn't exist. *I must be getting old. My brain is turning sappy.*

For a moment he was so caught up in the lie that there was silence at his end. He quickly returned to reality and asked if he could come by tomorrow with the balance of what he owed for Arrow. To his surprise, Sam said that wouldn't work. They would be busy all day and they were leaving for an out of town wedding early Saturday morning and would be gone until Sunday evening. Monday would work for them and he could bring the balance and make plans for Arrow until his family moved to New England. Her words completely caught him off guard.

Did he hear right? "That's fine. Monday it is. I have a few properties to visit on Saturday and Sunday so it works for me. I'm leaving for Florida on Tuesday, and Monday is the last day I can take care of this. I also need to talk to you and your husband about boarding the gelding at your farm until I find a stable closer to where we will settle."

Sam assured him that they could work something out for boarding and that she would look for him on Monday morning. If there was a problem, he was to call her.

He hastily said that he would see her on Monday around ten. A huge smile broke out on his face and this time it wasn't forced. Now he could move on with this whole debacle and finally be done with it. Luca clicked off the phone and pounded his hand on the desk in celebration. Finally something was going his way. He couldn't believe his good luck. They were going to be gone overnight until Sunday? Are you kidding me? What the hell, it was as if the sky had opened and a whole bucket of good luck had fallen onto his lap. When Sam said they would be gone overnight, he almost jumped out of the chair. He was pumped! This couldn't have worked out better. He would drive to the farm Saturday night and search for the horseshoes. He had a strong feeling they were in the barn, probably the tack room. If not, all bets were off and he would have to plan something more risky for Monday.

For now, the timing was perfect and he would have free access to the farm. He was stoked! It had been a stroke of genius on his part when he asked for a tour of the farm. Luca's clenched jaw began to relax as he remembered how easy it was to get an inside view of their home. Turned out it was one of the hottest and most humid days of the month and he had taken them up on their offer for something cold to drink. He was dripping with sweat and they were doing no better. After entering the cool house, they introduced him to their three dogs, and after fussing over them and petting each one, he learned that they stayed in the house at night. That would work out perfect. At least he wouldn't have to deal with barking dogs.

Luca focused on a fragment of the conversation he had with Sam about the overnight wedding plan. He had commented on how lucky she and her husband were to get away with animals to care for. She agreed and replied that two of their friends were coming by to take care of evening chores, and they would return early the next morning. Recalling his conversation with Denver he knew that evening chores were always completed before dark. That tidbit of information gave him the whole night to check every possible place the horseshoes might be. Touring the farm,

Denver had pointed out trails alongside the barn that led to the side of one of the fields and into a neighboring town. There was also another entrance to the fields and barns that was a distance from the house. Denver had cleared it when he came to live with Sam. He wanted it separate from the main driveway so that trailers, delivery trucks or tractors had easy access to the back of the property. The only barrier to the dirt road was a long chain fastened to two posts. Hanging from the chain was a large metal sign that said 'No Trespassing.'

Since the road was a distance from the farmhouse, the chain deterred anyone from using the road without permission. Denver had kiddingly told him that he didn't want teenagers using the road for parking or drinking. He wanted no one on the property without permission and he'd had a few run-ins with hunters who tried to use it to get to the other side of the mountain. A southern boy like Denver didn't take kindly to strangers not asking permission to cut through his property. They both talked about how times were so different and people could sue for anything and the home owner could be held liable if it happened on their property and it wasn't posted. The good old days when you could trust everyone were gone. Luca had nodded his head in agreement saying he was on the same page and that you can't trust everyone. He said he was always careful around strangers, but of course his wariness was very different from Denver's.

Luca thought about the chain. It didn't have a lock on it, and was only there to block the road and keep it private. He would drive in and take it down then hook it back up and drive further into the farm. Out of sight, he would walk the rest of the way to the barn. He had been very observant of the cameras and flood lights and knew where they were. This job was going to be a piece of cake. Pacing the room with his glass of JB in hand, he walked to a chair and plopped down. He ran his fingers through his hair. He was agitated, cranky, and tired. Everything was annoying him and he wanted to get back to Florida. He knew he couldn't outrun the Feds forever and he was ready to retire on an island in the Caribbean and enjoy the new boat he had placed a down payment on. It was time to get the hell out of Dodge with his life and money intact.

The last time he had met with Parker he hinted that this was his last scam and that he was thinking of retiring. Maybe that wasn't so smart because now his old buddy was pissed off that he wouldn't be available to partner up with anymore. He bet Parker was thinking he could outwit him, but he was privy to an important piece of information. Even if Parker did phone about his horse, he couldn't see her until Monday. By then, he would be out of town, back in Florida and packing up his things. And by the time Parker tried to move the money into his account, he would be on his way to a well-deserved vacation where his former partner would never find him.

Luca turned his attention to his drink, running his finger around the rim of the glass. Come hell or high water he was determined to leave the farm with the horseshoes in hand. He sucked a breath in between his clenched teeth and took a slug of the bourbon. The hot liquid began its work and he felt his body relax and the pain in his jaw subside. Maybe Lolly would be on tonight and he would ask if she would join him after her shift for a drink. She had refused every advance he had made, but now he was feeling lucky. Luca glanced at his Rolex watch. He had enough to drink, and it was time to dilute the amount of alcohol he had consumed with a steaming cup of black coffee and something to eat. He was ready for a medium rare steak and a large salad. Forget Lolly. She wasn't in the cards tonight. He was tired and hungry and after he finished dinner, it would be time for his massage appointment. He would beat Parker at his own game and be gone in a flash. They didn't call him the 'Teflon Don' for nothing.

Chapter 27

*B*ronwyn's phone call had placed Parker on high alert and he immediately felt a sense of urgency to head to the farm and claim Magic. Bryn's tone had been crisp, cool and to the point. There was no mention of anything other than the job, although he wished there had been. The tone in her voice said it all. She was over him, and was only reporting vital information she had gathered. Just the facts, and only the facts, were what she relayed to him.

At Jefferson and Rooker, Parker was well-liked and highly respected. He had a busy social life and often had dinner or drinks with colleagues. But the likable guy, single and self-assured, led a double life and his true identity was not one that anyone would suspect. This deep shadow life took precedence over everything including male friendships or forming meaningful relationships with women.

He initially met Bronwyn on a complicated job. They were thrown together under risky circumstances and after the job was completed they met for dinner and drinks. In his line of work a woman in the mix was not a wise idea. That night, Parker broke one of his cardinal rules. Never mix business with pleasure. But who can predict when love strikes? With Bryn everything was different and she was unlike any other woman he had dated. She was funny, amazing and fearless. Parker knew from the moment he met Bryn that he was in trouble, and he threw caution to the wind. Not only was she beautiful and smart but they both had the same mindset for their line of work.

Magic was supposed to have been the last horse trailered with the embedded numbered accounts stamped in her shoes and then his business with Luca would be completed. But when she went missing, he had to change plans ASAP and move at lightning speed to finish the job. Damn, just when everything was in place and he thought he could get back on track with Bryn, the mare had gone missing. And why had he been so stupid to risk Magic as the last horse for the job? What the hell was he thinking? Talk about arrogance. But then he remembered why he had chosen Magic. It was to solidify Luca's trust. If he sent Magic to Florida, it said a lot about team work. Luca knew that Magic was his prized mare and had insinuated that she should be the final horse trailered down south. Parker knew it was a test of loyalty and he had gone along with it to placate Luca.

When Parker had initially made the phone call to recruit Bryn, he knew he would need to grovel and plead his case to get her on board, and he knew he needed her more than she needed him. He had mulled over the predicament he was in and the big piece to his plan had to include Bryn. She was the perfect chess piece and had an uncanny ability to gather information without raising suspicion.

He and Bryn had worked well together on their first job. Her personality made people feel comfortable and her attractive smile could put anyone at ease. Bryn knew Magic and had ridden her many times while staying at his farm. Magic was her favorite horse and they had a special connection. They had bonded in some magical way and Parker knew he had to use Magic as the hook to get Bryn on board to help him. She wouldn't do it for him, but she would risk anything for Magic and he knew she would want to know as much as he did where Magic was and if she was okay. During their phone call he explained about the importance of the horseshoes and filled her in about crazy Luca. Thank God she had agreed to the plan and he hoped he didn't put her in any unforeseen danger. A picture of Bryn and Magic flashed thought his mind and he felt himself smile for the first time in days.

The job with Luca was dicey, to say the least, but Parker finally had a plausible reason to phone Bryn for the first time since their breakup. He shook his head and swallowed hard as he recalled the last day they were together at his farm. He had a chance to save what they had, but his mind went blank and his silence had spoken volumes.

After Bryn walked away, he was lost and out of sync with everything in his life. It was worse than the feeling he had when he had to tell a client there was a drop in the stock market and part of his investment strategy had bombed. Where his head was at in that moment with Bryn, he had no idea. Now he understood why he allowed the woman he loved to walk away. It *was* fear. It was totally crazy but he had to admit he was afraid of commitment. He was fearless leading a double life, which at times placed him in situations that would have knocked the socks off most men but stupidly he was afraid of pledging his life to the woman he loved. Once he recognized his misgivings and looked fear in the eye, he knew how foolish he had been. It was entirely his fault and as usual it was all about him.

The memory of that mistake was as clear in his head today as the day it had happened. They were sitting on one of the benches along the path to the pasture, a carafe of wine sitting next to them. She said she had something serious to talk about and he felt his heart sink. He knew exactly where the conversation was heading. She was ready to move on with or without him. She told him, tears leaking from the corner of her eyes, that he complicated her life and she knew there was no future with him. "I'm ready to find someone who will love me enough to make me a permanent part of his life, and evidently it's not you." In that moment he became a mute.

They had been a couple for a year and that was long enough to decide if they were going to take the next step in their relationship, or move on, and they had both agreed to that timeline. Still he wasn't ready to move forward, so of course he had chosen not to answer. 'When in doubt, do nothing,' was his motto. At times it had served him well, but not at that important moment. And worst of all, it wasn't as if he hadn't expected her to stay without a commitment from him. She had hinted many times that she was concerned about his unwillingness to take the next step, and she had waited patiently for him to open up and talk about their future. But Parker, a skilled avoidance male, always managed to change the subject and he had let Bryn walk away.

Since their breakup, he had focused on himself and gave a ton of thought to what had caused him to be afraid of a long term commitment with the woman he loved. There was no single reason he could come up with except his secret life, but that was an excuse that didn't fly. Bryn not only knew about his secret life, she was as deeply involved in a shadow life as he was. He had two choices, to either stare down his fear of intimacy and do something about it, or accept the fact that he would be a lifelong bachelor. The latter idea did not appeal to him. He wanted a home and family and someone to share his life with, but when he had needed to man up and tell Bryn he loved her he had choked, the words sticking in his throat.

Now it was his loss and he was sure she had moved on. Not only did he fail to *ever* bring up the M word, his silence said loud and clear that he wasn't ready to stay the course and make her a permanent part of his life. It was one of the most asinine mistakes he had ever made, and he believed she would never forgive him and his lack of sensitivity. He never said the words she needed to hear. Once he faced his own stupidity, he decided to beg her to come back to him, but the job with Luca came into play and was a priority. He had no choice but to push Bryn to the back of his mind because in his line of work there was no way he could concentrate on anything but the job at hand. He needed a clear head and all of his wits to work with his slimy co-conspirator. Luca was a hot head and if cornered, he would turn on his own mother.

Parker couldn't risk placing anyone in Luca's cross hairs, and if the dangerous man knew there was a woman in his life, he would use it to his advantage. Luca would use any leverage to get what he wanted, and his history of outwitting the Feds proved that he would stop at nothing.

Because of the mess he created, he was forced to keep his dealings with Bryn all business. He missed her, and he knew if she gave him a second chance, this time, it would be on her terms and he was ready for just that.

Chapter 28

Parker dove into the pool and began swimming slow laps. Using controlled even strokes he circled the parameter of the pool, every stroke removing tension from his body and mind. With each break in the water, his powerful arms swept him into a deeper state of calm and his mind began to clear. His breath became rhythmic and his body relaxed as it moved into a state of meditation. It was Parker's Zen time.

As he swam, Parker thought back to the first time he had looked at the property he now owned.

The estate, situated several miles off the main road, suited his need for privacy and his dream of becoming a top breeder of superior quarter horses. Fifty acres of rolling fields and meadows became the backdrop for a magnificent log cabin, two swimming pools, fenced in fields and large barns.

Immediately after paying the hefty price for the property, he moved forward at warp speed and transformed the beautiful land into his personal oasis and retreat.

Within six months, the property now boasted what he had envisioned in his mind's eye. Everything had been built to his specifications and a private landscaper designed and planted lush flower gardens along stone walls and pathways. White fences lined all the pastures and horses grazed in rich fields of green meadows. Built according to *his* specifications was an indoor riding ring, an outdoor training ring and a stately barn to house his prize horses. There was an opulent barn to store hay, a one-story barn that boasted a lavish tack room, and a separate foaling barn. Everything was built to his detailed plans. Parker had personally designed a huge indoor-outdoor swimming pool along with a seventy foot long lap pool, which was a 'must have' for him. The methodical soothing repetitions were his daily ritual, and many times elusive ideas occurred to him while swimming laps.

For Parker, gracious living in New England meant entertaining colleagues. A beautiful gray and gold-tiled hot tub was one of the center pieces of his well-earned life style. He entertained all seasons of the year, and during the warm days of summer the glass walls of the kidney shaped pool retracted and opened to the magnificent stone patio. Large round tables, topped with colorful umbrellas, dotted the patio, creating an inviting entertainment area. Flower gardens peppered the landscape and a long winding path led from the gardens to fenced pastures. The manicured trail was perfect for intimate conversations, with friends and clients. Stone benches were placed strategically along the pathway and garden shrubs and ornamental trees flanked each side. Gas torches were lit for evening walks, and several small ponds sported ornamental Koi and Goldfish. Parker had thought of almost everything, but his mind was constantly filled with new visions and ideas for his piece of paradise. He was a restless soul, his mind buzzing with ingenuity and inventiveness. Parker was a brilliant entrepreneur and his lifestyle was proof of his lust for life.

When they were a couple, he and Bryn loved the intimacy of the pathway along the gardens, and walked it at the end of each working day. The canopy of trees and bushes created a cozy retreat, and they enjoyed walking to the end of the path where it opened to white fenced fields.

Bryn and Parker often carried their glasses of wine, or frosty mugs of cold beer to the garden retreat, enjoying the privacy and solitude while sharing discrete conversations. The garden path was a perfect hideaway and during the winter it took on an entirely different ambiance with sounds of crunching snow replacing the twitter of summer birds.

Many of Parker's clients would have been surprised to learn that he was not only a shrewd businessman; he was a lover of gardens and horses. He was a selective in what he shared, but the few buddies he did have knew that he meditated daily. Meditation and swimming were tools in his arsenals of weapons that allowed him to relieve the stress from his clandestine operations.

Parker lifted his head from the water and exhaled. A gentle breeze passed over his face and he turned to float on his back. Floating lazily, the faint smell of roses wafted through the air and the stress of the day began to slowly vanish. He took in a deep breath, turned and swam lazily towards the steps of the pool. The laps had done their job, infusing him with a Zen-like peace and he was ready to implement his new plan of attack.

Parker glanced at the hot tub and although he would have

liked to have soaked in it, he didn't have time. He grabbed a towel, wiped the drips from his hair and legs and headed towards his bed and bathroom suite.

The spa rain shower poured over Parker's powerfully built body. He had been standing under it long enough to come out with the wrinkled skin of an old man. The laps had done their job and the cool shower helped pull his head together. His mind ran through each detail Bryn had described. Parker ran his hands over his wet face and tipped it up to the shower head. What a mess this was turning out to be. Why the hell couldn't Luca have waited for him, but then again when was Luca ever patient or predictable. He should have seen this coming and what was worse; he was one step behind Luca rather than a step ahead. It had turned into a cat and mouse hunt, and he was *not* going to be the mouse. Parker could feel the anger rising in him and wanted to take Luca by the throat and pick him up and throw him. Who the hell did this man think he was? Parker was running this operation, not a low class scum like Luca. He gave another rinse to his hair and then slicked it back to squeeze the water out.

Stepping out of the shower, he grabbed a blue towel sitting on the small stand next to the vanity. After toweling off, he wrapped it around his waist and headed to the bedroom to dress. Slipping on a pair of jeans, he padded barefoot to the kitchen. Water dripped from his hair and down the side of his face. He unconsciously wiped it away, his whole focus on the job at hand. Sitting down on a stool at the center island, he opened his lap top and tapped in his password. As he waited to log in, he leaned back on the bar stool, his hands behind his head and retraced the events of Bryn's phone call. They were a major cog in the wheel. "Man, I didn't see this one coming."

Running his hands through his wet hair, he got up, went to the refrigerator and took out a cold bottle of beer. He popped the cap and returned to the stool. The variegated brown granite was covered with stacks of paper work, his laptop sandwiched between two of the piles. Parker's laptops were guarded by strong firewalls and his passwords changed daily. They were also loaded with a special device that worked through a remote on his key ring and it alarmed if anyone, other than he, opened the laptop or meddled with it. With a press of the button on his key ring, all work was destroyed. That, and the security cameras and alarms that surrounded his home and property, kept everything safe and under constant surveillance. This laptop was used for his dealings with Luca and was committed to that job. After their dealings were completed, the laptop would be destroyed and a new laptop would be employed for the next job.

Parker never mixed his shadow jobs with his work at Jefferson and Rooker. An office adjacent to his bedroom suite was fitted with computers and monitors and dedicated to his business at their headquarters.

The long island in the spacious kitchen was where he chose to work on the Luca job. It was bright and opened into a grand dining area, but more importantly, it provided easy access to the coffeepot and refrigerator, two of the appliances he liked to be close to when he was working on a tight schedule. For Parker, who lived a double life, separating work spaces kept everything clean and neat. Each job required him to wear a different hat and take on a different persona, so distinctive work spaces allowed him to open one compartment at a time. It was a technique that served him well.

Parker swallowed the last slug of the beer and set the bottle on the bar. Things were now on fast track and he had to plan his moves carefully. He thought he had more time to beat Luca at his own game, never thinking the shady jerk would have the smarts to track down Magic. The scam was supposed to end in Florida but he could now see that it would end in Massachusetts.

Parker tapped a short coded message into the laptop. He hit the send button, and leaned back to wait for a reply. His private server was another arrow in his quiver of secrecy. As he waited, he thought about Bryn. He still couldn't get her out of his mind. She was meeting with the Steele woman tomorrow and her assignment was to find out for sure if it was Luca who booked the appointment to buy a horse. He was 99% sure it was, but in his line of work he could never play the odds. He needed to be 100% sure before he made a move. Everything was on hold until Bryn phoned him. So much was hinging on what she found out. If it was Luca nosing around, there would be a quick change of plans and he would use a new tactic to foil the bad ass but it was a risky strategy. For now, there was nothing he could do but wait for information.

Chapter 29

*I*t was Friday and, as planned, Bryn drove to Sam's farm for an afternoon of riding. As much as she looked forward to taking a long trail ride and stopping at Sam's friend Lyla's bakery, she was really on a mission to gain information about Mr. D'Angelo and what he was up to. She was certain it was Luca, but when she questioned Sam she would have to be careful not to appear overly interested. Once more, her instincts about his intentions made her very uneasy. Even though he used his real last name, she and Parker agreed that they had to figure out why he had gone to the farm on his own. For certain there was something dangerous about the game he was playing. Bryn was dying to know what type of story he gave Sam and what his manner was like. Although Bryn had never met the man, Parker had given her enough insight into who he was, and it wasn't good.. She arrived at Sam's at noon and the day promised to be slightly cooler than the last three days. Sam had the two sale geldings tacked up and they were tied to a short rail next to the barn. Bryn was dressed for riding, wearing jeans, riding boots and a blue jersey, her long auburn hair pulled back with a tie. "Hi," Bryn said as she walked toward Sam. "Where are the dogs? I miss their hellos, although Rudy and Roger let out a call when I walked by."

"Hey yourself," Sam replied as she gave Arrow a pat on his rump. "The dogs are in their pen. They sense when I'm going riding and believe it or not they stay quiet."

Bryn chuckled. "I've got to tell you, I love your dogs and your goats are very special. Thanks for asking me to go riding with you. I'm really excited about it. I haven't been on the back of a horse for some time and it'll be great to be out on a trail again."

"Pay no attention. Rudy and Roger are always begging to be let out of their pen." Sam reached for a riding helmet and handed it to Bryn. "Here, try this on for size. It should fit, but if it doesn't you can try this one. Your head looks about the same size as mine. You can ride Tex. He's great on the trails and on roads. Actually, both of these guys are but I noticed you took a liking to Tex when you were here."

Bryn's initial fabricated story was that she was curious about Curly horses and she was in the area for a conference and had found Sam's farm on the internet. She had a free day and was close by so she wondered if she could stop by and take a look.

Sam, always eager to show her unique horses, had been very accommodating. Unfortunately, meeting someone she liked and then deceiving her wasn't something Bryn had planned on.

Bryn felt a shiver of joy as she ran her hand down Tex's side. "He is *so* handsome. You read my mind." Tex nuzzled her hand

and she wrapped his long mane around her fingers exposing his liquid brown eyes. She kissed him on his velvet nose and immediately felt a connection with the gelding. It was the same feeling she had when she first met Magic. "I've always loved a bay horse and Tex is certainly one of a kind with his soft eyes and gorgeous curly black mane."

"That he is," Sam said pulling the helmet strap under her chin.

Bryn slipped the helmet on. "Fits perfect. Thanks. I appreciate it," she said tightening her helmet strap. "Wow, Tex looks great under saddle. I wouldn't mind owning him myself." Bryn ran her hand along Tex's side. "Aren't you the handsome man?" she crooned as she walked around the gelding and checked the stirrups.

"I set the stirrups to what I thought was your length, but try them out first," Sam said untying Arrow from the rail.

"By the way, both horses are still for sale, although the guy who came yesterday gave me a deposit on Arrow and said he may also want to buy Tex," Sam put her foot in the stirrup and swung up and onto the saddle.

Bryn gulped. "He did? Wow that was quick." Bryn mounted Tex and placed her boots in the stirrups. "These stirrups are set perfectly," she said waiting for Sam to say more.

"You're about the same height as me so I took a chance. Sam turned Arrow towards the path that ran alongside the barn where the trail began and Bryn clucked to Tex to follow.

Bryn rode up next to Arrow. "Did he ride either of the horses?"

Sam put her sunglasses on and tightened the tie to her ponytail. "No, he didn't want to, and in all honesty, he wasn't dressed for riding. Nice pants and a silk white shirt, and he wore very shiny black shoes. I hated to even take him to the barn, he was so perfectly dressed. Didn't seem at all like a horse person until he started talking and then there was no doubt that he knew his horses. But to tell the truth, at first, I didn't have a good feeling about the guy until he told us that he wanted to make his daughter happy with a Curly horse and I thought that maybe I misjudged him."

"Strange that he'd buy a horse without riding it first." Bryn's wheels were turning. What was Luca up to?

"I think so too, but he was an oddball kind of guy."

"Perhaps you should stick to your first instinct," Bryn said, sliding her hand along Tex's neck. "He doesn't sound like a friendly man. Maybe he's not the right person to sell either of your horses to. Look at this guy," she said leaning forward and rubbing Tex's neck. "I've always been a sucker for a bay horse and who can resist one named Tex. Still, I find it strange that he's buying a horse at first sight. And I wonder how could he buy a horse that neither he, nor his daughter, has spent time with. He must *really* trust what you say about Arrow and is depending on your word that the gelding is the perfect mount for his daughter."

"I know. Crazy, huh? Maybe he'll change his mind, but he did leave a deposit. On the other hand," she laughed, "I can still change mine."

Arrow blew through his nose, relaxed and was ready to move out. Tex followed suit. "I guess they want to get going," Bryn said as she gave a clucking sound and Tex took the lead.

Tex was a step ahead of Arrow until Sam gave the command, "walk on" and squeezed her legs against his side moving him up beside Bryn.

The riders continued chatting about the horses and Bryn

sighed and smiled. She was in horse heaven and for the moment she didn't want to think of anything else.

Sam lifted herself up, standing for a brief second in the stirrups, and then sat back down, finding her sweet spot in the saddle. "That's better," she said leaning forward and stroking Arrow's neck. "Getting back to the Luca guy, he told us that although he gave us a deposit, he had to check with his wife. He took photos with his cell and sent them to her and his daughter. If she agreed on the horse, his daughter could ride Arrow when they moved up here."

"This Luca sure seems easy to please," Bryn said with a shrug.

Sam nodded. "Almost too easy, I thought. But then, he went on about how he thought we were honest people and Denver assured him that Arrow was safe for a young girl and showed no compulsion to be anything other than a great horse. That seemed good enough for D'Angelo. You know, Bryn, he was a strange sort of guy but after selling horses for some time now, I have met so many different kinds of people that nothing surprises me. Plus, in our contract we agree to take back a horse that doesn't work out, although so far that's never happened. And he gave us a cash deposit and said that if his wife says yes, he'll return with the balance. So, he is following through. He wanted to come back today but we had riding plans and I told him we'll be out of town for a wedding so we can't see him until Monday."

Bryn's eyes widened in shock. "*What?* You're out of town until Monday?" she blurted.

Sam was caught off-guard by Bryn's startled concern. "Does it matter? What's a day or two?"

"Oh, nothing, I guess." Bryn composed herself, adlibbing as she went along. She took in a short breath and shuddered. What the hell? Sam told Luca she would be out of town until Monday? Oh my God. Tomorrow night is when he will make his move! Before she had a chance to ask more, Sam clucked to Arrow and he moved out into a trot. Tex followed close behind and Bryn found focused on him.

They trotted their horses along the lower fields and then slowed them into a walk.

Bryn was captivated by the beauty of the cut fields that ran along the side of the mountain. The horses moved into a gentle rocking motion and Bryn felt herself relaxing more and more. She was enthralled by the beauty of the landscape and was conscious of how much she loved riding and how much she missed it. Her eyes traveled across the rolling fields and white fences, and she found herself smiling as she fixated on the smells and sounds that filled her senses. Bryn reached down and ran her hand along Tex's neck. "Good boy, Tex. You are the best." Aware of her hand on his neck the bay horse dropped his head and gave a gentle snort.

The path along the field led to a long trail that wound through the back side of the mountain and down into the town where Lyla's bakery was. The bakery was about an hour's ride and Bryn decided to enjoy the day and question Sam about Luca over lunch. They rode past horses grazing in the fields and one, another bay Curly, trotted to the fence to watch them pass. Slowly but surely all of the stress from the latest news about Luca faded and all that mattered was the pleasure of the ride. They reached the end of the fields and entered the dense forest where the trail was lined with tall pine trees. For a while neither woman spoke, drinking in the stillness of the forest. The woodland floor lay thick with pine needles and the spicy smell of pine filled the air. The summer sun was shaded by an umbrella of tall oak and pine trees.

Bryn inhaled the musty fragrance of the wooded land and became lost in thought. For now and this moment in time, all was well.

They rode deeper into the forest, now and then the silence broken by the sound of the horses' hooves crunching down on twigs and leaves. A mile or so later the trail broke into a fork. Sam pulled Arrow to a halt and Bryn did likewise. Sam pointed to the trail to the left. "That trail leads along the back of the mountain and down into a beautiful valley. If you have time to visit again, we can head that way and carry a lunch with us. There's a beautiful meadow where we can tie the horses and spread a blanket. You will absolutely love it."

Bryn stretched her lips into what could pass for a smile, but she knew that another ride would never happen. "God, I would love that. You have no idea how much I'm enjoying this day and how much I appreciate your company. Unfortunately, it may be quite a while before I can return."

Frowning, Sam said, "Well, you never know when you'll be in the area again and you'll always be welcome at our home. As my Minnie says, 'People come into your life for a reason and the thread that connects you with them is there for a purpose.'"

"Your grandmother sounds like one smart lady. I hope to meet her someday after all you've told me about her."

"I'm sure you will. Follow me. We're taking the trail to the right. It comes out on the road that leads to Lyla's bakery." Sam clucked and Arrow moved out, followed by Tex.

"How far are we from her bakery?" Bryn asked.

"Only about another four miles. We'll come to the end of the trail and ride the road a short way. She has a wooden rail in back of the bakery where we can tie our horses. Lyla's a true horse woman, and she made sure that her customers could ride their horses to her shop. She has a huge sign in front that says 'Horses Welcome.'

Bryn laughed "Oh my gosh. That is too funny. I've never ridden a horse to a deli. I love it! Do a lot of people ride their horses instead of driving?"

"Yes they do. Both our towns are kiddingly called *Horse Heaven*. I think there are more horses than people living in our towns. It's not unusual to see other riders on the roads and trails and it makes living in both towns perfect for horse lovers. Actually I have a friend Addie who lives in Vermont and she goes into town with her pony and cart. She drives her pony through the bank drive-though and then takes the highway to get back home."

"What? How great is that! I can't even imagine doing that. She sounds like someone special."

"She is, and I admire her very much. She's a true horsewoman and a great friend. Watch out for that branch," Sam said moving Arrow around a large limb that was lying on the path.

Bryn eased Tex around the tree limb and moved up beside Arrow. She had a sudden thought. "I love riding Tex, and if that D'Angelo guy doesn't buy him, I think I will."

"See," Sam said. "You *will* be back again. I knew it. Hey, the trail widens just around the bend and we can canter a little."

"Let's go! Can't wait! Yahoo!" Bryn was in her glory.

Chapter 30

New England had been in a summer heatwave, and it had broken all records. The sweltering days during the last week were created by a Gulf Stream pattern that wouldn't break, and it was playing havoc on man and beast. Bryn and Sam talked about the crazy weather patterns as they rode through the shaded mountain trail. The words "Climate Change" was the topic of conversation with all of the newscasts, and on the lips of most of the people they knew. They didn't get into the politics of the issue, just discussed how much colder and snowier the winters had been and how much hotter than usual summers were. Sam mentioned reading science reports listing the causes for the more erratic weather and the dangers for the world economy with the disruption of the ecosystem. Bryn reiterated that whether one believed it was a natural phenomenon or man's own doing, she believed that fossil fuels were pushing climate change along at a fast pace. Sam told Bryn that she and Denver studied the NASA website regarding the expansion of the "greenhouse effect."

"Honestly, Bryn, my kids and their friends are really up on all of this, and they've convinced us to do the research."

Bryn asked Sam about the tornado that had plowed through her town and how she had fared. "It was a scary time," Sam said. "I have so much empathy for anyone who goes through a disaster and weather like this really unsettles me. Now, I never say never that another disaster won't hit home. I feel more vulnerable but not frightened. I guess as long as we're alive we have to be prepared for the unknown, and that's how I try and live my life."

Bryn nodded in agreement. She hoped she would never have to live through a major disaster, but like everyone she didn't feel she could live her life unscathed by some unforeseen circumstance.

An hour after leaving the farm, Sam and Bryn left the mountain trail and slowly made their way down a rural road that opened to Main Street. Several people waved as they rode by. Lyla's town, nestled between several mountain ranges, was a mix of old and new. Because there were so many horses, a special path was constructed on the side of the road to keep horses and riders safe. Horses did not have to compete with traffic, and Lyla's town was voted the most horse friendly community in Massachusetts.

Bryn took in the sites of the town as the horses clip-clopped along the horse path. They passed a large, gray granite library, a small grocery store and several Victorian style homes with large swaths of flower gardens set along stone walls. Further down Main Street they passed a Nail and Hair Salon sandwiched between a Hardware store and Antique shop.

Bryn was pleasantly surprised by the ambiance of the town and the friendliness of the people who nodded to them on the way.

They rode past a grassy park where parents and children were being entertained by a puppet show in a large gazebo. Several of the kids ran up to them excited to see the horses pass by.

A short distance from the park, Sam pointed to a beautiful white church with a tall steeple. "Lyla and Carver got married there."

Bryn was fascinated by the various buildings and homes along Main Street. "It's so pretty here. Are they trying to attract tourists? I haven't noticed a bed and breakfast, well, at least not on this street."

"Yes and no. I think this town shows good planning and it was voted as one of the ten most family-friendly places to live, in the state. The residents care about their schools, and are willing to pay for them. This town is more than a bedroom community, and although most people work in the city, they value their schools, senior center, library, parks and small businesses. People in this town support the businesses, but in return they have to agree to uphold a certain décor. Everything in Mansville is planned with a purpose, and nothing can be shabby. It's why people in neighboring towns shop here and dine here. The residents of Mansville have found that if the locals are willing to invest in planning and education, home sales go up and home owners reap the benefits. My town is using Mansville as our model for what works."

Bryn's eyes took in everything. "So, it sounds like it's a win-win situation for everyone. I think you're right. This should be a model for other small towns."

Sam nodded her head. True, but it only works if the people are invested in the community. Unfortunately, not all residents in all towns agree with a higher tax rate and don't have the vision that this town does. Our town is more rural so I do most of my shopping in this town."

At the end of Main Street, Lyla's bakery came into view. Lyla's shop was situated on the corner of Main and Meadow Road. At the corner, Sam turned Arrow onto Meadow and came to a halt behind Lyla's bakery. A large open field was filled with cars and a few pickup trucks. Off to the side of the building, a gigantic oak tree shaded a long wooden rail used for tying horses. They dismounted, removed their horse's bridles and replaced them with leather halters. A large metal water trough was set at the side of the building and they walked the horses to it. After the horses drank their fill, they tied them to the rail and headed to the front door. On the wall of the building a large sign said, 'Horses and Riders Are Welcome Here.'

"What a great sign," Bryn said pointing to the wall. "For sure your friend Lyla is a horse person. I can't thank you enough for taking me here and the ride was fabulous," Bryn said walking next to Sam to the front of the yellow building. The shop door was painted a deep blue and adorned with a white floral trimmed sign that said, 'GiGi's Bakery and Deli.' They stepped aside to allow two women to leave. One of the women said hello to Sam and asked if she had ridden her horse to the bakery. Sam replied that she had, and it was a gorgeous day for a trail ride. They exchanged a few more pleasantries and then left with a, "See you soon."

"Seems like you know everyone," Bryn said.

"Just a few fellow horsewomen. Not friends, but we all belong to the same network. Someone always knows someone that I know, and so it goes. It's a small-town thing I guess."

"Well, I love this place already. The color of the building is so cheerful and it gives off a happy aura."

"Wait 'til you see how she decorated the inside," Sam said, opening the door.

The large open space dazzled Bryn, and she was immediately immersed in the rich fragrance of freshly baked bread, mingled with the sweet smell of ginger, and cinnamon. She took in a deep breath and smiled as she gazed around the deli. The walls were painted a soft blue color and trimmed with white woodwork. White shelves and long white granite counters were topped with baskets filled with breads of all flavors. Her eyes settled on a long bakery display case holding a variety of pastries and an assortment of pies. For a moment she thought she might skip lunch and order dessert. Bryn found it amusing that one wall was devoted to the painting of a Mini horse playing in a field of buttercups and quickly realized that the wait staff's aprons were decorated with the same Mini horse. Their uniforms were identical, and each wore a blue jersey, jeans covered by a white apron, and white sneakers. Their hair was tied back with a blue ribbon and topped with a blue cap.

Near the entrance of the shop, the granite counter was neatly set with a stack of menus, a pile of white bags, four glass canisters filled with granola and a blue plate with a generous samples of an assortment of cookies. A huge menu hung behind the counter listed a variety of deli sandwiches, soups and fire stone pizzas. Bryn stood taking the whole thing in while Sam chitchatted with a woman she knew.

The cash register was at the end of the counter and two customers waited while a young woman with dark curly hair tucked under her blue cap was filling a bag with brownies. Bryn heard the worker ask one of them how their lunch was and if it was their first time at GiGi's.

On the opposite side of the room was a large brick oven. A young man was removing a fire grilled pizza with a long wooden paddle. He slid it onto a tray and returned with the paddle to take another pizza out of the oven. Despite the heat from the oven, the room temperature was comfortable and inviting. Bryn was amazed at everything her eyes took in. The deli was much larger inside than she had thought. She turned her head upward, surveying the wooden beams that crisscrossed the ceiling. Huge white fans whirled lazily overhead creating a slight breeze on her face.

The dining area opened through a high beamed archway. Bryn could see that Lyla had merged the old with the new, creating an inviting space. The shop was busy and she could see the dining area was lined with blue leather booths. Bryn was so focused on the décor of the room that she didn't notice the woman who came up to Sam and gave her a quick hug. "So this is your new friend?" she turned to Bryn and held out her hand.

"Hi, I'm Lyla," she said grinning ear to ear.

Bryn firmly shook the hand of the freckled nosed young women with the red curly hair. "I'm Bryn and I'm enthralled with your shop. It's absolutely amazing and I have Sam to thank for bringing me here."

"Thank you. It's all I dreamed it could be. Kind of a work-in-progress, but built with love."

"Everything here," Sam explained, "is organic and scrumptious. Most of the produce to make the salads and desserts comes from her garden or other gardens in town.

"I'm impressed," Bryn said

"Sam is my best cheerleader," Lyla laughed. "Follow me and I'll take you to your booth." Lyla led them to the dining area. "You can order and I'll join you as soon as we catch up. You hit the luncheon crowd but it should begin to thin out."

Bryn followed close behind Sam through the arched doorway of the dining room. "What time do you close?" she asked.

"We close at two-thirty, so we have enough time to clean up and get ready for the next day," Lyla said over her shoulder.

The floor was covered in a rich brown ceramic tile and the walls were painted the same color blue as the front of the shop. Tall open ceilings were graced by more white fans and Bryn could see small tables lining the back wall of the area. It was crowded, and they had to stop several times to allow wait staff to pass, trays filled with luncheon food and delicious looking desserts. Busy wait staff walked back and forth to a kitchen set at the back of the dining area, in an alcove out of customers view. The soft background music of James Taylor mingled with customers' voices, some eating and others sipping coffee or cold drinks.

It occurred to Bryn that Lyla had created an ambiance that engulfed a customer into a beautiful symphony of sounds and smells. The woman was truly gifted.

Lyla stopped at an empty booth and removed the reserved sign on the table. "Okay, take a look at the menu and I'll send someone to take your order. I'll be back later to join you. Enjoy," she said as she quickly moved away and headed towards the kitchen.

Before they had time to look at the menu a waitress appeared at the table. Smiling she said, "Hi, Sam, I'll be your server. Can I get you ladies something to drink?"

Bryn looked up at a tall attractive woman, her dark hair pulled back in a blue tie. "I'll have a glass of your strawberry lemonade." Sam had already told her about the variety of lemonade flavors and she was eager to try one.

"Hi, Lil." Sam knew the woman from her book club. "Make it two. Looks like you're busy today. What's the special of the day?"

"It has been non-stop but it's beginning to quiet down. Lyla is getting busier and busier. She's going to need to hire more servers if this keeps up. I can only do three days a week and it's more than enough for me, but I do love her and this shop. It makes it fun to come to work. Oops, forgot." She smiled. "There are two specials today. Thinly sliced roast beef topped with Swiss cheese on a small roll and a side of dipping sauce, or turkey, ham, tomato and Swiss cheese on a dill and cheese roll."

"I know what I want," said Sam.

Lil continued, "Our soup of the day is carrot, potato and onion simmered in a chicken stock. Delicious, as I am told by our customers. And as you know, Sam, our house salads and homemade dressings are always a great choice."

"I'll give you a minute and be back with your drinks," Lil said

Bryn unfolded her napkin and placed it on her lap. "So, how did Lyla manage to build such a beautiful deli and bakery?"

"Lyla's always been a baker. Before she owned the shop she was well known for her baked goods and her natural cereals. She sold them at farmer's markets and from her home. She always had a big garden and is a greenie. This is the deli and bakery she worked at before she bought it. It was called the Taste of Home Bakery back then. The owners Nell and her husband were retiring and Lyla was the perfect fit to carry on. She and Carver remodeled the shop and made it just the way Lyla had dreamed. She named it GiGi's after her Mini horse."

"So, that's the picture on the wall of her Mini? I've got to ask, why name a bakery after a horse?"

"That's a long story that I'll tell you some time. Lyla rescued

GiGi and she is very special to her. The initials GG stand for God's Gift, so when you think about it, this bakery has the same meaning."

"Oh, I get it now. I can't wait to hear the whole story when I come back, hopefully in the near future. So, if this guy Luca doesn't buy a horse, you'll let me know?"

"I will for sure." She answered. Sam leaned across the table and in a hushed voice asked, "Can I ask you something Bryn? In your opinion, do you think he's sincere about buying a horse or is he just a con man?"

Bryn's eyes widened in surprise. "Why do you ask that?"

Chapter 31

Parker had just completed his last lap in the pool and was drying off when his cell phone rang.

"Hey, what's up? Anything new? I got your message and was just going to call you." Parker wrapped the towel around his waist and sat down on the chaise lounge.

"Well, you won't like what I found out," Bryn said, taking in a short breath. "First of all, it *was* Luca at the farm, trying to find out about Magic and the horseshoes. And, of course, he had the perfect gimmick. He told them he was there to buy a horse for his daughter. Can you believe it?"

"That bastard is one ingenious guy. I gotta hand it to him. He actually made up a fake daughter?"

"Yes! You've got to admit, he is pretty slick," Bryn said.

Parker wiped the water from his eyes, trying to wrap his mind around what Bryn had told him. "So how did he find Magic?"

"He spotted Magic in one of the fields, and had the brass to ask if they also raised quarter horses. They told him that the mare was a rescue and they were waiting for the owner to claim her. He was smart enough not to show too much interest in the mare other than to remark that she was a fine looking animal and he noticed that she wasn't wearing shoes."

Parker picked up a small towel lying on the chair next to him and wiped the drips of water running down his face. His mind was racing as he thought of the consequences of Luca showing up at the farm. "Man, I should have seen this one coming. He'd never show up without a con ready. But, a daughter? That one almost makes me laugh."

Bryn kept on talking. "And a wife too! Can you believe it? That scum was on-game. He built a story to make them believe he was an honest family man and it wasn't difficult for Sam to describe him. She didn't like him from the moment he opened his mouth, and had a gut feeling that there was something about him that didn't ring true. But he went on and on about his daughter and wife and how they were moving back to the area and he had bribed his daughter, who didn't want to leave her friends in Florida, with the promise he'd buy her a Curly horse."

"I didn't know he had it in him to be that convincing. It's difficult for the idiot to act friendly or show any interest in anything other than women. He's the highest form of narcissism."

"That I believe. And to add the perfect touch to the ruse, he left a deposit on one of the geldings. Can you imagine that?"

"I've got to say, I'm impressed with his gall. Sounds like he thought this one out, *way* ahead of time." Parker got up from the chair, walked to the sliders and slid them open. "Hang on. I'm grabbing a beer. This con sounds like a movie. And to think he's trying to outwit me with this gem of bull. If I didn't know better I would think this is a comedy."

"Get your beer. I have a glass of wine sitting next to me. This story only gets better."

Parker placed the phone on the counter, opened the fridge and took out a bottle of Stella. He popped open the cap and decided to take out another one for good measure. Something told him this was going to be a two beer discussion, and once the call ended he would have a lot of decisions to make.

He padded back to the lounge chair and set the bottles on a small table next to him. "Okay, go ahead. I'm ready to hear the rest of this insane saga."

Bryn had opened up a small bag of Doritos while Parker was getting his beer. She took another sip of wine before she began. "So, Sam told me that when she first met Luca she was uneasy, but when he told her he was buying a horse for his daughter, she thought she had misjudged him. I wanted to tell her she was right about her first impression, but I couldn't say anything. I'm telling you, Parker, you've put me in a bad place and I hate it. I really like Sam and her husband, and now I'm worried. From what you say, Luca is a nasty guy, and I think he's a serious threat to them. How is he going to get his hands on the horseshoes without strong-arming them?"

Parker groaned. "I'm sorry, Bryn. I hate that I had to drag you into this, but you got the information I needed and I owe you one. Not to worry. I'll take care of Luca. I'm in a time crunch now but the next move will be mine. And your new friend should have stuck with her first instinct. She's right about him. He's a snake. What about her husband? What did he think of Luca?"

"Sam said her husband didn't like the guy and is still hesitant to sell him a horse. He would rather wait and keep the deposit until he meets his daughter and wife."

"Smart man. What's he like?"

Bryn finished the last of the Doritos and crumpled the bag, taking another sip of wine. "Very friendly, and from Texas. He's a cool guy and he looks like he knows his way around trouble. You would like him."

"I probably would. You're a great judge of character. What the hell, you liked me at one time," he laughed.

Bryn snickered. "Well, we all make mistakes, don't we?"

"Aww, that sent a pain straight through my heart. I wasn't that bad, was I?"

Bryn decided not to answer. This call was business, and she knew if she took the bait, it would get personal and she didn't want to deal with that. He had made his choice, and whatever they had was over. She quickly changed the subject. "Of course he brought up the fact that he noticed none of the horses, including the rescue, wore shoes. Clever way of gaining information don't you think? Sam said that she told Luca that the mare came shod but one was loose and her farrier pulled them."

"No one ever said my old buddy was stupid. He wouldn't be one of the Feds' Most Wanted if he wasn't clever enough to get away with worse bull than anyone I know. Tell me more about the shoes and what they did with them."

"Turns out, their farm is a drop-off place for discarded horseshoes. A daughter of Sam's friend has a club. The girls decorate the old horseshoes and sell them. The proceeds go to support rescue horses and a therapeutic riding program. The horseshoes are stored in a back barn until pickup. Sam brought me to the back barn to show me where they're stockpiled and I was hoping to see Magic's shoes. The pile wasn't very large, and when I questioned her, she said they had a pickup last week."

Parker got up and started pacing. "That's the craziest thing I've ever heard of. That pickup would have been after Magic arrived at their farm."

"I know, but I scanned the pile as quickly as I could without acting too interested, and they weren't there. But the shoes are unique and anyone who knows horseshoes would wonder about them. I think she would have set them aside for the owner of the horse. It wouldn't take a genius to look at those horseshoes and realize they weren't used for everyday riding. Unfortunately, I bet Luca figured that out too, and knew there was no need to check out the cast-offs."

Parker sat down. He leaned back in the chair and propped his feet up on a small hassock. He took a deep slug of beer and said, "Damn. This last deal was supposed to be so simple. So, what else have you got?"

Bryn looked down at her notes. She had scribbled them on her pad the minute she left the driveway. Sometimes the smallest details matter the most. "Luca also told them he may be interested in buying two more horses, one for him and one for his wife. How's that for covering all bases?"

"You're kidding! Did he ever sweeten the pot! He's buying time until he figures out his next move. He knows just how to work them."

"True, he even asked about the schools in neighboring towns."

Parker held back a laugh. "So, what are his fake wife and daughter's names? This I've got to hear."

"His fake wife's name is Lolly and his daughter's name is Margareta. He said he owns a computer software company and he had lived in Boston before. Now, he's looking at property near a private school where he's enrolling his daughter. Isn't that too funny?"

"Oh my God! If I didn't know the man, I could actually enjoy this. Lolly must be his latest girlfriend and Margareta must be some relative. He would only use names he had on the tip of his tongue."

Bryn finished her wine and refilled the glass. There was a lot more to tell Parker. "So, what do you think?"

"It makes sense that the horseshoes are still at the farm and if we figured that one out, I'm sure Luca has too. Your new friend has them tucked someplace safe and she hasn't given any more thought to them other than they're out of the ordinary, and the owner of the horse would want them back."

"Agree. She most likely still has the horseshoes. But that's not all. This last piece of information will give you something to think about. Better take another swig of beer. I have a feeling you'll need it when you hear about this *major* snafu. "

Parker sat straight up in the chair. "What's the other piece?"

"Sam and Denver are going to be away for the weekend at a wedding. They're leaving Saturday morning and returning on Sunday. A friend is taking care of the farm that evening and the next morning, but no one's staying there. What's more, Luca knows this because he said he'd bring the rest of the cash for the horse on Friday, but Sam told him about the trip and said he'd have to wait until Monday. Luca will have carte blanche at the farm, since no one will be home. And you know as well as I do, he *will* show up, and not leave until he has the horseshoes in hand."

"Damn. Do they have cameras around the property?"

"Yes. I spotted them and I'm sure he did too. Looks like they could be easily disabled and Luca could do that."

Deep in thought, Parker rubbed his chin. "Okay, I'll get back to you as soon as I figure out my next move. In the meantime, stay away from the farm until you hear from me. Don't try anything on your own. I know how you are," he warned.

Bryn leaned forward, trying to keep her temper in check. She didn't like the tone in his voice. "Not to worry. This is *your* gig, and I only said I would pass on information. You're on your own with this one. But I would like to know your plan. After all, I did help you against my better judgment."

"Understood." Parker got up from the chair, talking as he walked hurriedly toward the house. "I'll call you before I make a move on the dirtbag. Until then, thanks for your help, and I really mean it. Remember, as I said, I owe you one."

"Stay safe," Bryn said and clicked off her cell phone.

Chapter 32

*P*arker was all business. His mind was churning. He should have seen this coming. Parker walked into the bedroom, throwing the towel on the floor in disgust. He stepped into his custom built brown granite shower and tapped the touchscreen located at one end of the massive spa. Two walls of body sprays angled at his back and neck began their magic, relieving the knotted tension in his muscles. With another touch of the pad, the surround sound system began playing his favorite music. He tilted his head back and closed his eyes as four shower heads rained warm droplets of water over his body. As a river of water poured over him, the strain of the job began to diminish and his body finally began to relax.

The shower, preprogrammed, turned off and he slicked back his hair and moved to a massive granite bench set against the wall. With a huge sigh, he moved his shoulders back and forth against the hydro-sprays pointed at his shoulders and lower back. The shower sprays, set to varying temperatures and intensity, massaged his shoulders, and tight neck, lulling him into a deep relaxed state of mind.

After five minutes of hydro-therapy, he stepped to the end of the massive shower and pressed the touchscreen once more. Two glass walls moved into place and closed. This end of the spa was his personal sauna. Parker sat down on a wooden bench and was immediately enveloped in gentle steam laced with the soothing aroma of eucalyptus. This was the place where he did his deepest thinking and he chewed through every piece of information Bryn had given him. He had to give it to Luca. He was one sly bastard. Putting money down on a horse he would never take, and then suggesting he would buy two more was masterful and a great play. Make the people think he was an honest man and gather every bit of information he could weasel from them was audacious. That's how the best scams were played.

The Wolf of Wall Street had sucked in all of his friends through cunning and half-truths. He was the best scam artist known in the investment world, and he knew how to play on human greed. The Wolf took full advantage of the concept of intrinsic human fallibility to sucker people into his web of lies and deceit. Luca often quoted the Wolf, but laughed when the Feds finally took him down. D'Angelo reckoned himself as one of the best scam artists who continued to slip through the Fed's net, and so far he was right. A wealthy con artist, the crafty hustler lived in the shadows and knew just how to skirt the law. It took a daring opportunist for a scam to work, and Luca was all of that.

Parker breathed in the steam and pulled his shoulders back and forth to relieve any lasting tension. Scams! That's what separated the honest man from the dishonest one. It's what made their world work. Many unscrupulous bureaucrats made their fortunes that way, and so far it had worked for his old buddy, Luca D'Angelo.

If it wasn't for the imminent danger of cornering Luca at the farm, Parker would have laughed out loud. But he did find it amusing that Luca was stoked thinking he had one upped him. He leaned back, breathed in deeply, and thought about Luca. Parker knew *he* had the best play book; after all it takes a crook to catch a crook. He had lured Luca into a sucker-game, and had used the overconfident hustler's greed and arrogance to reel him in. Parker's eyes narrowed as he thought about the exaggerated, self-opinionated mobster's feeling of grandeur. "Well, that won't last long, loser," he mumbled as he stretched his arms overhead. "The thing you will never understand is that *I*, Parker Thomas, am the superior scam artist, and *you*, Luca D'Angelo, are going down for the count, and *you* will never see it coming." At last, he had something to smile about.

The first part of the con had been to persuade Luca to join him in a venture that promised him great wealth, more than he could amass on his own. Luca was a loner but Parker had convinced him to work with him in a foolproof scam. Parker knew how Luca's mind worked and to sweeten the deal and earn his trust, he had moved millions into the Cayman accounts using the horseshoe numbers. Just as planned, his co-conspirator was hooked on the easy money and Parker knew he would never walk away from the last numbered rip-off from Jefferson and Rooker.

It had taken Parker months to think about how to entrap Luca and it had worked. Well, until Magic went missing, but that was the only glitch in the overall big picture. Stupid Luca who thought the reward was greater than the risk and blinded by what he believed was Parker's incompetence. No doubt about it. It was a race to the wire and Parker was going to finish first.

After twenty minutes in the steam room, Parker had a clear head and a plan.

What Luca didn't know was that as soon as Magic went missing, he had been tracking her and using sophisticated programs, had acquired all the information he needed to know, especially about Samantha Steele and her husband Denver Maxwell. In fact they would be shocked if they knew how much he had learned. He knew what they had in investments and in their bank accounts, which college their twins were enrolled, and the names of their friends and grandparents. It was all part of the job. He had to know who the people were who had his horse and be one step ahead of the man they thought was a buyer.

During their last conversation, Parker knew by the tone of Luca's voice that he didn't believe he had lost the horse. He had pacified him with the promise he would call as soon as he had something concrete to tell him, but he should have known better. Luca was nobody's fool and stayed out of prison because he was always one step ahead of the Feds so why would he believe him? Luca mistrusted everyone, friend or foe. Parker knew from the beginning of the scam that Luca would try and outsmart him and keep the last numbered account for himself, but that would be the biggest mistake of the hoodlum's life. Parker stood up and turned off the sauna. He was ready to begin. Lips pressed tightly together and eyebrows furrowed, he was in the last inning of the game and he could see the home plate. *Well, buddy, so far, your ruse is working for you, well, almost.* He opened the sauna door and headed for the bedroom.

Chapter 33

Immediately after speaking with Parker, Bryn knew she had to do the right thing. This whole mess was going to blow up and she didn't want to take a chance on Sam and her husband being caught in the cross hairs. Parker was planning on surprising Luca at the farm. He said he would have backup and the word backup meant that Parker was planning for any possible outcome. What if Sam and Denver came home early? Maybe something would happen at the farm that Lyla, who was taking care of everything, would call them. Or maybe Lyla, at the last minute, would decide to stay overnight at the farm and she would run into Luca. What then? Bryn knew that she could not risk her new friend's life. What if by happenstance someone was at the farm when Parker and Luca met head on? Bryn felt herself shudder just thinking about that. Just before he had clicked off his cell, Parker said he "owed her one." Well, it was time for him to pay up. She picked up her cell phone and called Parker back.

After much convincing, Parker finally agreed with her logic. It was too hairy to base the takedown on the hope that no one would be at the farm when everything was about to come to a head. They would have to take a huge gamble and bring Sam and Denver into the conspiracy. But would her new friends trust her enough to believe what she would tell them?

Sam's cell phone rang just as she was putting the goats back in their pen. There was a ton of work to complete before their overnight trip and she wasn't ready. She didn't have her dress, Den's suit or their overnight bags packed. It was always like this. She had the false concept that time waited for her. Last-minute Annie, Minnie fondly called her.

"Hello," she said walking briskly back to the house.

"Hi, Sam. Well, you won't like what I've found out," Bryn said, taking in a short breath.

Sam could hear the demanding tone in Bryn's voice. "Bryn, I'm straight out. Can't it wait until Monday?"

Bryn's reply was clipped. "No. This is urgent and I really need to see you and Denver. I'm on my way to your farm right now and I should be there in a half hour. Is Denver home?"

"Yes, he is, but tell me, I insist. What's this all about? You're kind of scaring me."

"I can't talk over the phone, but believe me, you will want to hear what I have to say. Got to go. See you shortly. Tell Denver I'm on my way." To avoid more questions, she closed her cell phone.

Totally unnerved, Sam stared at her phone. Bryn had ended so abruptly, she didn't have a chance to ask anything else. She half jogged and half ran to signal Denver who was working on the tractor. Early in the day, Yellow Beast had backfired and died and all the cranking of the engine would not start it. Of course it had happened when she was working in the lower field. Just when she thought it was running like a well-oiled machine and the unreliable tractor had once again lulled into believing that it could keep up with Den's John Deere. She had to walk back up from the field and Denver had to drive his green tractor down to the disabled Yellow Beast, a toolbox tucked beside him.

By the time she reached the top of the field, she was out of breath. Yelling his name as loud as she could, she never gave thought that she could have called him on his cell phone. "Denver, Denver!" The horses heard her before he did and whinnied back before he turned his head. "Great, what the heck was I thinking," she muttered. She took out her cell and tapped in his number.

"Hey, darlin', is that you up there yelling like a crazy lady? What's the emergency?"

"You won't believe this, but I just had a call from Bryn who's on her way here to tell us something urgent." Sam was talking faster than she could catch her breath. "And it sounds very serious. She asked if you were here 'cause she needs to talk to you too."

"When will she be here? I'm just finishing up with your tractor. As of right now, Yellow Beast is kaput and it's going to take more time than I have to fix her."

"Forget the tractor," Sam was becoming more frantic as she spoke. Something about Bryn's tone said this was not good. "Just drive your Deere up and come to the house. I'll meet you there."

"Okay, I'll be there in a minute. You say she's on her way?"

"Yes, she'll be here in a half hour, and I hope she won't be long. We have so much to do before we leave and she insisted that this can't wait."

"Okay, I'll head up. It may be just about a horse or something. Don't get yourself all in a panic. Put your Sherlock hat on and I'll be right there."

Sam could picture the grin on his face. He loved to call her that when she and Addie were together. As she hastily walked back to the house, a sudden thought flashed through her mind. She didn't know why but the mysterious buyer from Florida, Luca D'Angelo, made her wonder if Bryn's insistence to see them *now* was all about him.

"Oh my God. I get it!" Sam was walking as fast as she could to the house. A shiver ran through her body. Her intuition had been right. Suddenly the pieces to the puzzle were falling into place. First, there was the rescue. Without a doubt the owner would have claimed the gorgeous mare by now. Second, there were the numbered shoes. She knew they were significant enough for her not to toss them into the discard pile for the girls. Third, there was the shifty-looking man who put a deposit on a horse he never asked to ride. And last but not least, there was Bryn who just happened to show up at her farm. Sam couldn't shake the feeling that Moxie knew her. There was no time to share her suspicions with Denver because just as she entered the kitchen, she heard Bryn's car coming up the driveway.

Chapter 34

Luca was on the road to Sam and Denver's farm by 10:30 p.m. As he turned onto Main Street, he saw that most of the businesses were closed except for a small gas station on the corner. He followed Main Street and hooked a left up the mountain towards West Ridge Farm. It was pitch black, not a star in the sky and the full moon was shadowed by heavy cloud cover. He had hardly glanced at the local weather forecast, but he heard something about rain after midnight and he planned to be in and out of the farm well before then. Worse yet, he hadn't noticed how difficult it was to maneuver the twists and turns, having only been at the farm during the daylight hours.

"Thank God for my GPS," he muttered. "I'd *never have* found this damn farm in the dark." He was driving too fast for the curves in the road, but he was wired and agitated, not a good combination. Every so often, lights from a house spilled out from the darkened landscape, but they were few and far between. "Why the hell do people want to live way out here? No streetlights and no traffic. What do these people do, close up town at dusk? This is no man's land."

Every now and then, his headlights reflected off some animal's eyes, giving an eerie glow to the darkened fields. At one point, he hit the brakes and came to a shrieking stop as a deer sprinted into the road in front of his Caddy. Luckily, he had caught the luminescent glow from the eyes before it darted in front of his car. He couldn't believe his good luck in not smashing into the dark shape as it bolted into the wood line. Just when he was ready to drive forward, four deer following on the heels of the first unexpectedly ran in front of his car. Luca couldn't believe it! It was a dangerous close call, and the rush of adrenaline made his heart almost jump out of his chest. Luca wasn't afraid of much, but he hadn't planned on getting killed by a wild animal shooting across the road, almost running into his car. "How ironic!" he said. He was exasperated, and the vision of death slamming him in the face flashed through his mind. Killed by a deer, and not another mobster was almost comical. Maybe someday he could laugh about his near miss with death by a wild herd of deer, but tonight he was in no laughing mood. He slowed the Caddy down to a crawl. He was not going to take any more chances on hitting a deer and damaging his rental vehicle when he was almost at the farm and set to move millions of dollars into his account.

After driving more than seven miles up the curved back road, he was alerted by the GPS. "You have reached your destination."

"Yah, sweetie, I hear ya." Denver had told him that the dirt road that led to the back barns and fields was a short distance from the farmhouse but could be easily missed since it was hidden by low shrubs and lined with tall pine trees.

Luca drove slowly, his eyes squinting and straining in the dark as he looked for the opening to the back road. He almost missed it, but his headlights caught the dark opening in the nick of time. He carefully turned onto the narrow clearing and pulled up in front of a heavy chain barrier. Putting the Caddy in park, he opened the door and stepped out. The headlights illuminated the chain that stretched between two trees and he unhooked one end and carried it to the other side of the road, dropping it on the ground.

Back in the Caddy, he put the car in gear and drove forward beyond the chain and parked again. He got out and picked up the chain and hooked it back to the tree. Luca didn't want to take any chances on someone noticing the chain down. Although it appeared the town and road was devoid of traffic or people, he knew that Sam and her husband had a lot of friends, and he wasn't about to risk someone driving by and seeing the chain unhooked. What if some kids decided to come by and use the path as a parking spot? Denver had mentioned that he was concerned about it enough to block the entrance.

He got back in the Caddy and drove up a small incline following the narrow road that Denver had cut in. For sure he did not want to risk anyone seeing his car parked near the entrance. Luca stopped the car and turned the ignition off. Fortunately, the headlights lit the path and wouldn't turn off for a few minutes. Luca got out, opened the back door and reached in for the flashlight.

He was feeling good about this job. Sitting at the bar slugging down a few shots, he had made a mental list of what he needed to get the job done. He had asked his new buddy, Dennie, the bartender, where the closest store was that carried hunting gear. He chuckled when he told him that one of his friends invited him to go turkey shooting but he hadn't packed clothes for anything but meetings. Dennie always obliging to the surly guest, gave him the name of a store about ten miles from the hotel. He picked up a large serrated hunting knife with a leather sheath to clip on his belt, a flashlight, hunting boots, short cargo pants, and a lightweight black hoodie. No sense in wrecking his Italian black shoes or tailor made white shirts. For good measure he had also bought a can of bear spray. Luca had tucked the small gun into the back of his cargo pants. It would be disposed of before he drove to the airport. His confidence was a mile high and he expected his trudge through the woods would be no more than a walk in the park.

Holding the flashlight in front of him, Luca carefully maneuvered the path toward the back barns. The wind was picking up and cool air was beating its way east, but Luca had no idea the quick weather change was imminent. He was dressed in light clothes, expecting no more than a few mosquito bites. After getting out of the warm Caddy, it felt to him that the temperature had dropped at least twenty degrees and he shivered. A roll of thunder sounded in the distance. "Damn, he muttered. "What the hell? I thought there was only a chance of showers. I should have paid more attention to the forecast. Got to get in and out of here fast."

Just then, he tripped on a rock and almost fell. He let out a four-letter curse and then began a deluge of curses aimed towards Parker and everything that drew him out into the dead of night to complete a job that should have been simple. Luca was out of his element. He wasn't in good shape and had never been alone on the back side of a mountain in the middle of the night. The rain was beginning to soak through his hoodie, and suddenly the sky opened up and began pelting him with buckets of cold water. He wiped the water running down his face; his body on heightened alert preparing for a wild animal to jump out at him. Stumbling again, he let out a four letter word as he caught himself in the nick of time. If his luck held out, the fear of being attacked by a bear wouldn't happen and he wouldn't fall, break a leg or hit his head. His imagination was running wild.

Luca started talking to himself to shake off the jitters. "Get a hold of yourself. Think, Luca. Stop acting like a numskull and start thinking about where to begin looking for the shoes." But he couldn't stop his heart from pounding. His breathing was coming faster and faster, and he had to control the urge to run. He stopped to catch his breath and cursed. A jagged streak of lightning lit up the sky, followed by a massive crack of thunder. Luca shivered. His arms and legs were covered with goose bumps and he tried desperately to shake away the heebie-jeebies. For a moment, he was disoriented, and he turned around, waving his flashlight from right to left. He was under siege by the weather and the wild animals he believed were lurking behind trees. Worse yet, he had the crazy thought that someone following him would reach out and tap him on the shoulder.

Screaming, "Stop it, Luca!" he tried to regain his senses and shook his flashlight in the air, railing at his situation. "It's those asinine deer that caused this. I'm still shaky from almost running into them. If another shows up I'll shoot it. That'll teach them."

A large bird swooped overhead, scaring the hell out of him, and his flashlight caught the eye of a creature scurrying to the side and into the undergrowth. "I don't belong here. I'm just an intruder in their home," he said, shaking his head in an attempt to find something to take his mind off the blackness that seemed to close in on him with every step. The beam from the flashlight was the only light in the darkness and the worrisome thought flashed through his mind that if it gave out he would be in deep trouble. His eyes tried to pierce the darkness but he couldn't see his hand in front of his face.

The only sound breaking the stillness of the night, other than his boots crunching on dead branches and leaves, was an owl hooting from a tree top. "That must have been what I heard fly overhead," he mumbled. Far in the distance, the owl's hoot was returned by another owl, sending a shiver down his spine. He was spooked and the hairs on his neck stood up. Fear was overpowering his usual bravado and he was angry that he couldn't control his emotions. He murmured a four letter word as he moved his flashlight from one side of the dense trees to the other and then back on the path in front of him. Luca was never a camper or a hunter and traipsing through the dense backwoods in the middle of the night was rattling him. He was definitely out of his element. The back and forth hoots from the owls were unsettling, and at the moment his usual self-control and overconfidence were nonexistent. He shouted out a four letter word as a twig from a tree branch slapped his face and barely missed his eye. Anger began replacing fear.

Mercifully, nothing ran in front of him that would cause him to freak out and he took in a deep breath, trying to concentrate on the job. It had better be worth all of this because he didn't relish the idea of coming back on Monday. How would he be able to persuade the Samantha woman to tell him what she had done with the horseshoes? That was the unanswered question.

Luca stumbled on a fallen branch and almost fell. He let out some choice cuss words and regained his balance. He didn't know whether to shine the light ahead of him or down on the path itself, but either way, the going was much slower than he anticipated. His mood was explosive and everything angered him. All of it! The sound from his boots crunching on broken twigs, the slap from the tree branch he hadn't expected, and the noisy hoot of owls. Everything was rattling him. Dripping wet, all he could think of was getting the hell out of the blackness and returning to civilization. Denver had pointed the dirt road out to him when they were on the tour of the property and for some reason Luca thought it was a short road that circled the back part of the farm. It had seemed so simple. Follow the road to the back barns, and then follow the path to the large barn where the tack room was. However, in the dead of night and pouring rain, he lost his sense of direction and the barns seemed miles away. Stumbling, tripping and soaked to the bone, he was slowed down by the darkness and by a dirt road he was not familiar with.

Finally, he was at the end of the wooded tree line and Luca could see the opening to the fields. Just then, a crashing sound came from the right side of the tree line. He stopped short in his tracks, his heart pounding. All he could think of was that it was the sound of a bear. Denver had told him there were quite a few bears roaming the back side of the mountain and a mom and cubs had run through his field just this spring. The bear population was growing and was becoming a nuisance in town. A driver had hit one crossing the road just last week. Luckily for the bear he was only grazed and the car wasn't damaged. Only a few bear hairs were stuck to the grill to mark the spot where the bear and car had collided.

Luca moved his flashlight where he heard the sound. Nothing! Neither bear nor other creature came into the spotlight. He turned the flashlight back on the road. Maybe it was a raccoon or some small animal out hunting, but the words "Danger! Danger!" rang in his ears. Buckets of water poured over him and his swagger, the essence of his character, was drowning in the deluge of rain.

Off in the distance he heard the howl of a coyote and the return calls of others. "What the hell?" Without even thinking, he began jogging, forgetting to be careful where he planted his feet. The chilling howls seemed to be closing in and he remembered Sam telling him about a coyote attacking one of her foals. He had half listened to her story, but now he wondered if a pack of coyotes was stalking him. With his free hand, he slipped his knife out of the leather sheath. Holding the flashlight and knife in one hand, he ran his knuckles over the hard gun tucked in his waist band. For now the knife gave him a sense of security but the gun was loaded and ready, just in case. As suddenly as they began, the howls from the coyotes faded and his mind settled on the task ahead. He slipped the knife back into its sheath and rubbed his left arm. The cold water made his chest feel tight and his arm began to ache. He shrugged it off and blamed it on the stumble that had almost made him take a header.

Luca blundered on and stopped for a moment to gather his wits and get his bearings. Another bolt of lightning lit up the sky and he realized he was at the lower hay field and was near the pastures where the horses were turned out. He had missed a turn in the road and had taken the long way around the farm. No wonder the hike had taken so long. He shouted another expletive and swung the flashlight side to side searching for the path that ran along the field. "Damn, there it is," he groaned and began walking back up the hill toward the barns.

He was finally headed in the right direction and he let out a huge sigh of relief as he wiped the water running down his face. The thought occurred to him that he should return to the car the shorter way. But he would need to walk up to the house and down the driveway to the road, and he was afraid to chance it. The house had security cameras situated on each end of the roof and porch and he wanted to leave no trace that he was there. He would have to go back to the Caddy the way he came, and the idea was not appealing. The only thing in his favor was that he had a better idea of the terrain, but he dreaded the trek back to the car.

It was still deadly dark and raining as he walked along the field and up the hill toward the barns. He came to a long wooden fence and heard a nicker from one of the horses in the pasture. Luca recognized their unease as he walked by. It was an ungodly, spooky night and he was on their turf. Luca knew that horses were always on alert and ready to flee danger in a split second. His flashlight caught a few of the dark shadows walking towards him. "Easy boys, just walking through," he muttered, quickening his pace.

Luca made it past the lower barns without a problem. The beam from his flashlight was still strong and his fear of wild animals began subsiding. At last he could concentrate on the job and he had a good idea on where he was. As he passed one of the hay barns a large floodlight came on and he quickly scooted to the side of the outbuilding. He wasn't worried about being seen, but it was good to err on the side of caution. The motion triggered light would go out in a few minutes and he believed he was the only unwelcomed guest on the property. A sudden chill went through him and he couldn't wait to get out of the rain. He was cold and the heaviness in his chest wasn't letting up. He needed to hurry.

On his tour of the farm, he had noticed the flood lights and remarked to Denver that he thought they were a good idea to have on the barns and the house. He could have cared less, but he was trying to make Denver feel comfortable around him. Denver had replied with a shrug, saying that they could be annoying when they were tripped by animals. That conversation gave him piece of mind because even if someone was at the farm it was not unusual for the lights to go on. Finally he was returning to the old confident Luca knowing there was one less problem to worry about.

Luca was feeling good. Even the rain was letting up. The powerless feeling he had walking through the pitch darkness was gone and he was on a mission. His flashlight lit the path and the going was much easier. The barns loomed ahead like apparitions in the night and for the first time since leaving the muddy dirt road he gave a sigh of relief. His lip turned up into a slight smirk. He had left the darkness of the unknown and was on his way to a fortune.

Following the path, Luca reached the main barn where the tack room was located. The goats let out a bleat and he turned his head toward the sound. He knew he was alone, but he had an uneasy feeling when they called out. They knew someone, or something was sneaking around their barn yard. "Stupid animals," he grumbled regaining his composure as he slowly pulled the barn doors open. Unable to turn the barn light on, he depended on the flashlight to light his way to the tack room. Horses, awakened by the intruder, nickered as he walked by their stalls. "Easy girls," he said automatically. Luca had forgotten the barn cats and suddenly the beam from his flashlight caught the reflection of a cat's luminous eyes. They lay stretched out on the barn rails, watching his every move. Their yellow eyes stared back at him, but none jumped down from their perch to offer a greeting. They instinctively understood that this was not a man to sidle up to.

Walking with purpose toward the tack room, Luca almost tripped over a cat that had jumped down from its high perch. He let out a curse and tried to kick it. Luckily, the cat moved before Luca's shoe found its rump. Even as soaked and cold as he was, he began to sweat. Ignoring the sensation of tipping to the right, he had a sudden desire for a cigarette and made up his mind that once back in the Caddy, the first thing he would do was to light one up. The tack room loomed before him and he moved his flashlight over the handle and opened the door. The room was large and neatly lined with saddles and tack. Shelves were stacked with see through bins of horse supplies and a small bench sat to one side of a tall cupboard. Luca moved his light along the walls where large hooks held leather straps and reins. Various hooks held bridles and halters with the name of the horse tacked above. "Cool, I knew she was a neatnik. This makes the search a whole lot easier."

On one side of the room, an over-sized calendar hung with postings of farrier and vet appointments. Next to the calendar was a white wall board with each horse's name and individual information. Luca hesitated when he saw the name Moxie and it brought a smirk to his lips. Moving his light along the wall, he stopped. There they were! Magic's shoes were hanging on a hook right next to the calendar and wallboard.

Chapter 35

Luca couldn't believe his good luck. He reached up and took the horseshoes down from the wall and moved the beam from the flashlight over them to get a better look. Sure enough, the numbers were stamped on the inside ring of the shoes. "I knew it! I knew it! I knew the Steele woman would save them for the owner." A half smile came over his lips as he slipped the horseshoes into the pocket of his cargo pants and left the tack room.

Luca was so puffed up with his own cleverness that the dark walk back to the Caddy seemed to flow like butter on a hot potato. The rain had begun to ease up and he moved along at a brisker pace. With his better sense of direction, each step made him more jubilant. He had beat Parker to the pile of gold and it felt so good that he didn't notice the second round of the massive storm pushing through. All he could think of was getting back to the Caddy and out of the miserable depressing situation he found himself in.

Big drops began to fall on his forehead and he pulled his hoodie tightly around his head. The ground, dry from lack of rain, was puddling in front of him and with every step he became more enveloped in murky mud. He was glad that he had thought to buy the rugged boots but he hadn't counted on being clobbered by the deluge. The rain was making it more difficult for the flashlight to provide the same sharp light as before and the path was becoming slippery.

"Damn," he mumbled. "Why did I buy the cheapest flashlight and the most expensive boots?" He muttered again as his wet boots stepped into a deep puddle. The wind was picking up and large branches were swinging crazily overhead.

A torrent of rain began beating down on him and a strong gust slapped his face. It was as if the clouds had opened for the second time and were releasing buckets of water on this one piece of land. Maybe if he hadn't spent most of his time in the lounge, he would have thought to turn on the television and have seen the flood warnings. His hotel was not in the path of the severe weather, but unfortunately the western part of the state was, and he was right in the midst of a slow moving storm. A loud crack of thunder overhead was followed by sheets of rain, and then bolts of lightning pierced the dark forbidding sky. The lightning was so bright that for a brief second the field he was walking beside was lit up like a flood lamp. The wind was howling and he felt like he was tumbling in a washing machine, as he was pushed forward and then backwards.

"What the hell is this! This is unbelievable," he shouted, almost tripping over a large downed tree branch lying on the path. What he thought would be a quick trek back to the Caddy was taking twice as much time as he anticipated.

Another clap of thunder sounded like it was overhead and another crack of lightning lit up sky. The vicious storm was slowly eating away the triumphant exhilaration he had when he found the horseshoes. The air temperature had changed from warm to cool and it was sodden with cold water. The battle between the heat wave and the cooler air driven in from the west was on, and Luca was caught in the cross hairs. Luca began to shiver again and the hoodie was little help. It was soaked with water and lay heavily on his head. His pockets were filled with water and the path was becoming a stream. Luca had never experienced a night like this and his temper grew raw. He had to keep going.

On the way to the barns, he had worried about being attacked by wild animals, and now, he worried about getting hit by lightning or a tree falling on him. He had a gun and knife to protect himself from a bear or coyote attack, but they were no match for Mother Nature. She was in charge now and he could only hope that he made it to the Caddy in one piece. He put his head down low and followed the dim beam of light, stumbling and cursing all the way. He squeezed his eyes to remove the water that now flowed over his face melding with the water streaming down and into his neck. He was a huge squishy sponge filled with water, but although soaked to the bone; he smirked as he touched the horseshoes tucked in his water-logged pocket. The nagging heaviness in his chest was becoming stronger but he mollified himself with the images of a double shot of bourbon and a hot shower waiting for him at the hotel. That would take care of everything. The vision of a warm car and the drive back to the hotel with the horseshoes on the seat next to him kept him going. It would all be worth it. The ugly weather was nothing compared to what Parker would experience when he realized that he, Luca D'Angelo, had bested him once again.

Luca slogged through water and stumbled on branches, shivering and cursing with each step. His shaky hand barely gripped the flashlight. He reached the end of the pasture where the turnoff to the dirt road was and stopped, moving his dim flashlight back and forth. His teeth were chattering and he was so cold that he couldn't think straight. He shook his head side to side trying to clear his foggy brain and began trudging through the water. This time he was careful to take the right path. He wasn't about to make that mistake again.

Wet, shivering, and cold, Luca finally made his way to the beginning of the dirt road where his Caddy was parked. Relieved and exuberant, he tried to yell out a, "Yahoo," but the cold had taken his voice and everything sounded garbled.

He could see the Caddy, but he had the gut feeling he was in real trouble. Each step was as if he were moving in slow motion. His arm was dead weight and as his hand touched the car he found himself gasping for air. He leaned against the hood to stop the shaking and fumbled for his car keys.

Suddenly, the dark night was ablaze with what seemed like a million lights. "Stop where you are and hands in the air!" a man shouted.

Luca instinctively reached for his gun but his hands were trembling so much he couldn't unsnap his pant pocket. His brain was moving ever so slowly, and with no control over his body or mind, he fell against the car and slid down into the mud.

As he moved into unconsciousness, everything began

fading away. Off in the distance, he could hear the sound of men's voices coming towards him. One of them sounded familiar, and then, there was nothing.

Chapter 36

October

The Toyota Tundra pulling the three-horse trailer sped along the highway. The fancy black trailer was empty, but not for long. The radio belted out the voice of Jason Aldean singing "The Only Way I Know" and Parker sang along. Bryn smiled as she listened to him singing without being conscious of just how good he was. Most of his clients would be surprised to know that he carried a great tune and was a natural at playing the guitar. Bryn believed that Parker would have chosen a career in music if his passion for danger and intrigue hadn't taken him into the dark underbelly of crime. This song in particular defined who he was and she understood why he was lost in the moment. She found herself humming along, enjoying the music and remembering how most nights, after dinner, they sat in front of the fireplace while Parker played the guitar and sang. Picking at the guitar in the evening was his way of lowering the stress of his demanding job. Her stress reliever was riding horses, and his was music. Once in a while she joined him in singing, but she was not gifted with the music gene so most times she just sat back and enjoyed the music. Bryn leaned back in the plush leather seat and tipped her head against the headrest, letting out a small sigh of contentment. She finally believed that life was good, and it was only going to get better.

Never in her wildest dreams would she have imagined that she and Parker would be on their way to Sam and Denver's farm in a pickup truck pulling a horse trailer. And the frosting on the cake was the huge diamond ring with a ruby center sitting on the ring finger of her left hand. She lifted her hand, moving it back and forth, mesmerized by the sparkle and glitter of the diamond. She turned her hand so that it caught the sun's ray. *I'm engaged,* she thought. *And I'm planning a wedding, although we haven't set a date.* Sam was right when she shared her views on love and commitment that day at the farm. How did they ever ease into such a serious conversation? It seemed like only yesterday and so much had happened since then.

Parker reached over and gave her hand a squeeze. "What ya thinking about, babe?"

"I'm thinking how happy I am," she said as she leaned over and kissed his cheek. "But my mind is still running over our last job. What could have ended in a disaster was a save, but I sure had serious doubts about it when you brought me in."

"I promised you I would take care of D'Angelo, and I did." Parker glanced at Bryn sitting next to him. She was as beautiful as ever. Her auburn hair was pulled back in a loose pony tail and although her aviator sunglasses covered her green eyes, he knew they were narrowed remembering the events that led up to the take down of the mobster. She despised Luca and had told him more than once; if she never heard his name again it would be fine with her. He didn't blame her. He had coaxed her to take on a precarious job, and she had once again come through for him. From the moment he had heard her voice on the phone he wondered if she would ever forgive him for being such a fool. She could have hung up, but he groveled enough to get her attention. How could he have let the best thing in his life walk away like he did? That would never happen again and he promised himself, and her, that he was in this for the long haul. He had a lot of kissing up to do in their renewed relationship and he would always work to make it up to her.

Bryn sat up and looked at him. She lifted the sunglasses from her eyes and placed them on top of her head. "I've thought a lot about that man and it hasn't been good. But in a crazy way, he brought us back together. I never would have given you another chance. I was with Don and didn't think I'd ever hear from you again. Hate to tell you but it was seeing how happy Sam and Denver were that made me more open to your advances." Her lips turned up in a mischievous grin before she added, "And of course I never really stopped loving you."

Parker glanced at her, knowing she enjoyed throwing the Don name at him. He couldn't stop himself from teasing her. "Well, he had no chance with you. Even before the job, I was going to find my way back to you. Did you think I would give up that easily?"

Bryn reached over and put her hand on his arm. "I know, which is why I could never totally commit to him. I always felt in my heart that we would get back together. I hate to admit this to you but just hearing your voice made my heart beat a little faster."

Bryn could feel her face flush. "I guess it's the adrenaline thing that keeps us bonded so tightly, well...among other things," she laughed. "Although this job was totally different from our last few, finding new friends and riding again made everything worthwhile. And because I agreed to work on the Golden Horse case, I have two friends, Sam and Lyla. Most of all, with the file closed, we can finally get on with our lives."

Parker lifted his sunglasses and looked directly into her green eyes. "Bryn," he smiled, "I couldn't be happier that you have two friends you can depend on. You are a fabulous woman and a loyal friend. Look at the risk you took to warn Sam and Denver. You cared so much you were willing to jeopardize the whole operation just to keep them out of danger. I have to respect that."

"I couldn't take a chance on something happening to them. I liked them too much and now we both have lifetime friends."

Parker nodded. "You were right. But I've always trusted your instincts." He paused. "Bryn, I hope you never doubt my love for you. Now I'm getting all sappy. Not good for a man like me. Don't tell my friends," he laughed as he slipped his sunglasses back on. "Ready to stop for lunch? I know a great little tavern in a town off this exit."

"Sure. We're in no hurry. It's a beautiful a day and I'm a little hungry."

"Good," he said turning the truck into the right lane to take the next exit.

"Oh, turn that song up. I really like this one."

"Hey, Soul Sister" filled the cab of the truck and Bryn began singing along, not caring if her voice didn't have the same melodic pitch as Parker's. The old saying "Sing as if no one is listening and dance like no one is watching" is how she led her life and it wasn't going to change anytime soon. Parker took the exit and then turned right at a stop sign. After a mile, the road narrowed, curved gently then straightened again. On the right side of the road they passed a sign with the name "Green Hollow".

"That's a pretty name for a town," Bryn remarked."

Parker nodded. "And the minute we enter Green Hollow you'll know why they named it that. The town sits in a valley between two mountains."

The road meandered along a ribbon of trees adorned with leaves of brilliant colors. At times the wooded tree line opened to large corn and hay fields. The fields lay fallow waiting for the winter snow to provide a bed of cover for the next spring growth. The summer harvest had been generous and barns were stacked with hay, and tons of corn filled the silos. Harvested corn fields were left with short stubs of corn stalks, a welcome stopping place for geese flying south. Parker slowed down for Bryn to watch a flock of Canadian geese picking at the leftover corn. The air was alive with honking, and a huge skein of geese filled the sky.

Parker pulled the rig to the edge of the field and stopped. Bryn took out her camera and clicked away taking photos of the massive flock of geese. Hundreds of geese were moving through the stubby corn rows and others were dropping from the air, graceful wings moving slowly until they found just the right spot to join the gaggle. "I have never seen anything like this. Although I've seen geese flying overhead and a few in fields, the sight of this many is overwhelming."

"It sure is," he said as he eased the truck back onto the road. "I was just thinking how I'd love to get married in the fall, but that's too far away. What about a winter wedding?"

Bryn raised her eyebrows wondering if they had enough time

to plan a wedding in such a short time. "Let's talk about a date over a glass of wine. Everything is happening so fast. You just proposed and gave me my ring. I hadn't thought we'd get married till next year."

Parker laughed. "True, but I think we've wasted enough time. How long can it take to plan a wedding?" He could see the look on Bryn's face, and it was one of surprise. Before she could answer he said, "Tell you what, you're right. But today is as good as any to set a date." He let the words sink in and kept his eyes on the road saying nothing else. Parker was a smart man and he knew her lack of immediate response meant she was thinking about it.

They were quiet the rest of the way to the tavern. The morning had been cool but the strong sun overhead promised it would warm quickly and by noon it would feel like summer had never left. The autumn day was made for dressing in layers. Jackets to begin with and soon they would be peeled off and all that was needed was a long sleeve shirt. As if on cue, Parker rolled down the truck windows allowing the warmer air to fill the cab. A slight breeze passed through the trees dropping a rain of red and yellow leaves onto the road. One flew into the open window and landed on Bryn's lap. She laughed as she picked up the leaf and said that she would press it and save it as a remembrance of the gorgeous fall day and their trip to pick up the Curly gelding she had fallen in love with on the ride to Lyla's bakery.

The leaves skipped in front of the truck, swirling to the side of the road as they sped along. Rounding a corner they came to a local fruit stand where several cars had pulled in. Brilliant orange pumpkins were stacked on both sides of the stand and an old wagon was piled high with gourds of different shapes and colors. Another wagon was filled with varieties of winter squash. Green

Hollow, like most New England towns, was ablaze in color. A large white wooden sign placed near the road advertised, "Locally grown fresh produce."

Parker slowed down and said they should stop and pick up pumpkins and squash on the return trip home.

Visiting small towns in New England was a pastime Parker had enjoyed during the time he and Bryn had split up. After their breakup, Parker had made up his mind not to date for a long time. He spent a lot of time soul searching and to fill the void that Bryn had left, he took a lot of day trips. Driving was his form of relaxation, and Green Hollow was one of the towns he had stopped for lunch.

Since getting back together, they had continued with the weekend drives, scouting out new towns and restaurants.

For fun, they had set up a large white board where they posted photos with the names of towns they had toured and the Inns they had stopped at. Parker, a history buff, enjoyed learning about old settlements along the New England coast line and in particular Cape Cod. They visited towns in the Western part of Massachusetts, touring Sturbridge, Deerfield and Stockbridge where they stayed overnight at the Red Lion Inn. There was always a small tavern or bakery or hiking trail to investigate and the more they explored New England the more they loved it. It was home and it was beautiful.

"I smell grapes, Bryn said.

"Me, too, but I don't see them. Must be wild grapes growing along the roadside."

"There," Bryn pointed. "Slow down. I see a bunch hanging from a bush on the side of the road."

Parker slowed the truck down. No one was behind him and the

sweet smell of wild grapes spilled through the window. Half kiddingly he said, "Wouldn't it be great to own a vineyard?" Before Bryn had time to answer he continued, "Maybe we can start looking at some farm land with open fields and rolling hills. I know grapes grow better on hill sides, but that's about all I know. But even so, I can picture it. You and me making wine and selling our own stamped bottles. What do you think Bryn? Can you see yourself owning a vineyard?"

Bryn laughed. "You know what? I can." She jumped on the idea before he could change his mind or just say he was only kidding. "Maybe we should begin visiting New England wineries and find out just what it takes to own one." Bryn grabbed Parker's hand. "The more I talk about it, the more I love the idea. We can talk to the owners. I know there's a lot to learn about making wine and choosing the right grapes for New England weather."

Parker was enjoying the whole idea. "Bryn, this is definitely a kick and I'm all in. You do the Google research and we'll put aside weekends for touring New England wineries. In the meantime I'll have my realtor start searching for a farm where we can grow the grapes. For sure we would need to be near towns where people have an interest in native wines."

Bryn could hear the passion in Parker's voice as he talked about working together at their winery. It was time to get out of their dangerous business and lead a more normal life. Since their last job the subject of doing just that had been tossed around several times. One thing for sure, any career change had to give them the same passion for the job, but without the risk.

As they continued brainstorming, the concept of owning a winery began to take on a life of its own. "I have a great idea," Bryn said. "Once we get the winery going, we could bring in local musicians and host wine tasting events during the summer months."

The longer they talked about owning a winery, the more Parker's enthusiasm grew. "How 'bout a wine club? It could attract followers of our fantastic wine and help us grow our business." Parker slapped the steering wheel. "Yes, yes, I can see this happening!" It was a future together that they could both be a part of. He was all in.

They brainstormed more about the varieties of wine they would make and what the label would look like, and the more they tossed out ideas the more ecstatic they became. "This could actually work," Parker said.

Bryn relished the whole notion of starting a business with Parker and she fed off his conviction that it could really work. All they needed was a deep desire to succeed and the determination to make it happen. The conversation continued and more ideas were floated. At last, talked out, they agreed to work on the vineyard project when they returned home. For now, they would enjoy a glass of wine and lunch at the tavern. With the vineyard plan put on the back burner, Bryn's thoughts returned to why they were on the road to their friends' farm. It was to pick up her Curly gelding and Parker's yearling filly. Thinking about the gelding made her almost giddy with excitement and she was eager to see her friends again.

The music of Train began the song "Marry Me" and Parker, a big grin on his face, reached for Bryn's hand, their lively chatter replaced with thoughts of a wedding. Bryn leaned back in the seat and gazed out the open window, her mind preoccupied as she watched a kaleidoscope of colorful leaves float down and skip across the road. Ahead, a mountain range burst with color, forming a ridge of dark and light as the sun poked between the trees. They passed an old farm where crooked fences wrapped around fields filled with herds of cows. Next to the pasture an aged red barn was stacked with hay, some of it sticking out of the loft door. Bryn was so deep in thought, she hardly noticed that they were entering the town of Green Hollow.

The road meandered along a short distance and charming black shuttered clapboard houses, each one restored and preserved, came into view. The tree belt was lined with massive oak trees, each one dropping red leaves onto the sidewalk and grass.

At a stop sign, Parker turned left onto the two-lane road of Main Street. The center of Main Street was devoted to the town green, an open expanse of land with large homes bordering it. On one side of the green a white church with a tall steeple stood next to a medium sized brick building. Parker told her it was the town hall and then pointed to the building next to it. "That's the library," he said

Next to a beautiful gazebo, a tall pole with the American flag fluttered in the breeze. A stone walkway spanned from one end of the green to the other, both sides lined with massive oak, graceful white birch and sugar maple trees. Bryn noticed several people walking their dogs and other folks were clustered near the gazebo, hands moving in animated conversation. Several people were sitting on stone benches drinking hot beverages in take-out cups. Parker said he had been in town on a weekend when the farmers market was in full swing. "Too bad it isn't Saturday. I know you would love it."

Bryn was fascinated with the town. It remained true to its historical roots and one could imagine the amount of planning it took to keep it historically correct. "This town is so beautiful. It reminds me of a New England postcard," she said looking out the window as Parker turned left at a stop sign.

"And wait till you see the tavern," Parker said. "You'll absolutely love it and the food is worth the side trip. Maybe we can stop here again on our way to visit vineyards."

Bryn laughed. "You are all in with this winery investment, aren't you? Doesn't take much to make up your mind to do something big. It must be your personality."

Parker chuckled. "Hey, missy. I don't see you dragging your feet. You like the idea as much as I do."

Bryn leaned over and kissed his cheek. "Yes, I do and remember the old saying, 'Great minds run in the same direction?' So consider yourself like-minded."

They were at the tavern and Parker began to brake. "Check it out. We're here." Set back from the road and surrounded by Maple trees, a large white sprawling building came into view. Yellow leaves floating to the ground reminded Bryn of tiny pieces of spun gold dancing in the wind. Bryn reached for her camera. "This is beyond amazing," she said as she clicked off several photo shots.

Parker swung the rig into a wide open space along the side of the tavern. He turned the engine off and they got out of the truck.

The view to the side of the building was eye-popping. Parker reached for Bryn's hand. "Walk with me. I want to show you something before we go in." The land meandered to the side and back of the antique lodge and large fields opened as far as the eye could see. Bryn removed her sunglasses and shielded her eyes with her hand. Herds of cows could be seen off in the distance and a tall mountain range was dotted with the colors of fall.

"Like it?" Parker asked, draping his arm over her shoulder and drawing her close. "This inn sits on 400 acres of land. There are cow pastures, hay fields and huge vegetable gardens. I asked all about it when I stopped here."

Bryn squinted as she took in all of the rolling fields spread out like a carpet, as far as she could see. "Oh, my gosh. This view is jaw dropping. All I can picture is long white fences filled with horses running through the fields. I could absolutely live like this and never want to leave. Can you imagine how it looks in the winter with the snow covering the fields? I can see us sitting in a sleigh, being pulled by horses. Can you imagine us on a winter night, the peaceful sound of our horse's hooves crunching the snow, bells jingling while pulling us through the fields?" Bryn couldn't stop talking about the beauty of the landscape and the pristine fields.

Parker wrapped his arm over her shoulder and kissed her cheek. "Yes I can, and this is exactly what I'm talking about. A home built to our specifications, fields for horses and our winery. Now you have even more to think about. Come on. Let's go in and talk about our future."

At the door of the tavern Bryn stopped to admire a plaque that said 'Circa 1756'. "I love this place already," she smiled.

Parker was grinning ear to ear. "Wait till you see the inside. And they have a bakery shop where the bread is baked in old style wall ovens. We can stop on the way out and pick up something for Sam and Denver."

The first thing Bryn noticed was the wide plank floors. Parker said they were the original floors and Bryn oohed and awed over them. Low beam ceilings stretched from the entry into a cozy dining room where a small fire crackled in the open hearth of a fieldstone fireplace. Waiting for the hostess, Bryn whispered,

"Parker, we have to bring our new friends here. They would love this place."

Parker nuzzled her neck. "So, let's set a date when we see them today."

Bryn had the urge to kiss him, but just then the hostess came into view and cheerfully said, "Welcome to the Red Oak Inn. Do you have a seating preference?"

Parker pointed to a table beside a window. It was the perfect spot for viewing the mountains and gardens.

They passed by other patrons eating or talking, their hushed voices interrupted now and then by low laughter or the clink of table ware. The aroma of wood burning in the fireplace mingled with the smell of baked bread and apple pie, the delicious melody of scents creating an atmosphere of comfort and relaxation. The wait staff moved through the room delivering food or taking orders and although it was busy, it was relatively quiet. Several couples were drinking wine, and it was apparent that this was a luncheon destination for business people.

Parker pulled out the chair and Bryn sat down sighing as she glanced out the window. "Thank you for remembering this place. I love it."

The waitress took their order for drinks and when she came back with their wine, Parker raised his glass and said, "Let's toast. To us, our wedding, and our winery."

Bryn raised her wine glass and tapped Parker's. Each took a sip of wine then placed the glasses back on the table. Bryn picked up her menu prompting Parker to lean over the table and murmur "The sea food chowder is delicious, and so are the popovers."

Bryn lowered her menu. Her eyes met his.

He studied her for a long moment and her cheeks began to

flush. Their legs touched under the table, and his voice, ragged with emotion, told her for the 100th time how much he loved and adored her.

Chapter 37

Bryn and Parker arrived at the farm in time for dinner but their first stop was to check out the two horses they had bought and were trailering back to New Hampshire. Denver and Sam walked them to the corral where the beauties were munching their way through the remnants of a small pile of hay. The women chatted all the way and the men followed behind deep in their own conversation.

Bryn was eager to see Tex, the bay horse she had ridden that warm summer day to Lyla's bakery and deli. Magic, the mare that had brought them all together, was the topic of conversation as they leaned against the corral and watched the two horses.

Sam and Bryn unhooked the gate and went in the corral to see Tex and the filly standing beside him. Parker smiled as he watched Bryn wrap her arm over Tex's curly neck and then give him a kiss on his soft nose. The buckskin filly nudged her arm looking for her turn. "Aren't you the pretty girl," Bryn cooed as she scratched her neck. "I can't wait to get them back to our farm, Sam," she said smiling ear to ear.

"I know how you feel and we're so glad that you decided to take them both. I know how much you love Tex but I must say, we were surprised that Parker wanted the buckskin. He owns such gorgeous quarter horses, and we thought he only favored that breed. You know how much Den loves his quarter horse, Jet. They are both quarter horse guys, although, Den has taken a fancy to the Curlies, that's for sure."

Bryn flashed a glance at Parker and smiled. "Well, he does breed a dynamite line of quarter horses, but he likes the ruggedness of the Curlies. I guess you were right when you said that once you meet one, you want one," she laughed. "Parker wants to train our new filly to be his riding horse for next year. Spirit will be his, and Tex will be mine. Right now he's riding Magic, but next year he wants to breed her, and Spirit will be ready by then."

"I like that name, Spirit. She does show a lot of spirit and is truly a remarkable filly. Willing and patient, she will make a great mount for him."

Denver and Parker leaned on the rails, watching the ladies and the horses.

Denver told Parker that he had just got back to the farm that morning. He had an overnight business trip to Pennsylvania, and he was glad to be home. He was still uneasy about leaving Sam alone and had limited his business trips to only one night a month.

Since the fiasco with Luca, he was more attuned to who came

to the farm, and thanks to Parker's suggestion, he now had cameras mounted on each of the barns and strategically placed along the access road where Luca had parked his car.

Parker agreed and understood Denver's reluctance to be away from Sam. He knew that as time went by, the apprehension would fade, but never quite be gone. "I've got some news to tell you and Sam after dinner," he said with a trace of a smile.

"Sure you don't want to tell me while we're alone?" Denver asked, his voice showing concern.

"No, it can wait. But the latest update will help allay any leftover anxiety about the whole debacle you found yourselves involved in, through no fault of your own."

Before Den could ask more, Sam and Bryn were at the gate. "Okay, cowboy," Bryn said, wrapping her arm around Parker's waist. "We're ready to eat. Let's go."

Sam had prepared grilled chicken and pasta for the friends. Everything was set on the long island in the kitchen. On the cutting board was a loaf of Italian bread, and next to it, a large bowl of salad. She had removed an apple pie from the oven when she heard their truck in the driveway, and the delicious smell wafted through the kitchen.

They filed their plates, and carried them to the kitchen nook, where colorful orange place mats and dinnerware was set.

"I'm so happy we decided to eat here rather than the dining room," Bryn said as she set her plate on the table. "Look at that view." I just love fall, and I think it's my favorite season."

The trees were filled with the colors of autumn, gracing the window with shades of showy leaves.

Denver opened the bottle of wine and poured a glass for each. They raised their glasses. "To good friends and great horses."

"Don't put your glasses down yet. There's one more thing I want to toast to," Parker said holding his glass up, "To our new vineyard!"

"What?" Sam asked. "A vineyard? Tell us more."

Parker and Bryn shared their plans of owning a vineyard and their enthusiasm was so palpable and contagious that Sam and Denver soon were caught up with their new undertaking.

"You both amaze me," Sam said. "Off on a new escapade and one that you have even *me* excited about."

"We've got a lot to talk about," Parker said nodding to Denver. "And the winery isn't the only topic we need to fill you in on. But for now, let's concentrate on this delicious food and the company of good friends.

"Here! Here! " They said in unison as they raised their glasses.

Dinner ended and plates were stacked in the dishwasher. Everyone had pitched in and with mugs filled with coffee; they retired to the great room to finish talking and planning.

Denver placed his hand on Sam's shoulder. "Sam, Parker's got an update for us on the summer of craziness"

"Can that wait for just one more minute?" Bryn pleaded with Parker. "This is more fun and we *will* talk about Magic and her horseshoes, but first can we finish up with the winery?"

Parker shrugged his shoulders and raised his hands towards Denver. "What can I do? She's the boss."

"Yah, that'll be the day," Bryn smiled. "But keep on letting me believe it. You're learning."

"I agree with Bryn. I want to hear more about the winery," Sam said. "We'll have more than enough time to talk about D'Angelo. Wait a minute, I'm getting a pad and pen to make a list of things to do." She returned with pen and pad in hand and took a sip of her coffee. "Okay, I'm ready. Bryn, I can picture a vineyard on a beautiful hillside in a small New England town."

"That's what I see," said Bryn.

Sam went on to describe the winery that Den and a group of friends had gone to several times during the summer. "It's so beautiful there, right Den?" she said looking across at him. "They host live music from local bands each weekend. We've gone with some of our friends and brought along chairs and munchies. But, you can buy sandwiches, hot dogs, salads and a bunch of other stuff from food trucks if you don't want to be bothered packing food."

Denver was buying into the whole vineyard idea and added," I agree with Sam. It is very beautiful and what a great view of the mountains they have there. And it's relaxing, sitting around listening to music and drinking wine. Although I kinda like the brewery tours a little more," he teased looking at Sam.

"Stop it!" Sam said with pretended anger in her voice. "You know you love it there and honestly he *is* becoming quite the wine connoisseur. The vineyard sells their wine by the glass, and also by the bottle. They also have a wine club and our friends signed up to have one of the house picks mailed to them each month."

Denver spoke up. "Oh, and one more thing. They also offer tours of their vineyard and their wine making process. It's quite the operation, and very interesting to learn about the type of grapes that grow in New England. I always picture vineyards in warmer climates."

"That's what I'm talking about!" Bryn said slapping her hand on her knee. "This is exactly what we envision. Our next step is to begin searching for the right location. Then we need to learn more about how to make wine and what kind of grapes thrive best in New England. It will all take some time, but it will be so much fun working on this venture."

Suddenly, Sam jumped up out of the chair. "I have a great idea and just the right location for your vineyard. What about Mansville, where Lyla's bakery and deli is? It offers hillsides for grapes, lots of farmland and a growing tourist trade. And the townies support businesses that promote natural products. What more could you ask for?"

Denver had a big smile. "I must say I agree with Sam. I travel a lot and looking at Lyla's town sounds like a great idea. It might not be your final choice, but it does have everything you're looking for. It has valleys and hillsides and lots of old farms that I'm sure you could set your sights on."

"Oh, my gosh. I love that town," Bryn said.

"And Lyla could offer your wines at her deli," Sam couldn't stop her enthusiasm. "We would live closer to each other and we could help," she added.

Bryn was caught up with the idea of living closer to Sam. She got up from the chair and leaned over to Parker and looked into his eyes. "Parker, you have to seriously look at Mansville. It has beautiful scenery and spectacular views overlooking the valley. I love that town."

Parker glanced at Denver. "What do you think, Den?"

Denver had been sitting back listening to all of the ideas being tossed around. "The ladies could be right about Mansville, and I think it's worth having you take a look. It has the flavor of a small town and it's growing, but it's a controlled growth. And the one thing they don't have is a vineyard and the girls may be onto something. It's a great place to begin looking."

Parker spoke up, a serious tone in his voice. "I have even a better idea. Would you two be interested in partnering with us in our new adventure? Bryn and I talked about it on the way here. You can say no, and our feelings won't be hurt and we don't expect an answer today. Just think about it."

Denver looked at Sam with a trace of smile on his lips. "What do you think, Sam?"

"Oh, my God! I love the idea, but you're right. We need to think about it and talk about it. We're pretty busy with our farm and our jobs, but with four of us, it could work."

Bryn was ecstatic and her voice quivered with excitement. "Okay, talk about it and then let us know. It will be so much fun working together. A new beginning and a new plan. After all we went through in July, this will make up for it. But, if it weren't for the mess we got you both into, we never would have met, so maybe there was a reason we were thrown together in a dangerous situation."

"Speaking of *that*, Bryn, before we talk any more about the vineyard collaboration, we need to update Sam and Den on the latest developments in the case."

Denver leaned forward in his chair and Sam's brows furrowed, as she suddenly became serious. He gave Sam a reassuring smile. "Yes, we've been wondering what has happened since we last talked. And I think it's time we heard the whole story. After all, if we are going to be partners, there shouldn't be any secrets between us in this matter. It did involve us, and it could have turned out really bad if everything didn't fall into place like it did. So, let's refill our coffee mugs, and Parker, I would appreciate it if you would start at the beginning."

"I agree with Den. We want you to fill us in on some of the

parts we still don't understand. Bryn, grab Parker's mug, and I'll bring Den's, and we'll get some more coffee."

As they walked back to the kitchen, both women were silent for the first time since they had sat down. Bryn and Sam brought the steaming mugs of coffee back into the great room and set them down.

Denver nodded to Parker. "Okay, from the beginning, please."

Parker took in a sip of coffee and placed the mug back on the table. All eyes were on him as he cleared his throat and began. "I knew Luca when I was a young boy pulling different scams. He was in the same type of mischief as I was and we were both good at it. The difference being is that when we grew up, we took our skills at conning and headed in completely different directions. At the fork in the road, where choices are made that can lead you to your future goals, I chose to use my talents for the good. I took the high road but at the same fork, Luca took the low. After I graduated college, I was recruited by the FBI. And because of my major in financing I worked on many cases involving money laundering. By the way, I really am gainfully employed at Jefferson and Rooker, where I have honestly earned enough money to live the lifestyle I enjoy. But I also take on side-jobs for the FBI requiring my particular skills. The Feds had been after Luca for years, but he always slipped through their fingers. Calling himself the *Teflon Don* was a slap in the face to the higher ups. He thumbed his nose at them so many times that he became a prime target and high on their list of racketeers they wanted to take down. Luca was also into some of the mob's dealings, but he mainly worked his own jobs. But, for all of his arrogance, he had his weaknesses, and they were women and money. And more importantly, he didn't get away with all of his scams by being a trusting sort of guy. Luca trusted no one, not even his own mother, who by the way, he treated very well and took very good care of."

Their eyes fixated on Parker, listening intently as he filled in the details of their harrowing experience and how they became major players in an FBI sting.

Denver ran his hand through his hair and Sam untied and retied her hair in an unconscious nervous reaction to the story. Finally it began to make sense.

Parker took another sip of coffee. It was so quiet that you could hear a pin drop, and no one said a word.

Denver leaned forward, arms on his knees.

Bryn and Sam sat up straight in their chairs, mesmerized by what Parker was saying.

Parker rubbed his chin and began again. "So, the Feds contacted me and handed me the case. At first I was hesitant. I hadn't seen Luca in years, and how was I going to pull this one off? My job at Rooker and Jefferson set the stage for the sting and since I knew how to work the accounts, I set up bogus ones using some of my own money and some of the Feds as bait to begin reeling Luca in. If Luca was a nice guy when we were kids, I might have thought differently about doing something like this to an old buddy. But he was never a good guy. He liked me because I came from the same neighborhood and he thought I had some loyalty because of it. But in no way was I ever like Luca. He was a bully and mean guy. More than once I had to knock him around and we had our battles, but he saw me as a buddy who thought like him." Parker paused again, rubbing his chin deep in thought. "But what I hated most about him was that he was a creep around the girls. There were rumors that he had done some really bad things and gotten away with them. I won't get into that, but use your imagination." Parker stopped and looked over at Bryn. "That's why I didn't want you to *ever* encounter him alone, Bryn. He was a treacherous racketeer and not one you would want to corner."

Denver's eyes narrowed, showing his intense dislike of Luca. "I get it, but how did you manage to get Luca to believe you were still a con and you wanted him as a partner?"

Parker recognized the look in Denver's eyes and he was glad the cowboy liked him. "The strategy was that I would *just* happen to run into D'Angelo at his favorite hangout. And once I told him what I was planning, and that I needed a partner I could trust to siphon millions of dollars from accounts where I worked, he was all in and took the bait. I made it so appealing and foolproof, he couldn't resist. And don't forget, I had a history with Luca and he trusted me. Well, for as much as Luca could trust anyone and only for that job. But, I knew he would try and keep the last numbered accounts for himself. That's who he is, and I sure as hell did not trust *him*." Parker paused. He could see that Denver had questions.

Denver looked directly at Parker. "So, after the D'Angelo takedown, you told me you were an FBI agent, but I didn't realize how far back you went with the guy."

Parker took in a short breath and began again. "Yup, we came from the same neighborhood, but that was it. The final takedown was set to take place in Florida and against my better judgment, to prove to him that I was trustworthy, I sent Magic down wearing the last pair of numbered horseshoes. But you know how that went. The trailer broke down and Magic bolted into the woods. Sam was right when she suspected that the numbers on the horseshoes were important. But luckily, she didn't know that she had stumbled onto something that would have been dangerous for everyone. If she had even hinted to D'Angelo about the numbered shoes, it would have been all over and the outcome would have been much different."

That thought sent a shiver down Sam's spine. "I had a hunch the numbers meant something special, so I hung them in the tack room rather than giving them away with the rest of the discarded horseshoes. And I didn't mention them to Bryn or D'Angelo. To tell the truth, I didn't think it was important to either of them. But, I felt there was something off about D'Angelo, and said as little as possible to him when he came to look at horses." Sam looked at Bryn. "What shocked me the most was when you told me you were an FBI agent? That one I would never had suspected."

Bryn got up from the chair and walked over to Sam. "Honest, Sam, I felt really bad that I had to lie to you about the real reason I was at your farm. I want you to know that this was the first case I had ever had a twinge of guilt about lying to someone."

Parker came to Bryn's defense. "And that's why she phoned and asked if she could warn you to stay away from the farm that night. She really saw you as a friend, Sam."

"I understand and please don't apologize. But I was totally shocked when we learned what was happening and that I had been in the company of a notorious criminal." Then to lighten the mood she said, "I mean I'm a woman sleuth and in another life maybe I would have been a PI. I should have listened to my gut when I first met him."

The seriousness of the conversation was broken and everyone chuckled at the thought of Sam as a PI. Denver smiled, put his arm around her and gave her a quick hug. "Honestly, Sam, I think you would make a great PI. So, should I just call you Sherlock from now on?" His smile disappeared as he turned to Parker, his manner serious. "Continue. I want to hear the rest of this."

Parker watched the couple joking back and forth. He admired their easy way of interacting with each other and knew he and Bryn had chosen the right couple as their new best friends. "So, now you know that the numbers on the shoes were used to transfer large amounts of money into offshore accounts. D'Angelo bought into the whole con because there was never a paper trail so the job seemed perfect. But, after all of my planning, several things happened that changed everything. Magic went missing, D'Angelo went looking, and I had to come up with a new plan ASAP. But first I had to be sure it was D'Angelo at your farm, Magic was there, and that you were safe. Bryn had to find out what was going on and had to be positive that you hadn't shared with him where the horseshoes were. We couldn't let you in on it because you would have known too much and could have inadvertently tipped him off. Does this make sense now?"

Den and Sam nodded in agreement. "So, what's happening with D'Angelo now?"

Parker leaned forward. "Well, you know he almost didn't make it. Major coronary at the car and he had a triple bypass. But, he's recovered and indicted and should be sentenced next month. I expect at least twenty years for racketeering and theft."

Finally Denver smiled. "At last some good news."

"But, that's not all," Parker said. "Here's the best part. There's a reward that's never been claimed for information leading to the arrest and indictment of one Luca D'Angelo. And the reward goes to you both, my friends. Because of your courage and involvement in the case, the eight hundred thousand dollars is now yours."

"What? You've got to be kidding! Are you sure about this?" Denver asked.

Sam felt dizzy. "Eight hundred thousand dollars," she repeated, shaking her head in disbelief. "We didn't even know there was reward money."

Denver tipped her chin up and kissed her. "You heard right darling."

"Yup," Parker said grinning ear to ear. "You will be getting an official notice in the mail and will be invited to our office to pick up the check, but Bryn and I wanted you to hear the good news from us. We hope this gives you something to think about when you decide to partner with us in our new winery." He winked to Bryn but she didn't catch it because she was too busy in the midst of a happy dance with Sam.

"Forget the coffee," Sam said as she looked at Bryn. "This is cause for a celebration and another huge toast."

"I'll get the bottle of wine for you girls and grab a couple of beers for us guys," Denver said, heading towards the fridge.

The four friends stood in the middle of the great room, glasses of wine and bottles of beer held high, ready for the toast. Denver spoke first. "To my wife, Sherlock and to our new friends Bryn and Parker. And to a future filled with new ventures, good health and great horses!"

"Wait, wait," Sam said. "I have another thing to add. To the end of one mystery and the beginning of my new career as a PI."

They clinked glasses and bottles and laughed. It was time to celebrate.

Photography by Diane Darin

Sandra J. Howell is a retired college professor. She and her husband live on a farm in Massachusetts. Her Curly horses have been showcased in area shows, newspapers, and Equine magazines. A foundation breeding program was established in Sweden with one of her Curly mares.

Check out her other equine novels: *Spirit of a Rare Breed*, *Saving GiGi*, and the heart-warming *Angels Club* series, not just for kids.

www.westridgefarmpublishing.com

Acknowledgments

This book was made possible through the support of my family and friends.

Thank you to my husband Dennis. You are my best proofreader and my greatest cheerleader.

Thank you to my friend Carol Fox who took the time to read and edit *Golden Horse*.

Thank you to Fred Pokrzywa for creating a fresh colorful website. You took a huge weight off my mind, giving me the time to finish *Golden Horse*.

Thank you to Courtney Vail for teaming up with me to write our *Angels Club* equine series for middle-school readers. You have created fabulous covers for our novels and are an amazing writing partner.

Thank you to my Tuesday Creative Writing group and our mentor Sylvia Rosen. Your encouragement and patience has made me a better writer.

Thank you to those who save our wild horses and who provide homes for rescues.

Thank you to our therapeutic riding programs for helping young and old through the magic of horses.

Thank you Doc Mike Stewart for the terrific care you provide for our mighty steeds.

And last but not least, thank you to my beloved horses for inspiring me to write equine novels.

A Special Tribute

Tribute to Wil, my devoted American Curly
Died: March 19,2016

S.Woodrow Wilson was born in Virginia and lived on my farm until he was 28-years-old. He was a yearling colt when he arrived and from the time he walked off the trailer he stole my heart. He was the best of his breed and was the sire of many foals born on my farm. Wil was shown in numerous horse shows and was also in Fantasia at the Equine Affaire. He was a magnificent representative of the Curly breed and his prodigy carried on his gentle traits and beauty. Wil carried children, beginner riders and family with care and dignity. He was gentle with youngsters and everyone who knew him thought of him as special. He was loved by all and is sorely missed.

Donations

You can help out with two very important needs that are dear to my heart: equine rescue and riding therapy.

Consider donating!

Blue Star
http://www.equiculture.org/join-the-herd.aspx

Dream on Curls Riding Center,
Springfield, VT
www.dreamoncurls.com

U.S. Wild horse and Burro Association, Inc
www.uswhba.org

Also, look for some organizations in your area where you can volunteer and get involved and be inspired.